Tjanting

RON SILLIMAN has written and edited 24 books of poetry and criticism to date, including the anthology *In the American Tree*. He lives in Chester County, Pennsylvania, with his wife and two sons, and works as a market analyst in the computer industry. Since 1979, Silliman has been writing a poem entitled *The Alphabet*. Volumes published thus far from that project have included *ABC*, *Demo to Ink*, *Jones*, *Lit*, *Manifest*, *N/O*, *Paradise*, *®*, *Toner*, *What* and *Xing*. Silliman is a 2002 Fellow of the Pennsylvania Arts Council, a 1998 Pew Fellow in the Arts and received grants and fellowships from the National Endowment of the Arts and the California Arts Council while writing *Tjanting*.

Tjanting

RON SILLIMAN

SALT

PUBLISHED BY SALT PUBLISHING
PO Box 202, Applecross, Western Australia 6153
PO Box 937, Great Wilbraham, Cambridge PDO CB1 5JX United Kingdom

First published by The Figures 1981
This new edition published by Salt Publishing 2002

Printed and bound in the United Kingdom by Lightning Source

Typeset in Swift 9.5 / 13

British Library Cataloguing-in-Publication Data
A catalogue record for this book is available from the British Library
ISBN 1 876857 19 6 paperback

SP

1 3 5 7 9 8 6 4 2

For Krishna Evans

Introduction

from *The Grand Piano*

Barrett Watten

The Turn to Language in the 1970s

"In the earliest times the intimate unity of word and thing was considered to be part of the bearer of the name, if not indeed to substitute for him," according to an authoritative account. "Of about to within which," was Ron's considered reply.

Of course, it's not so simple. It's not being so simple had enormous implications for how we would see the language-centered horizon of our unfolding, collective project. Was the turn to *language* in the 1970s the same as the collective unfolding of that pact? Or was it a moment of individuation that, against the unlimited and boundless space of *language*, would return us to tradition in the name of poetry, however modified as critique? What was it we thought we intended, if not what we meant?

"You are not I . . . ." Nonidentity is the term common to all. The limits of the imagination contradict wildly at a given time and place. A person thinks his nonidentity is either a loss or a gain, but it is never simply a fact. Tautology is assumed by the dominant; recognition is a hole in the face. "But the truly heroic element, the hero's activity, eludes our perception . . . ." The recognition of nonidentity is the first step in the appropriation of one's fate.

"Many and various mixes," as Larry Eigner wrote, in a singular demonstration of *language*. There is no one approach to this question, whose prospect, we would find out, might appear suspiciously reductive. This is apart from the question of the name—of the group, for instance—about which too much already has been written. Rather, the question is what was meant by *language* as the horizon of the work. And staring at language on the page, against the background of the page, printing that page, reading to various audiences from it, becoming known and knowing oneself in terms of its effects—*language* to us would come to mean what?

Proofs for the second edition of *In the American Tree* have just arrived, along with a request for a new introduction to *Tjanting*. Looking at my earlier introduction—which now betrays a painful stress of public incomprehension, which I sought to elevate to the status of a method, presented as an authoritative account to the reader, and all this as an introduction to another's work—I am struck by the violence of its style. The gaps between statements; the need to incorporate a wildly divergent range of references before saying anything that could be taken as assuming authority or knowledge, either of Ron's work or my own; the attempt to undermine any paraphrase of the work as a condition for entering into it . . .

Errors disappear; idiosyncrasies arrive. Idiosyncrasies are the mediating terms of the text. Peripheral information, life in the suburbs farthest out, the deformations of habit leave ghosts of evidence in the perception of the mass. In this area of language, incompletion can be eliminated simply by being named. Trivia and language-about-itself disrupt false boundaries of the self; abstraction is stated in such away that it assumes the objectivity of fact. "We awake in the same moment to ourselves and things" [Wittgenstein]. The deconstructive activity of the text finds the destroyed centers of other lives. Idiosyncrasy is the central term of an assertion of faith in the power of writing to construct.

[2]

I identify poetics, as an iconoclastic method, with the generative force of a negation. If not quite with negativity as a form of self-presentation, as if we had wanted to continue the project of doing away with epistemology almost to the point of doing away with ourselves . . . In one fell swoop of disidentification, an act of self-erasure would translate us to the encompassing horizon of language—a capaciousness precisely, at the same time, the difficulty of our address to another. Otherwise put, the interpersonal dynamics of our work, much like the task of introducing it to others, were pressured, stressed. To the point of deformation, a turning away . . .

A turning away from the center of shared concerns evinced, in fact, by the opening of Ron's work: "Not this. / What then." And in case anyone missed it the first time, the message repeats: "Not this." Not *this*: a denial or surpassing of the act of reference as a condition for the unfolding of the poem. The origins of a metalanguage, beyond the reciprocal canceling of proposition and context. A will to write oneself out of the thicket of particulars, toward the certainty of form. This would seem to imply a transcendental turn, a move to abstraction—if one that was never realized. (It would have been so easy to move toward abstraction, we could immediately have rejoined the company of art.) Not *this*: but not abstraction, either.

In *Tjanting* writing looks at itself first. Revision, self-consciousness, the insistence on the typical appear at all points. Verbal "input" is repeated and broken down in an extensive written continuum based on an iteration of sentences that could equally stand by themselves. New information is woven into a fabric of parts which begin to appear as units, divesting themselves of connotative roots. The writing makes a reality by taking itself apart; the new, created order finds information to be in the world.

"Not *this*": also a sense of going beyond the editorial horizons of *This*, the magazine I edited and in which all of us appeared. Retrospectively, there seems to be a collective horizon of emergence there. My first thought was, if I am not going to take this as a typical moment of betrayal, what could Ron possibly mean by that—? If we are going beyond *This*, insofar as it was a product of my labor and desire, and in a way that I thought coincided with that of others—what are we then going to do?

A provisional answer would be the rejected one: a return to the particulars of everyday life, to an experience that had been abstracted and derealized in the horizon of *language*. Particulars, not language or metalanguage or deixis, but the lure of the things themselves. Here we would rejoin tradition— at least, the tradition we most cared about: Williams's "No ideas but in things." That did not seem to be a going beyond of *this*. It follows that, wherever one reads the death of the referent in Ron's writing from the time, one may just as well substitute an endless chain of references to particulars of everyday life. A horizon of writing as material: "The muscles so sore from halving the rump roast I cld barely grip the pen."

links to the author

> "The concrete is concrete because it is the concentration of many determinations, hence the unity of the diverse. It appears in the process of thinking, therefore, as a process of concentration, as a result, not as a point of departure, even if it is the point of departure in reality and hence also the point of departure for observation and conception." [Karl Marx, *Grundrisse*]

Perhaps the problem with *this*, if not its demonstration in the pages of *This*, was that it did not capture the truth of Ron's method, his way of writing sentence after sentence: the totality of poetic form. In being so bogged down by particulars, one may never see the horizon of totality, the bigger picture, the encompassing whole. But isn't it precisely in the mode of negation—of refusing to accept the horizon of particulars, even though it is right in front of you—that the bigger picture starts to dawn?

It seemed that what Ron wanted was the reverse—a going

beyond *this* toward a kind of particularity that could no longer be merely called up in the act of referring. Not an obdurate, material fact, but a difficult relation of *language*. A purely relational determination, in the space opened up between things and the language used to refer to them. The gaps between words and things, rather than the positive existence of either.

"A semicolon is used to mark a more important break in sentence flow than that marked by a comma. 'The controversial portrait was removed from the entrance hall; in its place was hung a realistic landscape.'" In this directive, syntax provides a point of departure for a statement that can speak for itself. [*Chicago Manual of Style*]

The denial of *this*, of all acts of pointing to something out there that could be labeled "that," thus accedes to a relation—as precondition of the total form. The denial of *this* becomes a test of adequacy of the representation of others, as well. You are not in the place I had reserved for you. Relation is predicated on that which is *not*. I am led in the direction of saying, the adequacy of representation or the inadequacy of particulars is not the primary reason for that *not*. Nonreferentiality must then defer, before it enters into any relation, to that *not*. Not as an intentional act.

Not an intentional act. What is going on here? Wittgenstein turned inside out? Rabbit and duck marching hand and hand, toward the horizon of language? To what were we refusing to refer? Or were we more directly referring to a refusal—as an actually existing state of affairs?

"The hero is as if concealed in a concrete puzzle; he is broken down into a series of constituent and subsidiary parts; he is replaced by a chain of objectivized situations and surrounding objects, both animate and inanimate." [Roman Jakobson, "Marginal Notes on the Prose of Boris Pasternak"]

The decisive question has always been the adequacy of statement. Somehow this has been taken to mean, the adequacy of statement in relation to that to which it refers. But reference is everywhere in Ron's poem. What, then, is the meaning of that constitutive negation? The *not* that has bound us up in stitches, one might say.

Language must be the relation of an inadequacy, of a statement to itself. But statements are what I wanted to make. In the manner of certain visual artists, who made a statement by placing a pile of anthracite coal in the middle of a white painted cube, the gallery space. Who traveled to the Yucatan and photographed a sequence of mirrors they had installed there. Who were photographed leaping horizontally from the sides of buildings, in a negation of everyday life. In this sense, *language* has everything to do with strategies in the arts. By which we assume philosophical credibility . . .

> Outside on a billboard, a Camel ad proposes: "Where a man belongs." Perhaps this is in the tropics rather than on the corner of 16th and South Van Ness. Limits are what any of us are inside of; the limit one is staring at is somewhere else. In the nineteenth century the motive force of the material takes over from there; in the present, the materials have no motive force: they do not move. There is no option but for the imagination to turn back on itself. And itself will generally find itself lacking at that point.

I remember the "Information" show at the Museum of Modern Art, which I saw in 1969. One of the references of this work was to *language* itself. In the form of documentations of all sorts—lists, statistics, computer-generated texts, defunct categorical schemes. Used paperback editions of logical positivism, from A. J. Ayers to W. V. O. Quine. Logically absurdist definitions of art on the walls by Lawrence Wiener and Joseph Kosuth. The apotheosis of self-consciousness as art in Jasper Johns's *The Critic Speaks*. Language was being proposed as an expanded frame of art, and re-presented as art. The inclusive dates of *Six Years: The Dematerialization of the Art Object*: 1967–73. A defining moment in the movement later known as global conceptualism.

Conceptualism was an opening to a more possible world in the 1970s, a departure from the stasis of everyday life. In San Francisco, artists like Terry Fox, Howard Fried, and Tom Marioni put forward site-specific values for a self-canceling art. At the Verbal Eyes performance series at The Farm, poets were drawn into its orbit, on the theory that conceptualism and *language* had something to do with each other. Here was another route to the overcoming of reference: a video-screen blankness of language as surface to produce a bonafide art effect. Doug Hall's use of empty repetitions in performance: "They are bombing Afghanistan; they are bombing Cambodia." Poetry, of course, had long since known how to do things like that. We knew something more about language than its use in conceptual framing or generating abstraction, but the artists had the confidence of an externalized role. Then there was the question of whether the artists could comprehend the literariness of the poets' use of language, if they could put it to use. Strategies for overcoming reference in language diverge into the prerequisites for each art, even when each is concerned with the relation of the work to the world . . .

A bus ride is better than most art. . . .
   To enter the work might be possible anywhere, as one gets on or off a bus. It is possible, in fact, to read this book on a bus.

It was not just literary motives that led to the question of *language* as a problem in its own right; nor strategies for performance or site-specific art, either. Perhaps, it seemed, we could learn something about our use of language in writing through a study of language itself. Was this another entailment of the turn to *language*? Would we finally arrive at the ever-receding horizon of *language* as an object in itself, as something to know?

Immediately I applied myself to the study of language. This was not the same thing. In learning the distinction between the idea of language and the material of linguistics, I learned a great deal. *Language* for us was a process of ideological unmasking, an unlinking of interests from chronic ideas, reified frames. For the linguists, however, it was an object . . .

"Government spending is the source of inflation." Why does the small businessman think this? Because capital competes for control of liquid assets with the state. And the small businessman is last on the list for any spare capital to invest. But perhaps this need for constant new sources of investment capital is precisely the cause of the inflationary condition he is in. The small businessman participates in a conflict beyond his control. A mechanical adjustment occurs that effects all other levels of the state he thinks he is in.

In the 1980s, I had hours of discussions with George Lakoff. We met almost by accident, a phone call after an event at 80 Langton Street. The moment I realized whom I was talking to, I launched into an attack on the distinction between connotation and denotation as philosophically unsound. Connotations likewise have senses—or we cannot understand them. At least, that is what I remember having said. I had been reading Wittgenstein. Connotation was a lure, leading onward, into the unfolding of a desire to know *language*. George and I immediately met for coffee. The turn to *language* took me in the wrong direction for a while, in a detour to linguistics. I must continue to think of the meaning of that turn.

It seemed that, one way or another, *language* leads to everything. It has been good to me, this idea of language leading onward. But once I had learned that, I felt as though I ought to go beyond language. But what would that mean? Would going beyond *language* be the same as going beyond *this*? What is the scene of decision I would then find myself in?

A tjanting is a drawing instrument used for handwork in batik. The pun is exact: *Tjanting* (chanting) would seem to follow its predecessor as an oral form (*Ketjak*), but is in fact written toward writing considered as itself. The trace of the hand on the surface, then, is the hero of the text. "Action is replaced by topography." And as any handwriting betrays the continuity of the self, the science of tearing oneself apart becomes the pleasure of the text.

Language: is it predicated on the inexpressible? Of what we could not express? Of that which could not be taken in the mode of expression? Are you happy/sad, as Pizzicato 5 would say? What is the meaning of your expression? Do you express the base? What base are you writing your expression in? Would you like to return right now to home base? Do you think there will be any basis for that?

What would it mean to go beyond the inexpressible? To return to expression? Is this circularity the cunning of *language*? That an inexpressibility of language would return us to a condition of everyday life?

"Nowadays, we have a hard time predicting what it's going to be like. And what we do expect, we don't have ways to relate effectively to what is seen. So it's hard to tell a reasonable status quo from a viable opportunity for a change from a disaster area." [Steve Benson, quoted from *The Talks*]

We were surrounded by *language* that we ourselves had made. In endless readings of the endless text. At the Grand Piano, in machine-like style. Kit, Bob, Steve and the Brat Guts writing group. Carla and Steve's improvisations. The coruscating brilliance of The Talks. The lure of the blank page and the material condensations of type. The hand-stapled aesthetics of Lyn's letter-press books. Clark Coolidge, holding forth for days at 80 Langton Street. I remember encountering Coolidge at the beginning of the week in which he read two hours a night from his untitled "longwork." We were enmeshed in a collectively produced labyrinth of relations, made of incommensurate texts. A *language* that was primarily *not* about itself, but about . . .

The unutterable inexpressiveness of that *not*. I wanted to use that *not*, to put things together in a different way. This was not an abstraction. "A telephone pole is an edited tree." The constructivist moment, starting again and again, after that *not*. The opposite of Creeley's maxim of lyric accountability: "Not from not / but in in," which sent Robert Grenier turning endlessly into the page. Grenier's intensity indeed provided a point of focus for us, provoking a self-consciousness of *language*. At the same time, he was turning away from our concerns, toward an encounter with language in the world as individuating fate. A turn demanding a reinscription of particulars as immanence, almost in a religious sense . . .

"In this whole system development and underdevelopment reciprocally determine each other, for while the quest for surplus profits constitutes the prime motive power behind the mechanisms of growth, surplus-profit can only be achieved at the expense of less productive countries, regions, and branches of production. Hence development takes place only in juxtaposition with underdevelopment; it perpetuates the latter and itself develops thanks to this perpetuation." By extension, individual fates are relatively lost or found, moving from peak to trough on a stagnating, motionless base. [Ernest Mandel, *Late Capitalism*]

We were. In quest of the totality of method. Specifics: in 1977, I published *Decay*; in 1980, *1-10*. This Press brought out Ron's *Ketjak* in 1978; I worked on the production of *Tjanting* in 1980-81. In the same three or four years: Lyn's *Writing Is an Aid to Memory* and *My Life*; Steve's *As Is* and *Blindspots*; Bob's *7 Works* and *Primer*; Kit's *Down and Back*; Carla's *Under the Bridge*; and Grenier's *Sentences*. Work that had appeared in *This*, Tuumba, and The Figures and which is collected in *In the American Tree*. Our writing had gone through a transformation, toward the horizons of a constructive device. We would be patient, building our utopia in the Universal Mountains on the basis of that which is *not*.

Life continued as a parallel text: Paris, linguistics, C—, 80 Langton Street. Intensive focus and intellectual exogamy. Labor, desire, and the material text. Content—and what is that? *Language* as relation: *not*.

But self-consciousness fights back. The conversation of men working in any garage gives a demonstration of this. A mechanic knows more about the mechanics of statement than most poets. Increasingly, current art tells us only about itself; while capital is chipping away at our position, we have art to fill in the gaps. We generate performance artists because there is no drama in everyday life. Art is possible only as a window on the self-consciousness of the past. The mechanic accurately measures the helplessness of his fate, but where is the person whose self-consciousness has survived art?

These are the dots, those are the connections. They are being filled in, even as they are evaporating. Will we ever achieve the horizon of *language*? Or is the horizon of *language* only where we started from?
Between dots and connections is a statement. That is what I wanted to make.

"Not this. What then?" The writing is working on itself. The mechanics are operating on their own terms; to deal with them is to operate on one's own. The serial order of the work finding itself out is equal to the fixed attention to be found at all points.

Have you ever wanted to go beyond *language*? How would you describe your motives for doing so, in so many words?

From *The Grand Piano*, a multi-authored account of poetry and poetics in San Francisco in the 1970s, currently in the process of being written by Rae Armantrout, Steve Benson, Carla Harryman, Lyn Hejinian, Tom Mandel, Bob Perelman, Kit Robinson, Ron Silliman, and the present author.

Tjanting

Not this.
What then?
I started over & over. Not this.

Last week I wrote "the muscles in my palm so sore from halving the rump roast I cld barely grip the pen." What then? This morning my lip is blisterd.

Of about to within which. Again & again I began. The gray light of day fills the yellow room in a way wch is somber. Not this. Hot grease had spilld on the stove top.

Nor that either. Last week I wrote "the muscle at thumb's root so taut from carving that beef I thought it wld cramp." Not so. What then? Wld I begin? This morning my lip is tender, disfigurd. I sat in an old chair out behind the anise. I cld have gone about this some other way.

—Wld it be different with a different pen? Of about to within which what. Poppies grew out of the pile of old broken-up cement. I began again & again. These clouds are not apt to burn off. The yellow room has a sober hue. Each sentence accounts for its place. Not this. Old chairs in the back yard rotting from winter. Grease on the stove top sizzled & spat. It's the same, only different. Ammonia's odor hangs in the air. Not not this.

Analogies to quicksand. Nor that either. Burglar's book. Last week I wrote "I can barely grip this pen." White butterfly atop the grey concrete. Not so. Exactly. What then? What it means to "fiddle with" a guitar. I found I'd begun. One orange, one white, two gray. This morning my lip is swollen, in pain. Nothing's discrete. I straddled an old chair out behind the anise. A bit a part a like. I cld have done it some other way. Pilots & meteorologists disagree about the sky. The figure five figures in. The way new shoots stretch out. Each finger has a separate function. Like choosing the form of one's execution.

Forcing oneself to it. It wld've been new with a blue pen. Giving oneself to it. Of about to within which what without. Hands writing. Out of the rockpile grew poppies. Sip mineral water, smoke cigar. Again I began. One sees seams. These clouds breaking up in late afternoon, blue patches. I began again but it was not beginning. Somber hue of a gray day sky filld the yellow room. Ridges & bridges. Each sentence accounts for all the rest. I was I discoverd on the road. Not this. Counting my fingers to get different answers. Four wooden chairs in the yard, rain-warpd, wind-blown. Cat on the bear rug naps. Grease sizzles & spits on the stove top. In paradise plane wrecks are distributed evenly throughout the desert. All the same, no difference, no blame. Moon's rise at noon. In the air hung odor of ammonia. I felt a disease. Not not not-this. Reddest red contains trace of blue. That to the this then. What words tear out. All elements fit into nine crystal structures. Waiting for the cheese to go blue. Thirty-two. Measure meters pause. Applause.

A plausibility. Analogy to "quick" sand. Mute pleonasm. Nor that either. Planarians, trematodes. Bookd burglar. What water was, wld be. Last week I cld barely write "I grip this pen." The names of dust. Blue butterfly atop the green concrete. Categories of silence. Not so. Articles pervert. Exactly. Ploughs the page, plunders. What then? Panda bear sits up. Fiddle with a guitar & mean it. Goin' to a dojo. Found start here. Metal urges war. One white, two gray, one orange, two longhair, two not. Mole's way. This morning the swelling's gone down. Paddle. No thing dis crete. Politry. Out behind the anise I strad-dled an old chair. O'Hare airport. About a bit in part a like. Three friends with stiff necks. I did it different. Call this long hand. Weathermen & pilots compete for the sky. Four got. Five figures figure five. Make it naked. The way new stretches shoot out. Shadow is light's writing. Each finger functions. The fine hairs of a nostril. Executing one's choice. What then? Forms crab forth. Pen's tip snaps. Beetles about the bush. Wood bee. Braille is the world in six dots. A man, his wife, their daughter, her sons. Times of the sign. The very idea. This cancels this. Wreak havoc, write home. We were well within. As is.

[16]

Wait, watchers. Forcing to it one self. Read in. It wld be blue with a new pen. Than what? Giving to one itself. The roads around the town we found. Of about under to within which what without. Elbows' flesh tells age. Hands writing. Blender on the end-table next to the fridge. Out of rock piled groupies. Hyphenate. Smoke cigar, sip water. Mineral. This was again beginning. Begging questions. Seams one sees. Monopoly, polo-pony. Blue patches breaking clouds up in the late afternoon. Non senses. It was not beginning I began again. In Spain the rain falls mainly on the brain. The gray sky came into the yellow room. Detestimony. Bridges affix ridges. On the road I discoverd I was. I always wake. Not this. The bear's trappings. Counting my fingers between nine & eleven. Factory filld at sunrise. Three rain-warpd wood chairs in the back yard. Minds in the mines look out. Cat naps on the bear rug. Bathetic. On the stove top grease sizzles & spits. Lunch pales. In paradise plain rocks are distributed evenly throughout the desert. Electricity mediates the voice. All difference, no same, all blame. Lampshade throws the light. Noon's moonrise. Burn sienna. Feel the disease. Denotes detonation. Not not not-not this. The sun began to set in the north. Reddest trace contains red blue. Metazoans, unite. Of that to the this of then. Break or lure. Out what words tear. One ginger oyster between chop-sticks rose to the lips. All elemental crystal structures are nine. Helicopters hover down into the dust. The blue cheese waits. No one agrees to the days of the week. Thirty-two times two. We left the forest with many regrets. Meters pace measure. New moons began to rise. Applause drops the curtain. The elf in lederhosen returns to the stomach of the clock. Chiropractice. Furnace fumes. Crayola sticks. Each word invents words. One door demands another. Bowels lower onto bowls. Come hug. Sunset strip. Holograms have yet to resolve the problem of color. Thermal. This is where lines cross. Hyperspace, so calld. Mastodons trip in the tar pits. These gestures generate letters. Industrial accident orphan. Driving is much like tennis. Orgasmic, like the slam dunk. We saw it in slomo. Cells in head flicker & go out. Zoo caw of the sky.

Sarcadia. A plausibility. Gum bichromate. Quick analogy to sand. Not this. Moot pleonasm. Cat sits with all legs tuckd under. Nor that either. Table lamp hangs from the ceiling, mock chandelier. Trematodes, planarians. Featherd troops. Books burgled. Blood lava. What wld be was water. Bone flute. I cld barely write "last week I grippd this pen." Allusions illude. Dust names. Not easy. Green butterfly atop the blue concrete. Pyrotechnics demand night. Kinds of silence. Each is a chargd radical. Not so. Photon. Pervert articles. Extend. Exactly. Descend. Plunders & ploughs the page. Read reed as red. What then? With in. Panda bear claps. The far side of the green door is brown. Fiddle with a mean guitar. "I don't like all those penises staring at me." Go into a dojo. Mojo dobro. Here found start. Dime store sun visor. Metal urges worn. Only snuggle refines us. Two long-hairs, two gray, one white, one not, one orange. Spring forward, fall back. Mole's way in. Build an onion. This morning the blister gave way to pus & half-formd flesh. Hoarfrost. Paddleball. Tether. No thindgis creep. Tiny plastic dinosaur. Politry teaches just what each is. Cameroon tobacco wrapper. Out behind anise I stood on an old chair. Southpaw slant to the line. O'Hare airport bar. Sounds the house makes. About a bit in part of a like. Shutters rattle, stairs "groan." Three stiff friends with necks. Your own voice at a distance. Done differently. Monoclinic. This long hand call. 'Her skirt rustled like cow thieves.' Sky divides jets & weather. Far sigh wren. Got for. Bumble. Figure five figures five. Dear Bruce, dear Charles. Make naked it. Negative. Out the way new stretches shoot. A thin black strap to keep his glasses from falling. Light's writing is shadow. Rainbow in the lawn hose's shower. Each finger's function. Beneath the willow, ferns & nasturtiums. Nostril fine hairs. Stan writes from Kyoto of deep peace in the calligraphic. Executed one choice. Pall bearers will not glance into one another's eyes. What then? A storm on Mount Sutro. Forms crab forth from tide pool's edge. Refusal of personal death is not uncommon amid cannery workers. Snaps pen tip. An ant on the writing alters letters. About the bush beetles. This municipal bus lurches forward. Be wood. Several small storms cld be seen across the valley. The world in six braille dots. Gray blur of detail indicates rain. A woman, her husband, their daughter, her sons. A pile of old clothes discarded in the weeds of a vacant lot. Time of the signs. Some are storms. The idea very. Borate bombers swoopd low over the rooftops. This cancels not this. The doe stood still just beyond the rim of the clearing. Writing home wrought havoc. In each town there's a bar calld the It Club. We were within the well. Many several. Is as is. Affective effects. Humidity of the restroom. Half-heard humor. Old rusted hammer head sits in the dust. Clothespins at angles on a nylon line. Our generation had school desks which still had inkwells, but gone were the bottles of ink. Green glass broken in the grass. Every dog on the block began to bark. Hark. Words work as wedges or as hedges to a bet. Debt drives the nation. These houses shall not survive another quake. A wooden fence that leans in all directions. Each siren marks the tragic. Dandelions & ivy. A desert by the sea is a sight to see. A missile rose quickly from the ocean's surface. A parabola spelld his mind. He set down, he said, his Harley at sixty. It is not easy to be a narcissist. Afterwords weigh as an anchor. Cement booties. Not everyone can cause the sun to come up. On the telly, all heads are equal. In Mexico, the federales eat you up. The production of fresh needs is the strangest of all. I swim below the surface. Room lit by moonlight. Words at either edge of the page differ from those in between. An old grey church enclosd in bright green scaffolding. Left lane must turn left. A dog in his arms like an infant. Each sentence bends toward the sun. Years later, I recognized her walk a block away.

Downward motion means out. Watchers wait. In motel rooms the beds are disproportionately large. Self forcing one to it. Croatians were restless. Read into. Between hills, a slice of fog. With a blue pen it wld be new. Not wanted is not wanted. Than what? This not. Self giving one to it. Time lapse photography captures the sky. Around the town we found roads. A roil of deep gray cirrus. Of about under to within which of what without into by. A taut bend to the palm tree to indicate wind. Flesh at the elbow goes slack as one grows older, gathers in folds. Fireworks replay the war. By the fridge on an endtable a blender. A fly's path maps the air of the room, banging at the windows. Hand writings. Recent words have been struck. Groupies pile out of rock. An accidental order is not chance. Hyphenateria. On the wall hung abalone. Sip cigar, smoke water. Who holds what truths to be self-evident? Mineral water bubbles in a glass. Each mark is a new place. Again this was beginning, being begun. Stick cloves in an orange for incense. Questioning beggars. Under golden arches we gorged to heart's delight. One's seams seen. Not ink but point scrapes the page. Polopony, monopoly. At sea side a city of rust. Late afternoon clouds breaking up into blue patches. Pigeons gather round the writing. None senses. In the back of the Buick were sleeping bags, pillows. Is this not beginning I again begin? Orange Opel's dented fender. In the rain Spain falls mainly on the brain. Gold-leaf sign on the glass reads X-ray. Gray sky comes into the yellow room. Peeling leather off the tatterd jacket. Detestimonial. Predictable people wear Frye boots. Ridges attached by bridges. Waiting for that bus to come back this way. Pine koans. Uganda liquors. Each sentence stakes out. Knot this. Can cups fill a cupboard? Tamal is the name of a place in the place of a name. I was on the discoverd road. Caterpillar is a tractor. I am in each instant waking. To him her tone was at once tender and gruff from long years of rough intimacy. Not this. I saw my blood, a deep red, filling the vial at the far end of the needle. Ing the trappd bears. I wanted to catch a glimpse of her face, but she never turnd this way. Between nine & eleven counted my fingers. Each cloud has a specific shape. At sunrise the factory filld. Cut to montage of forklifts & timeclock. Back in the yard three wooden rain-warpd chairs. Scratch that. In the mines minds gape. Try to imagine words. Bare cat naps on the rug. Haze hued those hills on the far, gray side of the bay. Bathetic. Underground, the mock coolness of the conditiond air. Grease sizzles, spits on the stove top. Sand sharks swam past. Pale lunch. A city of four tunnels. In paradise desert rocks are distributed evenly throughout the plain. We saw the sails at sea. Electricity translates the voice. But what comes thru depends on you. Blame all difference, know same. Thru the window I see the apparatus of the modern dentist. Shade throws the lamp light. Light green lines between wch to write. Noon's rising moon. This one squints at a thick printout in his lap on the bus home from work. Sienna burns. Suddenly, in the hospital corridor, the familiar smell of balsa wood & model airplane glue. Feel a disease. Or, thru a window just after sunset, the faces of watchers turnd blue by the light of an unseen television. Detonates denotation. For an instant I was unable to remember how to get the change back into my pocket & pick the bag up off the counter. Not-not not-not not-not this. Crystals hung in the window to refract the sun. It began to set in the north. Ploughshares turnd into gongs may be playd without actually being touchd. Trace of red blue contain within the reddest. Each day's first cigarette tastes stale. Metazoans united. The true length depends on the size of the type. Of by that to the this into of then. Morning, mourning. Brick or leer. The buzz of flies fills the room. Out words what tear. Chinese coins with holes in the center. To the lips, thick & poised open, rose a ginger oyster between chopsticks. A blue glass ashtray filld with wooden match sticks. All 9 elemental structures are crystal. Each statement is a mask. Down into the dust hover helicopters. This script a scrawl. Wait for the blue cheese. A motorboat for the salt seas calld Twenty Languages. No days agree as to the one of the week. We make our deposit in the cloud bank. Thirty-two times two-squared. Black smoke of a structural fire belched up out over the docks. Regretfully we are leaving the forest. In a string net, a bundle of groceries. Meters face measure. Charging for lapis but giving you sodalite. Moons begin to rise anew. Cool coffee kindld thought. Applause curtains the drop. Me too in general yes. Back into the stomach of the clock went the elf in lederhosen. Certain sentences set aside, others set off. Chiropractical. Dr Heckle & Mr Jive. Furnish fumes. The red hook-&-ladder snakes around to back into the station. Crayola sticks streak a page. Like radios talking of radios to radios. Each word once the invention of another. These dark glasses serve as a veil. One door is the demand of another. Gulls fly, strung from hidden wires. Over bowls lower bowels. For "wires" read "wives." Hug come. Time flows, pouring forward from the past. Strip set sun. Vast vats of waste water aerate in the flatlands by the bay. Holograms have yet to tackle the problem calld color. Walking as tho one had to think abt it. Thermal, Tamal. Fresh odor of new dung. This is where the cross lines. Too late to catch the bus, they slap its side as it pulls away. So calld hyperspace. An old Chinese lady wearing a light-purple tam. Mastodons in the tar pits trip. An ashtray in the shape of a heart. These letters generate gestures. The shadow of buildings upon buildings. Accidental industrial orphan. The lines abt swimming meant sex. Tennis is much like driving. Fire escape forms a spine. Slam, like the orgasmic dunk. Drunk. In slomo we saw it move, try to. Against that cream stucco the gray flagpole has no depth. Heads in the cell flicker & go out. In that sandal I saw countless toes. Zoo sky of caw. A transmitter, like radar, atop each tall building. Transbay transit. The word is more & less. The history of the foot. The fogbank heavy on the beach like a slug. Stopping the car to make a quick phone call. You will never stop learning how to read. Hyper / formance. What really happend to the C. Turner Joy. Up & down scales on reeds. Not this. The words were in the page already. Summer without sun. I like white space. Truck towed tons of tractors, all yellow. Plotting the way ahead. Instrument landing. The flutter of clarinets. Boar bristle hair brush. Toilet's handle says "press." These letters more angular than I used to write. Congas in the urban night. Cans of beer & fear. Sunrise behind fog means light changes on the green steep slopes of the hillside. A small pen-like instrument used to apply wax designs. Cut. He staggerd about in the intersection, whooping & making wild gestures, then sipping from a can of beer, oblivious to the early morning traffic. Pain in the lower calves from hours of walking. Potato chips at war. With heavy hearts, we set out to follow the river to its conclusion. If he has no sideburns, then it's a hairpiece. When we got to where the clouds were, they were too thin to see. Industrial siren meaning lunch. Quips & players, or diamonds in the blood. There are clues nearby. In each major city, the ugliest mansion was the French Consulate. She & I strolld thru the rose garden. Nor that either. An architect's model of a rest stop. Tulis is not tulip. Shaking the brain awake. Each word is a wafer of meaning meant, minded. No fish imagines water. I surface at the center of the pool. A dress shirt halfway between pink & lavender. Tautness of the warp while on the loom. Each sentence is itself. Two fives & a nine. A nose that points slightly to the left. What I am writing is writing. Tics dig in. Wicker throne. Scratch that. Keep moving. Dressd to kill. Burgundy jumpsuit.

False start. Circadia. True start. Applause, ability. A run around a ring around of roses read. Gum bichromate. Jets swoop low over the destroyer amid bursts of anti-aircraft fire, dozens of bombs going off in the water, then rise up again & the audience cheers. Sandy analogy to the quick. The poem plots. Not this. Indented servant. Moot pleonast. Opposable thumb. All legs tuckd in, the cat sleeps. Mandibility. Nor that either. Cumulative tissue calld tonsil. Mock chandelier table-lamp hangs upside down from the ceiling. Pages of description. Planarians inch forward, trematodes retreat. Eat lady fingers. Trooping feathers. This to me is tmesis. Books burgld bought back. Roller is not coaster. Lava blood. Larva blood. What wld water be was. What you are reading is the dance of my hand. Flute bone. Brothers & sisters I've never met. Barely I cld write. Brown door, white door, green door, all along one wall. Allusions elude. Grip this. Names dust. That was last week or weak. Not easy. Pi. Mauve butterfly atop the ochre concrete. Footsteps on the stairs. Pyro demands night technics. Insert new modes of thought. Kind to silence. What then? Each radical is charged. The sound of a telephone dial, turning, turning back. Not so. Air is zone. Photon. Milk of Indonesia. Particles avert. Milk of amnesia. X tends. Warp is vertical, weft is horizontal. X acts. Ten million without power. D sends. Once I was a needle freak. Pages & ploughs the plunders. Any cloth or fabric structure. Read red as read. Ronnie 2 Baad. What then? This is another sentence. With inn. What gets seen thru a speculum. Claps the panda. Tofu turkey. The near side of the brown door is green.

Indirect sunset. Mean with a fiddle guitar. I like the shapes of thing. "Don't like all those staring penises." The tar-heater stands in the street, breathing loudly. Into a dojo go. Holes in the petals from unknown eaters. Mojo dobro. Rough tough cough. Start found here. Roofers holler down. Sun visor from a dime store. Words secrete letters. Meddle, urge, warn. Dog climbs up onto the couch. Only ray struggle finds us. Half heard. One white, one not, one orange, two longhair, too gray. Grinder buffer sander. Fall back, spring forward. Out of the rooftops grew types of pipes. Mole's way into. Brushing to rust-proof. Build a better onion. The man who invented spikes to go into the sides of phone poles. This morning the blister was replaced by tight, tender new flesh. Backstairs are a proposition. Hoarfrost. People who don't understand cats. Ballpaddle. Muted trumpet. Tether. What is the ocean's porpoise? No thid gnis crete. B complex. Plastic tiny dinosaur. Gary Moore, Henry Morgan, Bill Cullen, Betty White, Allen Ludden, Jack Narz, Gale Storm. Politry—each is, just what teaches. Poultry—features creatures. Wrappd Cameroon tobacco. Rough waves move quickly. Out behind fennel I stood on an old chair. Cantalope halves in the bay "look like the moon." Southpaws slant their lines. Chinese youth in the parks of North Beach. O'Hare airport bartender. Strokes of the pen. Sounds make the house. Pigeons fly past sleepers & sunbathers. About of a bit into part of a like. Bread crumbs in dry grass. Shutters groan, stairs rattle. Two bell-towers & 21 crosses go into the cathedral. Friends with three stiff necks. The war between grasses is ceaseless. Distancing your own voice. Trenchcoats in warm weather. Differently done. Down vest. Monoclinic. I see her walking in my direction. Long this hand call. Opcorn. His shirt rustld like cow thieves. Coming in by ladder. Jets divide sky & weather. Party conversation: familiar voices focus. Fart saw run. Kit grins to see me write. Get fur. At a reading, watch friends listen. Bumbles. Tweeze each letter. Five five figure figures. I hear foot-steps come up the stairs but no one arrives. Bruce dear, Charles dear. Kleenex is a trade name. It naked make. Unpoppd kernels at the bottom of the cup. Negative. Listening, they concentrate, stare. Way out the new stretches shoot. Star. To keep glasses from slipping, a black elastic strap. If it's speech you got to listen. Writing light's shadow. Flougher. Lawn hose' shower makes rain bow. These lines stretch in all directions. Each function's finger. Amyl bums the brain. Beneath the ferns, willows & nasturtiums. This is how the Dutch thought to spell it. Hairs nostril fine. Later he said he saw me just sitting there, waving a pen in the air, & thought a smile wld give me permission. Stan writes from deep peace of Kyoto in the calligraphic. Using a stage whisper to call cats. Executed choice one. Jerusalem artichokes, Canadian potatoes. Pall bearers look away. Campd on the couch in a light blue nightie. What then? Embeddedness, in bed with us. Mt. Sutro rainstorm. I hear faucets off & on. Forth from tidepool's edge crabs form. Bufflehead is a duck. Cannery workers commonly refuse personal death. Hear change in pocket to pull jeans on. Naps spend tip. Whisky with an "e." Ant alters letters of the writing. An old friend finds me at the Savoy. The about bush beetles. Pens prick the page. Lurching forward, muni bus. Newsprint on elbow. Bee wood. A hum in boiling water. Across the valley several small storms were at once visible. Scribble. The world six in braille dots. Cats bat the wind chimes. Blur gray of rain indicates detail. Blank page is all promise. A man, a bald deaf man, his wife, their silent daughter, her sons. Crazy to do this. In the weeds of a vacant lot, a pile of old discarded clothes. Any verb trails noun. Sum our storms. Only part of the table seen in the mirror. The signs of time. Inversions face affect. Idea vary the do eye. Tiny scars appear. Low over our rooftops swoop borate bombers. Porn jury giggles at throat. Not this cancels this. Wld you ouija? Just beyond the rim of the clearing a doe stands still. Soft contacts dissolve. Wrote home wrought havoc. Ought not to have. A bar calld the It Club in each town. Six separates this. Were we within? All words are some language. Several many. Jots. Is as is as is. Dry cereal chewing sounds. Effective affects. This drug enhances pleasure. Rest humidity of the room. Hair combd back to dry. Heard half-humor. Just who set George up. In the dust sits old rusty hammerhead. Write right into the binding. Clothespins angling from a nylon line. Weaver. Our schooldesks had ink-wells, but no bottles of ink. Bacteria under foreskin infects friend. Green grass & broken glass. This is one example. Each dog on the block starts to bark. Counts consonants. Hark. Not this. Words work as hedges or as wedges to a bet. Cloth spin. Debt driven nation. Our epic is the draftboard meets acid. Another quake shall not survive these houses. Think of cat to feed. Wood fence leans in all directions. This brain has no rough edges. Tragic markd by siren. Ducks that fail to fly. Ivy & dande-lions. Kibbles. Sea desert sight see. Elastic band about doorknob. Missile shoots from ocean surface. Articles are fibre. Parabola spells my mind. Cat's up. At 60 sets his Harley down. Not impos-sible to not think. Narcissism is not simple. Toes don't go straight. Afterwords weigh anchor. Spacey. Boot cement. Melissa is a missile. Everyone cld cause the sun to not come up. Food good. All heads are equal. Yolks slip from the shell. In Mexico, eat the federales. Love letters. Fresh production of strange needs is all. A woman dressd in nurse whites & a face just that pale. I swam beneath the surface, sun lighting the water. She, consti-tuting the assemblage. Moon lit by room light. Beware the pook—ump no rubbish. Words in the middle differ. Wire rope. Enclosed in bright green scaffolding, a freshly painted white church. Watch & traffic passes. Left lane turn left. Writing standing is not simple. Infant in his arms like a dog. Spine straight, one walks. Each sentence bent toward the sun. Wind makes hat delicate proposition. I recognized her years later a block away. Remember—you're asleep. This sketches, drawing itself out. Some weathers arouse a longing for years ago. A pair of small, silver, military jets zip past. Eyes, you hoped, were not lies. Cargo containers atop flat-beds behind cyclone fence. To the west, fog spilld over the hilltops. One spot at the bay's center where the sun shines directly. Hand or tongue to the eye adds mind. Man sees hoss. Hear airplanes above these clouds. The London of the west. Fishsticks wrappd in wax paper. In an of into by. Not this. Holds his shoulders like umbrella over spine, neck bobbing. Mexican hot chocolate. Cork, where once door's latch was, protects children. Furnace lights up with a whoosh. Written down, sight ceases. Sky blue eyes. Shoes form a platform. Run against light to catch the bus. Riding, writing. Heads of hair dot the air. Not this calls flaws forth. Boppo, boffing. Hi drawl it. Any glyph of words crafted twists in the ear. Bare feet cross linoleum. Engines rev. Indirect light of late afternoon. For whom prose is not without context. Mantis, end stop, the power of the poor. White ash at cigar's tip. Kites from far places. Eyes whose hue depends on clothing's color. Shingle Shoppe. Beard knots. Sails down, anchord in the bay. A chopper slides between islands. Huskies chase birds into water. Cameras dangle against belly. Fat men, slender wives, children run ahead. Wax paper cup in which cola has gone flat. Lavender & green in pigeon's gray neck. Kids buying chilidogs, skateboards in hand. Neck pulls in when pigeon sits. Out on the breakwater, watching whitecaps. Charterboats bob. Lower clouds move quicker. Black smoke of a tugboat. Gull just opend its wings & let the current lift it up. All trite when you see it, she said. Fly's eyeball. Odor of urinal cakes. Reading aloud is not speech. People try to imagine how to sit in chairs. Water in glass never its own color. Where you put the lamp shapes the room. The adroit tigers. A fire, smoldering, in the cigarette. Beer washd over the chocolate & down the throat. Plants move indoors. Concentration stopped at the lens of his glasses. Apples meet the bowl's curves. Ether, either. The height of pepper shakers. Lacuna coat. All shoes on some feet. Mountains, gardens, harbors. Brown bottle under ice plant. Where the talk took him. Difficult to recall the former ease of thought. Leaves the bathroom like a rainforest. More letters are than we know to write down. Scratch, scratch. Graffiti's day is by. Which gin, which tonic? All faucets drip little. Light is to language as. I had one foot in the sailor's grave. Your eyes dilated with anticipation. Old soap slivers sat in the blue plastic dish. Gums recede. Fingers print always in the region of the knob. The slow lift of any launch. Several words too many. Cut.

Not this. Outward momentum presses down. Several tiny cuts on his upper lip. Watch waiters. Two Yankees, two out, too late. The beds in motel rooms are disproportionately large, high up off the floor. Small white plastic fork whose handle ends in the figure of "golden" arches. Self forcing to one it. The distinction between crayons & small cigars. Less croations are rested. Blue sweater forgotten on a red chair. Read into reading. Residue of watercress netted in sink's drain. Between slices, a hill of fog. Hands never completely dry. It wld be with a new blue pen. Light wars. Not wanted is not not-wanted. Kitsums. Than what? Body remembers what brain forgets. This knot. Officer off-duty. Self given to one it. Sees bra strap thru blouse. Time lapse catches sky. See's candies. Around town find roads. In the shade flowers fade. Gray cirrus roils deep. The even weave of freeways. Of about to under to—within to which of what—without into by of by. Patterns of wire in library windows. Wind bent the palm. In the distance red hills where the sun has yet to set. Flesh gathers in folds at the elbow as one grows older. As city darkens, lights appear. War replays pyrotechnics. By the pink toilet a sky blue box filld with tampons. By the endtable on the fridge a blender. Red taillights sweep around the night freeway. Mapping room's air, fly bangs against windows. Coffee at the 5 Cooks cafe. Hands writing. Solo sax. Recently words have been removed. Towels on hooks on a door. Rockies pile out of groups. Green shade over a lamp (never used) hanging from the high ceiling of the yellow room, tassled. A chance order is not accidental. For an instant, cigar's tip is orange. Hyphenaterial. Clear in net. Abalone hung on the wall. Trombone slides in. Sip smoke, water cigars. Call Peg. Holds who what evidence to be self-truth? Cats on chairs asleep. In a glass mineral water bubbles. Late at night unable to tell blue pen from black. Each place is a new mark. Guffaws & chortles. Again beginning was this being begun. Plastic trash can containing old bath water. Stick an orange with cloves for incense. How he draind those around him in the 50's. Questing for boogers. Shadows cast cause depth. Under heart's arches we gorged to gold delight. Whispers in the next room. One's scenes seem. When he was in the army. Not ink but page pulls the point. Burger grill's griddle brick. Poloponius, molo ponies. Palm hits brow—agh! At city side a sea of rust. Glue-all. Breaking late clouds up into afternoon blue patches. Space heater. Writing gathers around the pigeons. This line leads to Uranus. Nun census. Silver fork upon a chippd blue plate. I saw sleeping bag, pillows in the Buick's back. The companionship of refrigerator's hum. This is beginning I again began not. Salt shaker tall as coffee's mug. Dented Opel's orange fender. Gray dawn. On the rain falls Spain mainly in the brain. Smudges forming fingertips on the back door's windows. X-ray reads gold-leaf sign on the glass. First sound of roommates beginning to stir. Grey into yellow comes sky to the room. Each page, once tree, soon shall be ash. Leather chipping, flaking off the tatterd jacket. A woman who wears sweat pants. Detestimonialist. Don't sneeze on cat. Predictable boots worn by Frye people. Potholders old & dark. Ridges by bridges. Knife blade streakd with butter. That bus coming back this way. Rough surface of cat's tongue. Pin koans. Clutter of seeds, oils, spices atop the side board. Uganda Liquors. Pedestrians scamper across in the sun. Stake each sentence out. Call this 5 Corners. Knot this knot. Ball bounced into the panda plant. Cups fill the cupboard. Aliens from other planets are perfectly visible. Tamal is a half-name in the place of the name. The squeak of faucets. I was on the road discoverd. Ash "tray." Yellow caterpillar tractor. Ashtray fills up. Waking is in each instant I am. Across, then down & across. Her tone to him thru long years of rough intimacy was at once tender & gruff. Begin each letter at the top. Not this. Pit bull's spittle as it snarls. I saw a burgundy filling the clear vial at needle's end, my blood. Liquid detergent. Ing the trap bears ed. Roach holder made of a matchbook. She never lookd this way, whose face I sought a glimpse of. Free write each day. My fingers counted between nine & eleven. Any symbol is a contrary seen in a positive light. A specific shape, complex & nameable, to each cloud. Sky pilot. Factory filld with sunrise. Scraping paper, leaving tracks. Forklift to timeclock of montage & cut. Call this tracing. 3 wooden rainwarpd chairs in the (back) yard. Fence is a verb. Scratch that. Each word in Max 3 meant polis. In the mind mines gape. Tell that to the Possum. Words tried to imagine. Coffee ground spilld on the stove top.

Bare nap rugs on the cat. Mouth open, take a deep breath, say Ah. On the far gray bay side haze hued the hill. Rush of footsteps upstairs. Bathetic. In a middle that is not yet the middle. The mock coolness of the air-conditiond underground. Hours alter colors of the page. Grease sizzles, spitting on the stove top. Words vary. Swam past sand sharks. An idea of land's end. Pale luncher. An eternal groove around record's center. 4-tunneld city & 7 its hills. Owl light. Impaird eyes, desert rocks are attributed evenly throughout the pain. Red water. We saw on the sea sails. Stoppage makes the line. Translicity elects the voice. Cowabonga. But you dependent for what comes thru. Call it dogface. Know all blame, same difference. Doors "ajar." I glimpse the machinery of the modern dentist thru windows. Pills on my Tarot. Shade throws the light lamp. Pacific Palisades. Write between light green lines. Beer in waxed cups. Noon's rise mooning. Someone must make awnings. On the bus home from work, squinting at a thick printout. On a bus in dawn heavy fog, on my way to meet Taggart. Smouldering sienna. One ideogram, meaning lunch, middle or China. The familiar smell suddenly of balsawood & Testor's in a hospital corridor. My nose, seen as a waterfall. Disfeel an ease. Cary Grant on the face of George Washington. Or the faces of watchers thru a window at sunset, their skin blue by the dim light of the telly. Once on the bus, took his shoes off. Detains, denotes detonation. His eyes enlarged by his glasses. I was unable for an instant to remember—how put change back in pocket, how pick up bag off of counter. That this is not readable misses the point. Not (not-not) nor not-not this this. Firestone. Crystal in window refracts the sun. Horizon, horizontal. It starts to set in the north. A salt flat is the most basic condition. Gongs out of ploughshares may be touchd without being playd. Rain coats the pavement. Contain within the reddest trace red blue. Limitless ooze in left nostril. Stale taste of first cigarette each morning. Words fossilize on the instant of writing. Metazoans untied. Meaning is like light, its day passes east to west. The true type depends on the length of the size. Bottle caps & scraps of gum. Of by that under to the this of into then not. Beaver fedora made by

Stetson. Mourns morning. Isogloss, no, idiogloss. Lure or break. The body is a garden. The room of flies filld by buzz. Yoko. Outwards what tear. Cro-Magnon profile. Holes in the center of Chinese coins. In spite of that white cane, I see him watch me. To the thick (poised open) lips, ginger oysters rose between chopsticks. 3 women wearing aprons. Wood matches fill the blue glass ashtray. Make a note of it. 9 crystals are all elemental structures. The tension reveald in the back of her hand, wch she leans, rests, on. Each mask is a statement. Shaped canvas, pulld over the skull. Dust hovers down into the helicopter. One sits with spine straight, the other hunches forward. Script scrawld this. From the ceiling hangs a cord, from the window, the tip of a metal ladder. Cheese for the blue weight. A finger touching the cheek means listen. Salt motor boat, Twenty Languages. Holding the sphincter, releasing the bladder. One days weak as to the no of the agree. Listening to the dance, not watching. Deposits made in the cloud bank. Sun behind the high rise. Thirty 2 times two to the 4th power. A museum for words. Over the docks belchd black smoke of a structural fire. A woman whose nose has no profile. We are leaving the regretful forest. Longer is thinner. A string net bundle of groceries. I hear Chinese nightingales. Meet her face, miss her. You don't recall having lit this cigarette. Sodalite exchanged for lapis. Myrna Loy scrunches nose. Moon begins anew to rise. Treble in one line foretells terrible in the next. Cool thought kindled coffee. Letting the truck roll before starting the engine. Drops curtain the applause. Holds onto the bicycle tightly with her thighs. Me in too general yes. The black man with tattoos. Back into the stomach of the elf went the clock in lederhosen. Keeping the stroller from rolling on the bus. Set certain sentences off, set others aside. Surrealism is disproved. Chiropracticality. The lean of books on a shelf. Mr. Heckel & Dr. Jive. One is, was isn't once. Few furnishings. As was, wasn't, be came. Backwards into the station snakes red hook-&-ladder. Here was first, but here. A page streaked by crayola sticks. An other is among others. Like radios of radios talking to radios. Head, pelvis, spine, in a line. Each word of another once the invention. Objects symmetrate in the mind. This dark veil serves as glasses. This room (around) surrounds one. One door demands another. Vibes echo off windows, walls. Strung from hidden wires gulls fly. All this & this too. Bowels over lower bowls. Wall paper demonstrates peeling. For "wife" read "wive." Door slams. Hugs come. Chair will topple if pushd. Flows of time pour forward from the past. Spoon drops onto linoleum. Strip set sun sit. Taking steps taken back. In the flatlands vast vats of waste water aerate by the bay. One is because began caused beginning once again is once. With holograms no true color. All extents & purposes. Having to think out how to walk. To talk now in words from mouth. Thermal, Tamal, tulis. Down in her mucklucks. New odor of fresh dung. Our roses are not Greek roses. Where is the cross lines this. The impersonality of the motel shower. They slap the side of the bus as it pulls away, having faild to catch it. To leave a moving vehicle, leave running. Hypersocalldspace. Here now the news. Light purple tam atop an old, bent-over, Chinese lady. Downtown it's hot as the Mojave but at the beach a thick fog chills all. Mastodons trip in the pits, drip tar. The way some men browse in hardware stores. Heart shaped tin tray gathers ash. They have to patch the infant's eyes shut before they can turn the "billy" lights on. These generators let gestures. A glass of fresh water thrown into the ocean quickly loses its integrity. On buildings shadow buildings. Orange decor means fast food. Accidental industrious orphan. It's the firehouse is burning. The lines about swimming mean sex. In summer, letters are more scarce. Driving is much like tennis. Whenever I sip, the air & carbonation rush up, away from my lips. Spine formd of fire escape. That was a terminal concept. Orgasmic slam, like the dunk. In the wind a cigar will continue to burn. Drunkt. All odors out of seven variables. Move in slomo we saw it, try to. Sitting, to shit, pull shirt tail up. Gray flagpole against cream stucco has no depth. Who broke the moon? Heads go in the cell & flicker out. Either way Pound comes out to be my grandmother four times. Countless in that sandle I saw toes. Sisters show same features reach new totals. Sky of zoo caw. On the bay masts sway. Atop each tall building a radarlike transmitter. Recording in the studio means play guitar sitting down. Trans itbay. Seaweed in the salt foam. Less is the word & more. Wake of a white yacht. The foot of history. A disease of the gums recalls the body. Sluglike fogbank heavy on the beach. All birds fly in one direction. To make quick phone call stop car. A tampon & milk cartons floating on bay's water. Learning to read does not stop. Joggers shouting at pigeons. Hyper form. Sails slack await wind. What befell the C. Turner Joy? On such days, sit upon rooftops, clothes off, sip beer. Read scales down & up. Antiphonal the fox is false. Not this. The weight upon the postman's shoulder, blue shirt, pith helmet. Were words already in the paper? Stooping to slip mags thru a mailslot. Some are without sun, summer with. Old men in a sushi bar talk horses. Like white I space. Cafe brunch, sausages & iced coffee. Tons of yellow tractors, towd by a truck. No day without its mark. The way ahead, plotting. Light filters in a fern grove. Landing instrument. Odors of eucalyptus, pine. Clarinets flutter. Brown layer of twigs & fern dust on the glade floor. Boar hair bristle brush. Rush of traffic scatters gutter's papers. "Press" sez toilet's handle, metal button. That cane not as an aid in walking, but against the possibilities of urban life. Less angles in the letters I used to write. White tennies gone gray. Congas in the modern night. This shop will be on vacation. Fear cans of beer. She has to pull herself onto the bus. Light changes on the green steep slopes of the hillside behind fog means sunrise. From his sleeve hung metal hook. Small & pen-like, to apply design in wax. Jaw's motion, as she chews a stick of gum. Cut. Shaking the beer can to gauge what remains. Whooping amid wild gestures, gesticulations, he stumbled about the intersection, blind to the morning traffic. The uniform pressure of photocopy. After walking, pain in the lower calves. About a flagpole pigeons gather. Chips at war. Empty fishbowl water stagnant. Sadly we set forth toward the conclusion of the river. Each face forms around its own asymmetry. If no sideburns, then a hairpiece. Holding pen down, veins at the wrist stand up. When we go to where clouds are, they're too thin to see. New laces, to tie new shoes. Industrial whistle meaning lunch. Is

Ponge here? Diamonds in the quips, players in the blood. "Nixt" the teller hollers, meaning next. There are near clues by. A peculiar excitement is felt for summer rain. The ugliest mansion in each major city, French consulate. Our form does not yet exist. We stroll thru a rose garden. The moon stayed full for 3 days, followd by lightning. Nor that either. Call me Baba Lou. Architect renders a rest stop. We saw ourselves driving straight into the storm. Tulis is not Tunis, tulip. Bright pink shopping bag, reading "Gump's." Shaking awake the brain. Tish. Mind each wafer was a meaning meant, a word. People struggle, attempting to shut bus windows. Fish imagines no water. One sees segments, slices. I surface at pool's center. This room, these people, determine these words. The dress shirt midway between lavender and pink. Her hair layerd, her eyes heavy. Warp taut while on the loom. Working in a restaurant just to get by. Sentence itself is each. Walking slowly home at dawn. Two 5's, one 9 & a 2. Not that. A nose that lasts. More cats with extra toes begin to appear. What writing writes. How one's arms figure in the dance. Ties dig. The language of lighting cigarettes. Wicked throw. One's time taken. Scratch that. Garbd in tennis whites. Keep moving. Her limp is a signature. Killd dressing. These recurrences were campsites. Burgundy suit jump. Shrill brakes grip hard, pedestrians leap back. Sun means no sky is neutral. The privacy of public occasions. Each must invent the world before conforming. Not this. Bags of groceries carried on the bus. Not that. In the panhandle, where life began. I smell cinders. A mist that sifts in the air, passing for rain. This was the hegemony of afternoon. The milk truck turnd over, its cabin crushd. On the street one sees windows, imagines thru them. The violence one feels, one's life described. Not that. One about a bit of under when. Cat pries the door ajar. Rub-on sticker rubbd away, letters linger, au. Steam from a full sink rises. Dry flowers in a blue glass. Kitchen table in electric light. Coffee in a see-thru mug. Paragraph like violence done to body. Boards creak, birds twitter, horns go off in the street, auto tires shush in the rain. Cat braces itself, hisses. Rockets at first thought to fall over. Ike's jack-o-lantern grin. The inability of many to accept their lives. What then? Excess milk in scrambld eggs drains off. These days are any. To look at the brown smudges on his t-shirt closely was to see the face of the polar bear. Shambling might get one there as well. Voices first, faces form. "Energy is moods." His eptness is in. One forgets, voice carries where others are not seen. Journal, our urn. Holding a match at the tip of one's fingers. Z-form, the rungs of fire escape connects landings. Downstairs, hushd voices, scurrying footsteps. day's rise raises eyes. In a crowd of listeners one moves motion, lights cigarette, opens beer, others follow, forms a ripple till silence settles. The somberness of red tennies in the dark. Begins in a room stanza. Calls size ambition but demands a specific relation, withinness. How force attention? This is the road. Not this. Rain stops at sunset, people emerge into night, excess nervous energy. A Chinese waiter quick with the dishes. Later will wonder what brought that up. The noise in chairs, of chairs. Glass is a conductor. Lampshade never precisely centerd. Jaw begins by ear. Tear streets up to alter habit. Oregano & dillweed is daily information. Neck at certain angle means listen. A way of rolling sleeves up indicates class. One tooth you cannot bite down on. What brings that to this? Not this. Can you tell a writer by the length of their fingers? Window steams opaque. Smells: wet pine or wood smoke. Above, painters on a scaffold brush library windows yellow-green. These cars are the vocabulary of traffic. Fire's smoke soakd up into fog's cloud. Clerks in an elevator exchange chatter. Television camera jocks mill around, idle in station windbreakers. Any city built of electrical wires. If it carries a map, it's a tourist. The particular vulnerability one sees in the eyes of a woman as she emerges from a restroom in a public place, registerd as hostility, the glare. Newman—"the stone is a piece of paper." The uniform stern houses of the mining town. Prose is what you do with a typewriter. My name is Jack Hammer. Steel trapdoor in sidewalk opens to reveal store's basement. Fishkites whip in the noon breeze. How we are who we are. Sit at a bus stop in sun, drink beer from a can in a sack. Cigar smoke encircles head. Sun on one ear, the other in shade. Fading signs in appliance stores.

Plastic flags—red, white, blue—on radio antennas (antennae) in a used car lot: no negamos credito. Is this a formal vocabulary? Lexemes of an afternoon. What then? A black Volkswagen without fenders, muffler, roars past. Women holding handbags must bend their arms. Shopping bag from which egg carton sticks out. Old red newspaper truck. The champagne of beers. Meaning ekes out. Pinball lizard. The morning of mark-ups. The way fingers half curl in sleep. Specific heights. A point to a word, words? The muscle of gut knotted. Predictability to craft or as consequences haunt? Thot to make letters stand for. From the air that segment of the bay is red squares. Against the entropic body, thrust words in air. As if to state the universe in sentences. The loud grind of the rotating dryers, the inevitable bad ventilation —the laundromat. This was the winter without weather. Each door hinged inexactly to its frame. Someone must have thought play gray paint "prettier" than wood. Quickly one gets to the consequences, choice narrows down. Jerry walking backwards straight to the new. Collage fails to abolish illusional gestalt. These are not samples. Hard edged as the hedges of a ruling class garden. This bristling. Never have learnd just how long to wear my trousers. What salt air wind does to house paint. Shatterd windows, antique chandeliers. A habit out of mineral water. Chippd dime. He purchases time as others do socks. Crushd cigar box. Row of chartreuse top-loading washers. Summer with no heat. At the edge of each medium lies theater. In the era of micro-waves lipstick got redder. First milk bottles disappeard, then Tootsie Rolls. Drawstring pants were then in fashion. Freak storms causd airplanes to meet unexpected mountains. What you learn about others as they do their wash. I found myself missing the delta. The asphalt came right up to the linoleum. People wore their hair as if they had just been swimming. All conversation seemd to be in the middle by the time you arrived. Punctuation limits the conflict of words. All lawns had begun to grow imperceptibly quicker. Dogs were more easily provokd. Even newspaper headlines began to look like hieroglyphics. It was more difficult to climb the steps to the house each day. The rhythm of consonants had begun to sound like primitive drums. The whimper of vowels was intolerable. The neighbors' salsa was constant. You took to the street.

Pestilence. False start. Someone went thru the building, checking each door to see if it was lockd. Circadia. Blue patches began to show up between the pre-dawn clouds. True start. Colors seemd cleaner. Apple awes ability. The dog sits & extends a paw. A runt around a rag of ruses road. A wreckingcrew way of writing. Ate by gum chrome. That one lived in an abstraction, call it egg nog, call it art. Over the destroyer & amid puffs & bursts of anti-aircraft fire gull-jets swoop, then rise, droplets of bomb plummeting while the audience whoops & cheers. When I lookd again, I saw the old museum guard was holding onto a lollipop. Sand & logic to the quick. Toxic smell of new paint. Plots the poem. Blur roar proposed as speech. Not this. Almond chicken, beef in hot sauce. An indented serve. We run into Lewis in a new multi-colord knit cap. Mood pleonast. Larry categorizes saxmen by richness of tone. Posable thumb. Flammable means im. All sleeps tuckd in the cat legs. Each imagines what the other means. Man day billited. Deep space of postcards. Nor that either. "I am here where I am & that's fine." Cumulus issue calld counsel. He wants clothes at all times without color. Upside down from the ceiling a table lamp hangs, mock chandelier. Photographs of objects I have no words for. Scription. Dried flowers in an old cup. Forward inch planarians. One of several types of quark. Lady eat fingers. The idea that type has a face. True pink feathers. This is how the painted desert came to be. Tmesis to me is this. But this is not this. Books bought burgled back. Ciphers & cinders. Roller is coaster knot. Calls the ivy creeping Charlie. Lava in the blood. Cat with a bear face. Larva in the blood. Each new blank page like the ridge above another valley. Water what wld be was. Behind the piano hides a tiny sculpture. Reading the dance of my hand. Reality no touchstone. Bone whistle. Goy will not understand an amulet. Never met all the brothers & sisters. All subjects resent socio-interpretation. Write I cld barely wld. Shrink row. Brown, white, green doors all along one wall. What makes them pick you out as the one to hassle. Elusions allude. Blue skateboard, red wheels. Grips this. All the cardboard one sees in the streets. Name dusts. In uniform, heads individuate out. Last week was that weak. Reading sounding, you translate, inject & find familiar eyes staring back. Not easy. Nor each. A pie square. I think here. Ochre butterfly atop the cream concrete. Screen doors banging in gray dawn wind. Foot falls on the stairs to the back porch. GPO OM NEW YORK, NY. Pyro demons might technic. Thot will not stop, will not replay. Mode new inserts. Bowl of plums by a bowl of flowers. Kinda sigh lens. Pulls long red scarf from ear. What then? One hears not wind but what it touches. Each charge is radical. Being letters together. Phone dial, spinning, spinning back. Fish kite means first-born. Not so. Not exactly. Air is sewn. Means son, first-born. Photon. Dare to be simple. Milk of Melanesia. Mute hand moves, leaves thot's tracings. Particles avow. Prisms hang spinning slowly in the bay window, in the sun. Milk of am knees ya. Spaniel gives a grunt. Tends eggs. Rainbow crossd my page. Vertical warp, weft horizontal. Orange-yellow flowers dying in an old beer bottle. Ekes acts. Sun's warm on the back of my neck. Millions powerless, in the dark, Kit wanders about the airport. Window's edge marks the page, light's patch to form a wedge, the line between shadow soft, not drawn. Deep sent. No such thing as postmodern. One's eye needle was a freak. One who writes by erasure. Pages the plough, plunders. Fly in sunlight shines blue. Any structure, cloth or fabric. Writing as writing, who will see it? Red reed as read. Whoops of distant children's laughter triggerd sudden recall of Tahoe summers in the 50's. Ronnie 2 Baad. No two engines rhyme. What then? I stood at the end of a long vacation. This sentence is another. Three 8s

in clear plastic holds beers together. Inn width. Two friends of mine, very different, in identical tennies. All life seen thru a speculum. A small can of Dutchboy paint atop a larger one. Slaps the panda. Socks present a formal problem. Tofu turkey trot. Shark rubbd wrong way becomes sandpaper. The far side of the green door is brown. Christmas decorations entangled in antlers. Direct sunset in. Candelabras disguised as cacti. Mean with a get tar fiddle. Type forms its own margin. Eye of thing like the shapes. The sociology of bed-clothes. "Don't all those staring penises like." Nothing to do but doing. The heavy breath of the tarheater in the street. A far jackhammer's gentle insistence. In tow the dojo goo. Child, I thought wind gauged earth's spin. Holes eaten in petal by the unseen. Ceremonial cannon echoes, two chances to count each out. Mojo soho dobro. Legs lookd tan but the face Japanese. Rough tough cough stuff. Man in a cowboy hat & levi cutoffs shouts into a public telephone. Here start found once. Heat's haze erases features. Roofers holler at foreman. Kids scamper quail-like. From a "dime" store a too-small sun visor. Information is what it does. Dry letters cake into words. The effect of the shadow of phone wires in daily life. Middle, arch, worm, hart. "Nature," she said, chewing gum. Dog plops on couch. I see a jetliner fly behind houses. Ray only bruise struggle fines us. Motorboat cuts white path in bay. Have herd. Head colds punctuate life. One, one not, one, two too. Small gray transformer atop phone pole. Sand buff grinder. Ideas form a paste. Fall spring back forward. The order of order. Types of pipe atop rooftops. Phlegm like Rockefeller has money. Mole's way, way in. Imagine all these cars mean people. Rust-proof brushing. Wind whistled over open bottle. Onion-build. Modern siren's multiple wavelengths. Sailor to have figured spikes into the sides of phone poles. Crushd cigarette filters in the clover. Only a memory now to which I give the term "blister." Pulleys on a roof lift tar. A proposition of stairs. Can you remember learning writing? Hoarfrost. For a second before it dries sun shines in the ink. Cats impenetrable to people. All this grass bends in one direc- tion. Trumped mutant. Shadow of my hand over these words. Paddles battle ball. Not my house I hope to wch sirens roar. Tether. Each word leaves a scar. Porpoise is the ocean's what? One sees anger shaking trees. Nod thic nis grete. A wooden dish containing four bruisd, rotting yellow pears atop the kitchen table. Be calm plex. Shredded wheat afloat in a bowl of milk. Plastic dinosaur tiny. Getting close does not mean reaching the other side. Gary Moore's crewcut, Henry Morgan's sarcasm, Bill Cullen's limp, Betty White's noxious laugh, Allen Ludden's dull glare, Jack Narz' slick, Gale Storm's name. Any term such as moniker stilts. What teaches each is just—politry. Periplum equals intrinsic form. Cameroon wrappd tobacco. Once-red flowers in the teapot wilt. Quickly rough waves move. Times changed. I stood out beyond fennel on an old chair. What then? In the bay cantaloupe halves "look like the moon." Constant oral habit. A southpaw line slants. Pepper mill. Chinese youth in North Beach parks. A certain precision bred by exhaustion. O'Hare airport bartender's girth. Bottle of olives. Pen strokes. Not this. Sounds mark the house. Held at an angle by an arrangement of thumb & two fingers. Over sleepers & sunbathers sweep pigeons. Too often the young mistake the condescension of elders for deterioration. About of bit a bit into part of a bit like. Kielbasa in a cafe in the plaza, cool constant tone of the fountain. Bread crumbs dry grass. Juggler on a unicycle circulates citrus. Stairs shutter, rattle groans. A certain expression defining tourists, uncomprehending gape. Twenty-one crosses, two bell towers, form the cathedral. This rhythm flattend by the presence of steel drums. Stiff friends with three necks. Pigeon's red "feet." Between grasses war is ceaseless. Parka of walrus intestine. Your own voice growing distant. Uncut blue so-calld dragon robe. Warm weather trenchcoat wearer. Gradually 'beads' of sweat greasd brow. Difference down. Wintergreen smell of urinal. Vest down. The hard edge of far things after a summer storm. Monoclinic. Gulls asleep atop untended motorboats. I cld see her walking in my direction. Again I came back to Twenty Languages. This hand long call. Galvanized smokestack. Cop porn. Distance gathers. His cow rustld like shirt sleeves. Forklifts cross a shipyard. Ladder by coming in. Neonatal. Whether jets divide the sky. Between twin antennae on a line hung a faded bass flag. Familiar voices focus party talk. Mocking hawking shrill call of gulls. Fart sore won. Helicopters like black bugs afloat in the air. Watching this Kit grins. Behind the breakwater swimmers gather. Ked fur. It appears to approach without getting closer. See friends hear

him read. Why crips "choose" city life. Bumbles. Joggers on the
water's edge. Each letter tweezd. That essence of syntax wch is
nostalgia. 55 figure(s). The small slender banana-shaped leaves
of the eucalyptus. Tho footsteps approach no one arrives. These
terraced houses once hills. Ah dear Bruce Charles. The vacant-
ness of any commuter campus on a weekend. Is kleenex a name
trade? Just who question what makes a month? It make it make.
Rat with mange scampers. At cup's bottom unpoppd kernels.
The social history of skirts. Mecca-tive. These words against
wind. Listen stare concentrate. Skin keeps me in. The new way
out stretches shoot. Having no friends his age botherd Jack.
Star. Call this hall Smith. So glasses don't slip, elastic strap. Blue
ball in the middle of nowhere, to assign all meaning. Listen if
it's speech. High city hillside. Writing shadows lightly. These
lines, furrowd, fill. Phlougher. Any semi-literate understands it
better. Rain makes lawn hose' shower bow. Grass blades dig into
my back. Stretches these lines in all directions. In the tropics
each large animal requires one to two dozen acres to survive.
Fingers each function. Settles into mulch, peat. Brain burns. In
a corner over latte rummy players finger cards, cigarettes in
saucers. Beneath fern, willow & nasturtium. Jerome, was it, first
to read without moving lips? How the Dutch think to spell. Page
fills the way clouds gather. Find nose hair drill. Children enter
to watch gamblers. I was, he said, just sitting there, pen poised
in air, his grin to grant permission. That full moon anxiousness
filld the room. The calligraphic in Stan writes from deep peace.
A tall wood walking stick bejeweld by a glass doorknob. To call
cats stage whisper. Familiarity in the eyes of a beggar. Executed
choice one. Acrid odor of cigarette filter burning. Jerusalem
artichokes, Canadian potatoes, scab grapes. Skirt curtain. Pall
bearers glance down. Four prongd snail head. In a light blue
nightie campd on the couch. Empty shell nobody home. What
then? Digests words. In bed with embeddedness. That stillness
at record's end. Mountstorm rain sutro. Not a laxative. I hear
faucets off. One steps into the irrevocable. Pool forth from tide's
edge crabs form. Two irreducible languages between wch we
quarreld. Bufflehead duck. Wore his glasses, nothing more,

wading into the sea surf. Commonly personal workers refuse
cannery death. An aircraft carrier surrounded by sailboats. Pull
jeans on, hear change in pocket. The solitude of the one clothed
person on a nude beach. Naps pend spit. Referential sentence
but deliberately obscure, concerning being whippd by lettuce
in a film calld 'sweet Lust.' An 'E' with whisky. Are colors true in
that period between sunset & dark? Writing of letters alterd by
ants. On the far side of the bay the sun was still up. At the Savoy
I ran into an old school pal. Reading rewrites this. The above
butch beadles. A light pink in the east sky just as sun sets. Muni
lurching forward bus. Then the hills go flat & gray. Print news
on elbow. Tattler tattoo. Sea wood bee wld. Profit is an asym-
metrical structure. Boiling a hum in water. Full moon red as it
rises. Several small storms were at once visible across the valley.
At dusk the east horizon is a rainbow, green, blue, magenta,
pink. Scribble. The democracy of porn. The braille world six in
dots. As days pass heat hazes the clear sky. Wind chimes turnd
cat's toy. Sudden heat in a cool climate elicits extravagant
behavior. Indicates blur gray detail of distant rain. As bus
emerges from neighborhood into downtown area the charac-
ter of passengers changes. Blank promise is all page. An old
man in a dark suit & jet dark sunglasses under a black fedora
eating a cheap burger at a fast-food stand. The crazy lady, her
silent man, their grim daughter, her freaky sons. Mustard stains
chin. This to crazy do. The inevitable bath powder odor of an
import outlet. An old discarded pile in the vacant weeds of
clothes of a lot. These blue stools bolted into the tile floor. Verb
any noun trails. That was my template. Strum our norms. The
blue guitar is tacky. In the mirror table fragment. Now you are
inside. Sighs of the thyme. Ketchup, catsup. Force shun infer
effect. Waiting writing. Idea do the ferry eye. Ducks turnd tail
up in water. Tiny appearances scar. Feathers blow about in the
sand. Low over roofs swoops borate bomber. His gesture is back
of a finger brushing under tip of nose. Giggle jury porns at
throat. Cauliflower farts. This cancels not this. The curve of the
crack in the windshield's glass. Ouija you wld? Fox-hunting
hound bags master. Just beyond clearing's rim stands a doe still.

Maté in a blue pot. Soft can contacts dissolve. The shadow of italics passes. Wrote havoc wrought home. In a dark blue suit but brown shoes waits for the light to change. Not to have ought. Victorian houses in a low morning fog. A bar in each town calld the It Club. The old woman on the bench dozes, waiting for her bus. Separates this 6, six. Four plastic milk crates in the street, to mark off a place to park. In with we were. I catch your drift. Are all words some language? A warm summer stillness in pine trees. Several many most. Crackd black pepper pops between teeth. Jots. Long green stalk of an avocado plant. As is as is as is. Dog sleeps where sun falls thru the open window. Chewing dry cereal sounds. Pushing carrots into the juicer. Affected effects. Chinese streets, narrow, sloping. This pleasure enhances drugs. I sit hunchd in a doorway while tourists pass. Red humus city of the room. Cigarette smoldering on a brick step. To dry combd hair back. Gawkery. Herd half humid. Later I see a long gray-white ash. Just who George set up. Around wch, the wet stain of tar. Rusty old hammerhead lost in the dust. Find somebody. Right into the binding, writing. Noses red with summer. From a nylon line angle clothespins. Not spin. Weaver. Ginger candy. Schooldesks in our day bore empty inkwells. All this carving not this. Friend infected by bacteria under foreskin. Under shirt & vest, I feel beads of sweat roll down chest. Green glass, broken grass. My reflection in store window across street. One example was this. Lap is a desk if I make it. Each bark on the dog starts to block. Alley shadows shift as sun moves west. Consonants count. Passersby eye this. Hark. Where poor people go to spend money. Not this. Membrance. Words wedge or the hedge, the bet. Mother as explanation sez "that's all there is to it." Pins cloth. A smudge on lens reshapes world. Drives debt notion. Storefront windows coverd with butcher paper, sounds of hammer & buzzsaw. Draftboard epic meets acid. Thus gossip bonds. Quake another these not houses shall survive. Dog left in parkd truck whines. Thinking feed cat. Vermont maple syrup over french toast. Fence leans wood in all directions. These curlicues add up. No brain edges this rough. Postcard weather. By markd siren tragic. After midnight man on bus falling asleep over newspaper crosswords. Ducks that fly to fail. I feel today. Ivy, dandelions, creeping charlie. Seashore smell of cocoa butter. See desert sea cite. Congas & radios punctuate the park. Kibbles. Black bee nibbles at clover. Around doorknob bands of elastic. Today's letters large & sloppy. Thru ocean's surface missile shoots. Fire sirens in all directions. Articles fiber forms. Congas & cowbells. Mind parabolic. Old red rowboat beachd in sand. It's up cat. Sleep in clover, wake stung. Set at 60 Harley down. Old woman sits shrouded in the sun. Not to not think impossible. Amid different musics. Is not narcissism ample? The way bees swing on flowers stalks bend. Don't toes go straight? Bird flaps wings furiously, then soars. After anchor weigh words. Dragonfly's four wings. Spicy. Thin band of white flesh across her tan back. See boot men. Kids battle with old palm fronds. A missile is molester. Kids leaping from swings at height of the arc. Sun cld cause all not to come up. False moves attest the rest. Good food wld. Bullhorn's tone but no clear words. Equal heads are all. All scouts wear scarves. Out of shell drips yolk. Lone red kite high in the blue air. Federales eat in Mexico. All this flat stuff. Lovers let. Book "jacket." Strange production of all needs is fresh. Jet & dragonfly appear to collide, slide by. Woman's face pale as her nurse whites. For a brief instant the lone cloud in the sky turnd into a rainbow. Sun lit the water's surface, beneath wch I swam, lungful breast-strokes. A second later there was no cloud left there at all. Constituting her assemblage. She walkd, carrying her sandals in her hand. Moon lit room light. I lie awake, hearing foghorns. Ump no pook—beware rubbish. Night sky is not without its changes. In the middle words differ. The taste one wakes with. Rope wire thread. These words jump around like fleas. The white church was no longer surrounded by green scaffolding. The soupy air of an indoor pool. Pass & traffic watches. Busdriver's lady friend rides along. Left left turn lane. Poetry—I quit. Not simple standing writing. Morning's glare as fog burns off. Arms on his dog like an infant. In coffeehouses I like to watch them write poems. Straight one spine walks. Smoking universal joint. Toward each sun bend sentence. The clarity of

[44]

fatigue. Proposition of hat renderd delicate by wind. Swift tufts of fog. A year later I recognized her blocks away. Boughs & eros. Remember your sleep. All of religion condensd into a single glance of a cat. Drawing itself, this sketches out. Beaus & errors. Nostalgia fills this weather. Not this. Zipping by, two small, silver, military jets. The sentence does not occur in nature, save as writing, tho something very much like it does. You were not lies hoped eyes. My sunglasses set forth a border. Beyond cargo-container-containing flatbeds a cyclone fence. A pen with a chippt-tip scratches badly. Fog to the west spilld over hilltops. Read as wld spelunkers their descent toward earth's hot core. Sun shines directly on one spot at bay's center. Unvoiced, becomes "pay," a whole other realm of speech. Add hand or tongue to eye, get mind. Word shuffle pricks ear. Hoss mans sea. Big dog sleeps in store's door. Above clouds planes are heard. True waking requires ablutions. Of west London. They will stand on the bus rather than sit beside me. Wax paper wraps fish stick. What did I just think? In under an of into by. Straw babies. Not this. Writing toward the stain in the page. Neck bobbing, shoulders go over spine like an umbrella. Anything cld get in there. Hot Mexican chocolate. Red chalk. To protect kids, cork where once door's latch was. People milling, waiting to use the john. Lights furnace up with a whoosh. Above the old Victorian an American flag whips in the drizzle. Sight ceases writing down. A glass of red wine wch, regardless of how much you drink, never empties. Eye blue skies. My body smells like cut grass. Plat sure forms a foam. Sun-crackd red paint table tops of an outdoor cafe. Run against the bus to catch the light. Swirls in a wood or glade of letters. Riding riding. Mutt stares wistfully at my iced cappuccino. Dots in air of heads of hair. On the screen one boxer was red, the other green. Forth this not calls flaws. All the psychology kept in. Boffo bopping. Ink sinks into wood pulp. Hydro light. Solitudinous. Any crafty glyph of word twists the ear. Air. Cross barefoot linoleum. Dogs got no place but the gutter left to shit. Injuns rave. All that structure behind billboards. Late light of indirect afternoon. Thought occurs in the whole body. Prose for whom context is not without. Fear governs the marketplace. Mantis, stop, the poor end of the power. The second week of September, 1752, did not exist. Cigar tips white ash. This was a kind of information. Far kites from places. A spill on the page that might be a word. Clothing's color depends on eye's hue. Gradual decay of penmanship. Shop shingle. The body leaves one no options. Not beards. Bad teeth means never forgetting them for a second. Anchord in the bay, sails down. Language drifts, ebbs. Between islands glides a chopper. Write in one's sleep. Huskies in the surf, romping after gulls. A bad bourbon hangover settled into a single infected tooth. Against belly, instamatics dangle, bob. The presence of the past calls forth nausea. Portly men, twiggy wives, towhead children run ahead. Each instant is an occasion. Cola flat in wax paper cup. Moonburn. Pigeon's grey neck shimmers green & lavender. Angles of the amphitheater. Skateboard-bearing children purchase chilidogs. Fog in the tea garden's pine trees. If pigeon sits, neck contracts. Catching tarantulas with Trotsky. Watching whitecaps beyond the breakwater. Storks, bills raised, gulping adders. Charter boats bob. A fever in the jaw, in the gums, in the left nostril. The quickest clouds are lowest. The bipolarity of walking. Tugboat's black smoke. Hangover like clamp on head. Current lifted the gull up, its wings out to ride it. Because she's leaving they reject her. When you see it, she said, it's trite. Nothing here I didn't know at ten. Fly balls eye. To have reachd out wld have complicated both their lives needlessly. Urinal cake deodorant. It was a dull pulsing pain that never went away. Is not reading speech aloud. The large old house stood empty. People imagine sitting down. Later I don't recall writing it. Water never the color of its own glass. Listen up. Room shaped by lamp's place. The discarded, chewd-into apple of life. The distraught tigers. The blimp floats over the city. In the tray, a fire smolders in the cigaret. The instant, mid-twilight, when streetlights go on. Over melting chocolate beer flowd down into the throat. Fever in the gums. Indoors move plants. Writing as diminution of a first idea. At the lens of his glasses concentration stoppt. We unpackd as quickly as we cld. Bowl's curve meets apples. Reading each other's work & stealing. Nether, neither, tether. Chronic time. Dimensions pepper shakers partake of. Tending themes. Lacuna coat. Fact is a made thing. Some feet in all shoes. Ideas pass hours. Mounters, guarders, harbors. Anger raises a golden wall. Ice bottle under brown plant. These gestures in the place of thought. Taken where the talk went. We blare with transistors from our stoop. The former ease of cogitation was difficult to recall. In my brother my own flaws sought a new order. Left in the rainforest of the bathroom. I crouch on the sidewalk to write. More than we know down are letters to write. Big hairy rats with dicks this long. Scratch, scratch. Eats like a machine. By day graffiti is. Credit Peg. Tonic wch gin what. Words, like a shadow, cross a stain on the page. All little faucets drip. Object constancy & the long distance phone call. To light is as language. Years later, to sit in this yard one last time. One had I sailor in foot's grave. As tho you understood every word. Anticipation dilated your eyes. You cld pick an ant up between your fingers without crushing it. In the plastic blue dish sat old soap slivers. Sky is in the clouds. Gums die back. An airplane heading somewhere high in the twilight. Always, in the vicinity of the doorknob, fingers print. Kerouac's distaste for the comma. The lift of any slow launch. If for instance we had learnd to write words from the middle. Too words several many. Awareness of muscletone is calld proprioception. Cut. Always we are suffering from this case of ourselves. But whether the plural term was rhetorical was determind by what it meant to sit soberly in the dillweeds at dusk. Wooden ladders ran up the sides of these houses. Cats kneaded the furniture appreciatively. Clouds seemd to smear up in the sky. Because of its distance & the intervening traffic the sound of their argument had the prosody of rain. The silhouette of an airliner threaded itself between the clouds. Twilight is the only true light. Now the orange cat stalks the snail. These were terms simple as our lives. Ambivalent too. His piano carried across the tundra. Himalaya cha-cha inn. When the pressure on the bridge of his nose was sufficient, it bled. Each cloud colord according to its height. Pipes alongside houses with no visible purpose. That was outside. Helicopters hovering above the nude bathers. Cauliflower & consternation. A bird with a toy whistle. My cat stares me in the eye & wonders. It was a type of music. But to each note a psychology clung. Mornings were no easier with the memory lessend. Suddenly, as the sky turnd a deep blue, the lowest clouds took on a golden glow. Letters were easier then. But it was like being around grandmother, waiting for the anger to reveal itself. It was entropy's hour. In the distance, the homey strings of firecrackers. Each dog identifiable as to location & pitch. Neighbors dragging garbage cans out to the street. This would be the last time they ate together. It was as tho the sky "was afire." Cats liked to wander about the rooftops. It is always nearly over. It is a sentiment with wch to disagree. Our voices dissipate at shorter distances each day. Random burst of giggles calld a conversation. As the tribe gathers night falls. Also cats walk along fencetops. Birds are closer cousins than you think. This was a series of disengagements calld poetry. One enters the form as into a village. The first law is that of surrender. The one in the yachting cap is calld chief. One cld catch a chill here & marry. Eventually the ice will join the drink. These were new toys on wch to chew. It was a special moment, his clearest writing & wld not last long. When the last light dies in the clouds night has fallen. I hear the dog collar (dog caller?), not the dog. When it gets hard to see you invent it. From the kitchen came the sound of a basketball dribbling. The turkey sat in the pan of its own juices. It was one of those shirts you own but never think to wear. What is the sound of water in a drain pipe? I write sentences. Beyond these simple houses the white city rumbles with decay. It is dark in the bushes. Blimps have become commonplace above our upturnd heads. Sexism is being less afraid of a big dog if it is being walkd by a woman. Just riding the bus entaild a massive effort. The sequence of pigeons in the eaves is intended as a message. Some of the finest poetry of our time has been written in a Donald Duck t-shirt. This we call parallel. Knowing the distinctness between seventh & ninth grade: fourth period means lunch. Saab story. Sonnets by guitarlight. A long spoon informs my frappe. Industry echoes. It is a salon too full of rich, slender young black women. Then it's not. The go players proceed silently. The spaniel leaps up into the leather chair. That you be correct is less important than that you be specific. Children resist logic, pounding on mother's shoulder. What then? This is a nic fit. The shirt settles lightly over the sunburn. We will remember with difficulty how it was spelld. Film cranes oversaw each intersection. When you come back later none of it's the same. That there are pelicans in Minnesota surpasses the imagination. It is a game children call four-square. A pleasant sort of numbness as prelude to feeling. An inexplicable pillar not at the center of the rotunda. While you read this you continue thinking, composing your own poem as you go. The blue light flickerd. It was a species that for centuries had sat in one chair with its hind feet raised into another, gazing into books. Somewhere heretofore unexplored. Thus it happend that we had enterd into an undeclared game with secret rules, whose payoff wld be unknown, tho specific. Birds hung in the trees like drops of water. Simile became a mask. Under the overpass was a tree with a door in its trunk. At the next table a couple sat arguing, in intense low voices, the role of the zodiac in love. In the background a ukulele gave way to vibes. Perhaps somewhere it was morning. These were false assumptions. This was bebop. His eyebrows converted into accent signs. Saxophones sigh. It was time again for the busboy to move around the room, gathering in the debris. There was a dispute as to what was psychotic. This was the reason you cld catch a line drive in foul territory. & what did that mean? Not this. What then? Telephones rang above the music. A waiter paged the name 'Crystal.' Soon it wld be modern. You will be prevented from running for office. This was only one-half step from the fortune of a Chinese cookie. One time the letters will slant, then later they will be straight & slender. You have to cancel. She has to steam broccoli. The rain falls at an angle. This brings to our attention a sequence of 'A's. Later he will change this, or he already has. The kind of person who brings his sleep-ingbag with him into the cafe. Dogs mill at the door in their banishment. She said, "I have a morbid fear of buses." He said,

"Why don't you sit down." This was in the middle. If the woman carrying the nursing manual sits opposite you at the table, this is a warning, but will you know it? What are rosehips? Even the drugs in our time are poisond. Each is a context as well as the subject of one. Travel traces the self across space. There was no one in the room not listening to one another's conversation. But May is the cruelest month, if you think carefully. Mixing acid with speed, smack with strychnine. This was how we came to free ourselves of literature, that we might resume writing. Boats heaved about in the storm. The children pedaled home. A page was turning, revealing a calmer, blanker time. It raind all night the day I left, the weather it was dry. He cld feel the damp dawn chill on the page as he wrote. Morning surrounded the house. Her trip left him immersed in solitude. The cyclamen bloomd in its red way. These are not solutions. It was like trying to find the word wch has somehow slippd your mind. Each street had a uniformity that was submerged in the symbolism of shaped trees. You cld see Lewis on his porch, shouting at the coyotes. There were telephones in every room. Gradually night streamd into day. How soon before the new world bobbd into view? Sitting on the damp steps finally soakd in. He reminded himself why it was important his shoelaces match. These instances seemd almost too far apart to bridge. One never saw a clothesline pulld exactly tight. Jays chirpd. He thot of television antennas as hands reaching out. There was a place north of here where they grew right out of the ground. So there wld be no mail today. Nor any predictability in spelling. Jazz of foghorns filld the bay. The whoosh of cars. The round leaves of nameless bushes. Not this. What then? The tomato plant dying back into the compost. An uneasy truce between cats. Cartoons seemd more accurate than the news. I sat on the edge of a foundation to a long missing greenhouse & wrote these down. There was dillweed & berry vines. Ivy coverd the east fence, nearly pulling it down. Poppies shot thru a pile of rock. The landlord stood at the door, twitching in anger. Even the revolutionary word, if it revolves, will have a reference. This is memory's role. This is what coffee does to your skin. When it rains the skylight becomes a waterfall. We sat around the kitchen table, laughing & smoking this pipe. The pen's shadow writes these words also. Scraping at a limit I cannot break. The rustle of birdwings. An albino cockroach we playd with for awhile. The sound of scissors cutting yarn. This passage is like a vacation. This enclosed porch-on-stilts will fade from my mind. Was this the tunnel that led circuitously to the center of the earth? Had they discoverd literature lockd in a buried chest? Cats rubbd up against their legs. Look closely & you will see the scratches on this lens. They cldn't. Distances extended. The grey patch on the horizon was the Salton Sea. The shadow before them was their own hand. This is ocotillo. These chairs meet a function. Walking, as tho that solvd life's problems. So one writes to discover who is doing the writing. & these connectives are less a style than pointers in that direction. The wind rises as the sun sinks. Here the ocean is like a pool & the swimmers wear red-orange caps. A shovel slants, forgotten in the garden. This then was nearly the bottom of the thing. But the problem was you cld not stop. So it escapes you. If only for once night wld hold still. Against your flesh the feel of new sox, new shorts. Light remains only in one corner of the yard. The blight in these trees is cultural. & tomorrow there will be a new job in a windowless basement room. You find your friends phoning less often. All this seems a bit much for just an ingrown eyelash. From here you can hear the cannons. Leaves are beginning to clog the gutters. Either we are at the edge or the middle. Amid buses & bustle, the fog burning off diffusing light, the withdrawn glances of people barely awake yet on their way to the day's labor. Thus paths crossd still another time. These eight trees grew sullenly in the shadow of the law school. His beard had the natural attribute of appearing trimmd. So she read her works quickly & "not without cause" he murderd his wife. This was this is. As if it was the building that cast its shadow. Cars adhere to the code of traffic. No birds colonizd this grove. There was time yet. In the distance chatter appeard more substantial. You shld not stare into the eclipse. Mirrors mean nothing to the pets. This is where Curtis works. But timing makes all the difference. I had determind to become invisible & I very nearly was. We stroll these streets deep in conversation. I am no less a stranger here, "turista." One stands naked in a three-piece suit. The saxophone lists the sentiments. This is the cat's meow.

Then it was the tide's turn to turn. Not this. Retracing my steps in the dark. Downward momentum presses out. The old men sleep on the Civic Center lawn. Several tiny lips on his upper cut. This was a new, more confusing time. Wash waders. A row of flagpoles without poles. Yankees out late too. A banana bruisd into sugary pulp. High up off the floor in motel rooms the beds are disproportionately large. Different hands for different glands. Handle of a small white plastic fork that ends in "golden" arches. These are the metaphysics of morning. Forcing self to it one. One & many. The small distinction between crayons & cigars. Shit is a toy. Vest croations are lessend. This red journal fading into black. Red sweater forgotten on a blue chair. Shit is a weapon. Reading read into. The morning is the magician. Sink's drain netted residue of watercress. Take brunch in the cafes. Hill of fog between slices. People take this as behavior. Never completely dry hands. A fly beside the coffeecup. Pen it wld be with new blue. Snow in Cullowhee, autumn in the park. Was light. Wind penetrates this sweater. Not not wanted is not not-wanted. This hill on wch I so often sit. Kitsums. Hands smear these words. What than? A little cloudy here, as befits the occasion. Brain regrets what body formembers. An old man in a baseball cap, pushing a bicycle up the slope. This knot this. It was October, meaning eight, the tenth month. Off officer duty. Somebody wrote me. Given self to won it. This is a pilotlight. Sees thru blouse bra strap. All good writing approaches sleep. Time catches sky lapse. You almost think you know it. Sees can these. We have faild to change the record. Find around town roads. Two & two forms the next highest number. Flowers in the shade fade. Gas heat dulls one. Gray roils cirrus deep. He was it. Even the freeways weave. It seemd to wear a copper bracelet. At of about to into under to by—in within to which whereas of what— above without into under by of about by out. I was written. Wire mesh library windows. He only liked large plants. Wind the palm bent. A row of flagpoles without flags. Sun where the red hills has yet to set in the distance. This dance. Flesh as one grows older gathers at the elbow in folds. Rimes orange with chimney with month. Darkens as city lights appear. This pen point is a blade. Pyrotechnics replies wore. I call this flowerlight. A sky blue box by the pink toilet filld with tampons. The solitude of the only dog. End by the table on the fridge a blender. The sun looks over my shoulder. Tail red lights free around the night sweep way. The hinge of this door 'mews' as I shut it. Fly mapping room's air bangs against windows. I am alone here now. At the 5 Cooks Cafe, coffee. Counting the airplanes in the sky. Writing hands. In this way history repeats itself, always new. Sax solo. The ungainliness of the language angles this. Words have recently been removed. Flushing halfformd shit. Towels on a door on hooks. Not this. Rockies group out of piles. All these false starts. Hanging from the high ceiling (never used) of the yellow room, tassled green shade over a lamp. & then went down to the ships. An accidental chance is not order. Chamomile as if with a 'K.' Cigar's instant is for a tip orange. Water is boiling by mistaken design. Hyphenaterialsclerosis. It figures. In clear nets. A one-legged man at a pay phone. Hung on the abalone wall. First aid kind of bandage stuff. In slides trombone. It's only one out of I don't know how many. Cigar water sips smoke. Who's they? Peg calls. Studies in the American brain. Self what who holds truth to be evidence. These days the weather seems meticulous. Chairs on cats asleep. The order of plants in the forest is the inverse of architecture. In a mineral glass bubbles water. In a pistol we have the perfect machine. Unable to tell black pen from blue late at night. Thus the further from home we get, the larger it looms, reeking of roast beef & scotch broth. Each new mark is a place. This is the tundra. Chortles, guffaws. That is the roar of a garbage truck. This being begun beginning was again. It is not easy to find your way here without the trail of crumbs. Old bath water contain in a green plastic trashcan. You don't hold the pen so much as pinch it. For incense with cloves stick an orange. Some sentences carry literature within them. How in the 50's he draind those around. My name the pejorative. Boogying for quests. How does one mill steel? Cast cause shadows depth. Although this noise was new to us, we understood it to be music. We under gold delight gorged to heart's arches. A shit that takes for hours until ass & legs are numb on the edge of the now warm porcelain seat. Whispers in the room next. The blind woman in the library. Won seams scene. This is not thought. He was in the army when. Language was like light, coming into existence all at once, but now it is like some other 'thing,' detaching limb from limb, as if the sun had turnd to charcoal, cold chunks dropping into the sea. Point not ink but pulls the page. Such solitude, tho not by choice, proved good. Griddle brick burgers grill. Each morning he mounted the page. Moloponius, poloponies. The bow on bough was a razor drawn over the strings. Agh—palm slaps brow. This was the probation of stones. Rust sea at city side. Rust tea cups. Glue-all. In the dream the house means the rented self. Breaking blue late patches into noon after clouds up. That wch is straight forward draws blood. Heat spacer. A perfect copy of a roll-top desk. Writing around the pigeons gathers. This was to be the day. Uranus leads to this line. A woman in a blue nightgown raises her shades. Send us nuns. These words fade from as I write them. Blue fork upon a chippt silver plate. Wondering whether he & they or they & they ever were lovers. I saw pillows bag in the sleeping Buick's back. After the bourbon's gone, continue to drink the melting ice. The hum of refrigerator's companionship. A nostalgia in the odor of Melba toast. Beginning is this begin I again not. Coherence in contradiction expresses the force of a desire. Coffee mug tall as salt's shaker. Chance will never abolish a throw of the dice. Orange dented Opel's fender. We were waiting for the phone to not ring. Gay drawn. Fridge rattles with electricity. Brain on the falls rain mainly in the Spain. Carolyn Hall & Mary Korkegian. On windows back door smudges forming fingertips. I recognizd the voice but cld not name it. Gold-leaf reads x-ray sign on the glass. This is the economy of alphabets. First stir of roommates beginning to sound.

Imagine the world in wch butter knives are possible. Room to the sky comes yellow into gray. Matinee. Each ash, once page, shall soon be tree. Words ebb on a line. Jacket chipping, flaking off the tatterd leather. Weaving the world in one's spare time. A sweat who wears woman pants. Salt shakers in the form of running backs. Detestimonialistical. Roar of jets in an empty sky. Cat on don't sneeze. These flaws are the law. Frye people worn by predictable boots. Writing on the can. Old potholders & dark. Why this is here. Bridges ridges by. She talks Strunk & White. Butter streaks knife blade, see? Thumb pushes crumpld tissue over ass. Bus coming back this that way. A surgeon to the page. Of cat's tongue surface rough. Having to be going. Been goings. An ashtray only atop the table. Atop the sideboard, clutter of seeds, oils, spices. So do it, so do I. You gander lickers. Many is the time. Across the sun scamper in pedestrians. Day breaks. Sentence each stake out. The shadows of people loom in their windows. This corners 5 call. In the ream of the senses. This knot this. Dark, crush: inch, obey. Panda ball bounced into the planet. Caffein tickles frontal lobes. Cupboard filld with cups. Dawn light in the bamboo curtains. Others from visible planets are perfectly alien. This is Tuesday. Half name of Tamal in the place of a false name in a bad place. Faucet's squeak. An engine turns over with chilld morning difficulty. Road was discoverd on the eye. The blue day before Wednesday. "Ash" (tray). Names a letter before L & M. Caterpillar yellow tractor. A dream of big trucks. Fills up the ashtray. Only what is calld can be recalld. Waking in each I am instant. A green chair in a cream room. Down, then across & a cross. Is that the end of the sentence? At once tender thru long years & gruff with rough intimacy, to him her tone was. Thus the memory of rocking chairs. Each letter begun at the top. The day after the white day. Not this. What then? Spittles a pit bull snarl's. A cat in the coleus. My blood I saw burgundy filling clear vial at needle's end. Clumsy coma. Liquid deterrent. Old lamp. Ing the ed trip bores. Involuntary seizures of the right eye. Match holder made of a roach book. The careful displacement of ordinary objects. She whose face I sought a glimpse of never lookd this way. High-heel footsteps on the sidewalk below. Each free day write. What it means to be in the Carolinas. My fingers counted between eight & twelve. Here was a city without pigeons. Any positive is a symbol seen in a contrary light. He wanted to scratch her beard. To each cloud a specific shape complex & nameable. No end to this writing. Pie skylet. The noise of water as it boils. Sun with factory filld rise. Rules are made to be. Scraping tracks, leaving paper. Drinking the three of cups. Cut to timelift & fork-clock of montage. Steam falls. Tracing this call. Pills in mouth, forgetting how to swallow. In the 'back' yard 3 (wooden (rain-warpd)) chairs. An new. Verb was a fence. Will wld be was. Scratch that. Is a fence. Polis in each max word meant 3. Thus threedom. In the gape mind mines. What it is to do this on a rolltop desk as always I have imagind. That to the possum tell. Verb is in France. Imagind words to try. 3 my people. Stove coffee spilld on the ground top. An herb is in pants. Bare snap rug on the cat. None plus puss fuss football. Take open a mouth, deep breath, say Ah. Third as in fan sea. Haze on the far side hued the gray bay hill. See how she sits. Up steps of rush foot stairs. O posed to my picture. Bathetic. Wanting to get to the next page because. That is not yet the middle in a middle. Who slept on our front porch last night? The mock underground of the air-conditiond coolness. A small distinction between the popcorn pimps & the johns. Colors alter hours of the page. Cannot believe I wrote this. Stove sizzles, spitting on the grease top. Matriculous. Very wyrds. P(roof). Sand swam sharks past. Order argues ardor augurs. An end of land's idea. & an ideal lens. Pole launcher. Watching the cat dream. Groove an eternal around record's center. Until one day finally. City for tunnel & seven its hills. The back brain does all the work. Light owl. Rime soap. Imp or dice, dessert rocks or a tribute to even law throw out the pine. The resistance of wakefulness. Wed rotter. The Special View of Mystery. Sails we on the sea saw. Tricks of the morning. The line product of stoppage. Wet rotor. Elects a voice translicity. Reed waiter. Bowa conga. With her tongue pulls softly at his foreskin. But for what comes thru you depend. Rude wider. Call dog it-face. Harpsichord at one end of the flat,

boogie at the other. Blame all difference, same know. Many t-
shirts hang from a line. A jar doors. Adjourn the convening. I
thru windows the modern machinery of the dentist glimpse.
In the dawn light dust gleams in the air of the room. Bills on
my pharaoh. Sentences must be hard-edge. Shade lights the
throw lamp. Many dogs sleep on porches. Pacific Palisades.
Adjusting our eyes to the martian air. Light between green lines
write. Few chairs are not worn in the seat. Waxd beer in cups.
Tequila to kill the sensation. Noon's moon rise nine. A worm
floats in the glass. Make someone awnings must. The worm is
bleachd & dead. Home from work on the printout, squinting at
a thick bus. One hears diesel's whistle. On my way on a bus in
heavy dawn fog to meet Taggart. It is impossible to explain blue
eyes in nature. Smoking sienna. Gradually sentences shrink.
One China, meaning middle, ideogram or lunch. Often words
occur as fossils. Suddenly the hospital smell of testor's &
balsawood in a familiar corridor. You never write the letter 'o'
in the same way twice. My waterfall, seen as a nose. Half the
world in double-parkd cars, honking for the rest. This feels &
needs. I pop my knuckles for pleasure. George Washington on
the face of Cary Grant. Jack hammers signal day. On the blue
skin faces of watchers thru a window the dim light at sunset
of the telly. Many words move where thought went before. Once
took his shoes off on the bus. The model for this was art.
Detonation denotes detainer. Think of clouds as specific.
Glasses enlarged his eyes. He sat on a chair's edge to note that.
How up off counter pick up bag, put change back in pocket, for
an instant I was unable to remember. Letters are the shells of
insects. That this misses the point is not readable. Few glasses of
milk are completely drunk. That not (not-not) nor not (not this)
this. The asymmetry of a small dog leaping up steps. Flyer's
tone. I often forget what I am in the middle of saying. Sun on
the window refracts the crystal. I get dizzy at the top of a new
page. Her rising horizontal. A good reading exhausts attention.
In the set it norths to start. Many sit on the library steps,
mumbling the Bible aloud. A basic flat is the most salt condi-
tion. Processd steam billows out of the sewers. Touchd gongs

out of ploughshares may be without being playd. The jet trail rapidly diffuses in the sky. Rain means coat the pave. Some puzzle out crosswords. Containd within the trace red reddest blue. Slivers & fountains. Left limitless ooze in nostril. These weeds form a lawn. First each taste of stale morning in ciga-rette. Culture means fingernails can be clippt. On the instant of writing words turn to ash. Between my ears you can count the clouds. Metazoans tied. Often drunks attempt to warn us. Meaning passes east to west. I said this facing east. The length of the true size depends on the type. First he puts the nickel in, then he checks to see if they've chalkd the tires. Scraps of bottle caps & gum. Next door, neck store. That of by under to the then of into not. The street weeper. Fedora by Stetson beaver made. As caffein pours into the system. Mourning morning. Plants without names for them. Idiogloss, no, isogloss. Jellied seaweed curld around the chopsticks. Lurid or broken. Adore abide states & beef hermit. The garden has a body. The invariant char-acterization of a plane curve. The flies' room buzzd by fill. Tilting the clear glass skyward. Yoko. & a vector pointing to three-space. Tear out what words. Thought is embedded. Pro-Magnon crow file. Things being equal. Coins in the center of Chinese holes. The legitimate definition of dogs. I see he watches me in spite of that white cane. AKA. Between chop-sticks rose ginger oysters to the moist edge of thick open lips. Pacing is writing. Three apron-wearing women. Piano solo of the rain. Blue glass ashtray filld with wood matches. A chimney out of wch three pipes stick. Note a make of it. These days at Tom's house. All nine crystals are elemental structures. My sunglasses atop an envelope to be sent atop a green sweater upon the table in a room two floors above the street. She leans (rests) on the back of her hand, its tension reveald. An eggplant the size of crook-neckd squash. Each statement is a mask. Papaya pickles. Over the skull, pull shaped canvas. Photograph of your pregnant friend, wearing only a halloween mask. Down into the helicopter hovers dust. In a far room I can hear music & a hammer. One hunches forward, the other sits with spine straight. They seem to walk with jagged hurriedness. This script scrawld. What morning is to the cyclamen. From the ceiling from the window hangs the tip of a metal ladder cord. Dust on the window is the lens. Chew for the please weight. Thicker strokes of ink. The cheek touching a finger means listen. Tom clears his throat. Salt boat motor: Twenty Languages. A basketball left lost in the ivy. Holding the bladder, releasing the sphincter. Exactly like a beach. As to the no of the degree one days week. Shadows in that room mean people. Watching the dance, not listening. What seems possible in morning is not possible. Make deposits in the cloud bank. The far spires rise high over the near houses. High behind the sunrise. We live embedded in a curvd space. Thirty 2 times two to the 4th power doubld. Perhaps doubld. Words for a museum. The grain of this table pointing north. Black smoke of a structural fire belchd over the docks. Many believe fingernails to be an alien form of life. A nose whose profile has no woman. An ashtray unemptied for weeks in an otherwise meticulous house. Forest is leaving the regretful we. Once there, brush your hair. Thinner's longer. My home is my book bag. Bundle of bananas, oranges, cans in a string net. Tuesday morning. Hear Chinese nightingales. Morgan sips scab beer. Face her, miss her, meet her. Each must follow his avocado. Don't you recall having lit this cigarette? The lines in the air pull tight. Lapis switchd with sodalite. Kids hurl bottles at the side of the bus. Myrna Loy's scrunchd nose. Blue bowtie. Anew moons begin to rise. Hazel eyes. Terrible in one line foretells treble in the next. A crane constructs a fountain. Coffee kindld cool thought. It was not my hand that shook, but the page. Before starting the engine let the truck roll. State Office Building, S.O.B. Drop curtains the applause. Dried puke paints this street. Holds her thighs tightly onto the bike. Sheedy Drayage. Yes to me in too general to. No arm stuck out of that sleeve. The tattood black. Old man still likes to wear his hard hat. Back into the elf of the stomach went the clock in lederhosen. These strokes turn into words. On the bus keeps the stroller from rolling. Walks down the plaza with his hands forming fists. Offset certain sentences, set others aside. Man in a tan suit. Dis so realism is proved. Light in a moving object slows toward the red wavelengths. Chiropracticalamity. The disorder of bed covers. Of the lean books on a shelf. Pedestrians wait for the light. Mistah Heckle, Doctah Jive. Underneath the half-drawn shade, I see nostril, lips & jaw in profile, moving rapidly in silent conversation. One who was isn't once is. Language is our special doom. Few furnishings for such a large flat. Skillets, pans, pots hang in a line on the wall. Came as was be wasn't. Still photograph of a waterfall. Backwards snakes lemon hook-&-ladder into the station. Colonel Mustard in the conservatory with the candlestick. But here was here first. In what sense is this a ledger? Crayola sticks streak a page? What is your theory of morning? An others is among other. Tamara O'Brien calls to ask me what I'm doing. Of radios like radios talking to radios. A banal guitar makes the lyrics profound. A line thru head, pelvis, spine. A new page like an empty beach. Each invention once the word of another. The message of morning is morning. In the mind objects symmetrate. Scratch that. Dark glasses serve this as veils. What then? One room (around) surrounds this. Evidence where a thought passd. Demands one another door. A chill dawn. Windows off walls echo vibes. Pauline Oliveros in an auto racer's jacket. Fly gulls strung from hidden wires. Back roads to far towns. This & all this too. I write facing North. Over bowls lower bowels. Large dog climbs the steps. Peeling demonstrates wallpaper. Encoding the page. For 'wive' read 'wife.' Unpacking the sentence. If pushd, chair will topple. I am not embedded in a three-space. Slams door. Number of days it takes to cross the room. Hug comes. Pauline Oliveros in a tibetan hat. Forward from the past pour flows of time. So I watch women walk every wch way. Onto linoleum drops spoon. Powdered bleach somehow left spilld in the gutter. Strip sun set sit. Scraping words into dirt with a stick. Taking taken steps back. Jeans worn with cuffs rolld to show boots off. By the waste bay in the vast flatlands aerate vats of water. Shadows cross the windows in the dark rainy dawn light. Again because one is because began causd beginning once again is once begun. Even a large tree bends to the storm. True with no holograms color. Windows rattle in their framework. Purposes

& all extents. In an otherwise dark room the light of a color tv. Out having to think how to walk. Birds' flight in rain wastes no motion. Words from mouth now to talk in. Thus to define green, round, peachy. Tulis, Tamal, Thermal. The card arrivd from Tuba City. In her down mucklucks. Dental matchbook. Fresh odor of new dung. Several kinds of gyroscope. Greek roses are not our roses. Symmetry of the crosswords. Cross is where the lines this. The shadow of a neighbor stands in a window. Shower of the impersonality motel. Advertisement inserts in the Sunday paper. Having faild to catch the bus as it pulls away, they slap at its side. A small piece of skin torn on the inside of one's cheek. Leave running to leave a moving vehicle. Rain blurs an unclean window. Nonhypersocalldeuclideanspace. Noodles. The news here now. Naked at the window, a towel to dry her hair. An old, bent-over Chinese lady, light purple tam atop. The hurdygurdy of calculus. At the Mojave it's hot as the beach but downtown a thick chill fogs all. Phone wires sway in the wind. Drip mastodons trip in the tar pits. The aftertaste of toast. The way in hardware stores some men browse. The stain of water on the wood shingles. Tin tray heart shaped gathers ash. Say 'the dead' as if they exist. Infant's eyes patchd shut before 'billy' lights get turnd on. A loose football between the legs of grown men. Let these generators gesture. In the natural light of year's first storm. A glass of the ocean thrown into fresh water quickly loses its integrity. Who cld imagine her lying beneath that fat man? Buildings on building shadow. Bag lunch in a plastic bag. Fast food means orange decor. Style is territorial. Industrious accidental orphan. Fluorescent light glare of the cheap diner. What's burning is the firehouse. Up hours before out of the house to speak first words of the day. The lines about sex mean swimming. Lights of the office phone blink on 'hold.' Letters in summer are more scarce. This is winter. Much tennis is like driving. Throb of the space heater. Air & carbonation rush up, whenever I sip, away from my lips. I pace. Fire escape formd of spine. Fork rests on a plate where once food was. That concept was terminal. You can tell when water runs in other apartments. Slam like the orgasmic dunk. Sun shines thru cherry medicine on a windowsill. A cigar in the wind will continue to burn. All these houses with elaborate back porches not visible from the street. Drunkt. Hinged window banging in a strong breeze. Out of seven variables all odor. Red inner leaf of the coleus. Try move in slomo we saw it to. Pelicans seldom fly inland. Pull shirttail up, sitting, to shit. Yarmulke hangs on a door. Cream flagpole against gray stucco has no depth. Non-specific argument in a nearby flat. We broke the moon. The whoosh of passing traffic. Flicker heads out in the cell & go. You come out of the john & the sun is that much higher. My grand-mother either way comes out to be Pound four times. A small bowl of steaming rice. Countless sandal I saw in that toes. Boards, birds. Sisters show same totals reach new features. Morning cradles the numbers of light. Scaw kye of zulu. All that remains are puddles in the sidewalk's cracks. Masts on the bay sway. Chippd gutter. Radarlike atop each building a tall trans-mitter. Ethan shouts at Fred. Play guitar sitting down, recording in the studio. Motorcycle rider glides her bike slowly thru the streets. Trance aybit. Mustard jar full of pens. Weed in the sea salt foam. Look up to see hummingbirds on a phone pole. Less the word. More lore. White yacht's wide wake. Roofers unload rolls of tar. The story of his foot. To the west the sky is flat. A body disease the gums recall. Write this down in a red note-book. Foglike slugbank heavy on the beach. A smudge of grease at the left margin, a thumbprint. One bird flies in all directions. Junk language. Phone to make quick stop call car. Orange plas-tic ruler, metric along one edge. Floating on bay's water, tampon & milk cartons. Natural confusion of gulls. Does learn-ing to not read stop. A lawyer younger than I in a bowtie. Pigeons shouting at joggers. One after another, shades rise in the morning landscape. Form hyper. They hang pulleys from the rooftop. Slack sails await wind. What is sadder than a hook-&-ladder? What befell the C. Turner Joy? How does the spilld ink sort? Sit on such days upon rooftops, clothes off, sipping beer. Buckets of tar lift skyward. Reed up & scales down. Read scab. Antiphonal is the false fox. The nostalgia of clotheslines. Not this. Opaque glass of a bathroom window. Pith helmet, blue

shirt, the weight upon the postman's shoulder. The room of
numbers / is very old // & filld with mirrors / folding in on one
another // to form a book/of dances in the head. Words were
already in the paper. Birds twitter amid foghorns. To slip mags
thru a mailslot, stoop. The irreligion of a noun not rememberd.
Summer without sun some are with. Sentences recede the
instant you think of them. Talk horses with old men in a sushi
bar. The strain in the balls the morning after. White like I space.
Barefoot on a hardwood floor. Cafe coffee & iced sausages
brunch. The sounds from behind the bathroom door. Towd tons
of yellow trucks by a tractor. Shoes for a Shanghai peasant. No
mask without its day. This brings it all back. The way, a head,
plodding. I can hear the pen as it scrapes the page. Fern filters
in a light grove. The morning shouts of children. Landed instru-
ment. The first blue thru the fog. Odors of cypress, eucalyptus,
pine. The real hardship of any love. Clarinets flatter. Next to
Iowa is Minnesota, wch we do not believe. Brown dust of fern &
twig layer on the glade floor. Large stool in a small bowl. Boar
hair brush bristle. Reading the paper, sipping French roast in
the aftertaste of breakfast. Gutter's papers scatter in traffic
rush. Simmering soup steams the windows. Toilet's metal
button handle sez 'press.' I only smoke facts. Against the possi-
bilities of urban life & not as an aid in walking, that cane he lets
rest between his legs as he sits on the bus directly behind the
driver. Central City Service Station. Less letters in the angles I
used to write. As if a dance in wch two figures, moving sepa-
rately, come together. Grey tennies bleachd white. Spoon scoops
away bruisd parts of banana. Night in the modern congas.
Meaning scars speech. On this shop will be vacation. Cakes of
dry snot on the inside of the nostril. Beer cans of fear. Digestion
gonna kill me yet. She pulls herself up onto the bus. Sun shines
on the kitchen sink. Changes behind fog on the steep green
slopes of the hillside means its rise. Invoking counterfactuals,
we enter the realm of possibilia. Metal hook hangs from his
sleeve. The pulse at the base of the skull counts one & one. To
design in wax apply small & penlike. Have to have had. As she
jaw's motion chews a stick of gum. Rough stem of a 'spider'

plant. Cut. Ice thread of a jet trail. Gauging the beer can to shake what remains. Sun's first light is orange, then whiter. Whooping & blind to the morning traffic, he stumbld about the intersection amid wild gestures, gesticulations. I don't know why you insist. The uniform photocopy of pressure. Familiar twitter of an unknown bird. Pain in the calves after lower walking. Cups sit in the sink "soaking." Gather pigeons about a flagpole. The civilization of adolescents: low-riders sitting in a parkd car with the radio on. At war chips. The baby is on duty, that's stupid. Stagnant fish empty water bowl. Blue-grey & green-gray. We set forth sadly toward the conclusion of the water. Time is its own sound. Each asymmetry forms around its own face. Writing on the horizon line. If no hairpiece, then sideburns. A bird that sounds like a cigarette light failing to ignite. Veins at the wrist, holding pen down, stand up. Shadows of ferns as favord forms. Clouds are too thin to see, when we go where they are. & then went down to the shop, set key to deadbolt. Tie new shoes with new laces, faces. The scrape of a fork—man eats alone. Ponge is aqui. The total logic of fog. Industrial lunch meaning whistle. The body's inertia on a cold day. Blood in the quips, players in the diamonds. Demand each sentence be written. The next teller hollers meaning next. First she pens paragraphs, then removes sentences from them. By are there near clues. Mesmer. Peculiar rain is felt for summer excitement. Some eyes are windows, others curtains. The ugliest French mansion in every major consulate city. This room is organizd by a flowerpot on one corner of the desk. Yet our form does not exist. The sound of a fluorescent lamp. We rose thru a garden stroll. An apple is left on a table. For 3 full days lightning stayd, followd by the moon. A small white office at the foot of the basement stairs. Nor either that. Up is followd by the pressure of forward. Baba Lou me call. One eye on any side of the nose. Rest architect renders a stop. An old porn shop with the magazines wrappt in clear plastic. The storm we saw driving straight into ourselves. This is just one example. To us, tulip, turnip is not tuneup, tunic, tulis, Tunis. Hard & fast. "Gump's"—bright pink shopping bag. Apropos of opacity. Awake the shaking brain. Ears parallel to the skull. Tish. Imagine a gin image. Mind each meaning wafer was a word meant. Rash of flash cameras. People shut bus windows, attempting to struggle. In the early morning brain. Water no imagines fish. Words in a new house. One segment sees slices. At nine, it is nearly nine o'clock. At pool's surface I center. A hand reaches out to pull the door shut. These words, this room, determine(s) these people. Slowly, we invent the house. The lavender pink midway between dress & shirt. Lightning over Bernal Heights. Her hair heavy, her eyes layerd. The quantification of dance into figures of chance surfaces in time as a theory of rhyme. Taut loom while on the warp. A vessel in the jaw expanded to twice its size. Just in the restaurant to get by working. Excess milk in scrambld eggs means a runoff. It sentence self is each. Codeine knots the stomach. Dawn slowly walking at home. The organization of the beard. Five ones, nine twos & a two. There is no joke to the poem. Not that. An orange cat meows at a glass door. A list that knows. Western fog modes. More toes with extra cats begin to appear. Pour coffee into waiting mouth, warmth in the esophagus. Writing what writes. I can feel poisons in my blood. How one's arms dance in the figure. A little Cessna swoops by. Digs tick. Staring at last into the bottom of the glass. The lighting of language cigarettes. Pain in the jaw as a mode of law swollen with vengeance. Wicked throw, a mean curve. A wedge over traveld blotter. Taken one's time. Now where rain was, sun is. Scratch that. Slow forward motion of thought. Tennis garbd in whites. The way a gas flame 'pops' off. Move keeping. The reason of morning tilts. Her signature is a limp. That certain even sensation of body warmth meaning fever. Dressd ing kill. Thin glass of a bulb snaps under the ball of my foot, encasd in a shoe. Recurrent camps there were sites. Boy sits at a busstop, basketball trophy in his lap. He burden suit jump. The silent sight of Witnesses selling Watchtower. Hard shrill brakes grip, back leap pedestrians. The stress in the mouth & eyes of the family gatherd on the sidewalk in front of the mortuary. Neutral means no sun is sky. The bass in the stereo in the downstairs flat. The occasions of public privacy. From here I watch cars drive to the

top of that hill. The world must conform to each before invent-
ing. The type of the baskervilles. Not this. Cld familiarity of
mode make this problematic? Carried grocery bags on the bus.
Or is it too compositional? Not that. Word is the inverse of
number. Life began where in the panhandle? Toothache with-
out the tooth. I send smellers. To render a fixture a socket. A
sifting rain mist that passes in the air. You can see the electric-
ity sitting in the clouds. Of this, afternoon was the hegemony.
Call this score daybreak. The milk truck, its turndover cabin
crushd. Dial the weather just to hear a voice. One imagines
windows on the street, sees thru them. Sweater & fever to keep
me warm. One feels life, one's violence described. Small cloud
of fog behind the eyes. Not that. Fumbling with an umbrella at
a street corner. One of under when about a bit. There is such a
sentence F such that this is not it. Ajar door back pries cat. See
head as lump muscle. AU letters linger, rub-on rubbd away.
Curly Q. Rise from a sink full steams. Yo soy bean. Blue flowers
in a dry glass. On a postcard mounted on the wall by the sink
two fieldmice beneath a mushroom nibble chestnuts as a blue
jay looks on. Light table in electric kitchen. Sweet hominy. See-
thru coffee in a mug. An old nail sits next to a blue sponge.
Body like paragraph done to violence. Sun sucks the dew up.
Boards twitter, birds creak, auto horns shush in the street in the
rain, tires go off. Mind possessd of its own inertial, like time
stops. Cat itself hisses braces. Old red star. Fall at over thought
to first rocket. Speech reflects chromatic aberration. Jack's Ike-o-
lantern grin. Even now I am thinking something quite different
from these words. The inability of lives to accept their many.
After rain thick drops of water hang from the underside of
phone wires. What then? Words hammerd out of air admit
light. Scrambld drains off in excess milk eggs. Make your
nostrils flare, one at a time. Any days are these. Because we are
here & might remain. To see the face of the polar bear was to
look at the brown smudges on his t-shirt closely. Processd colby
cheese melted into the sizzling eggs, speckld with caraway &
oregano. There as shambling might get one well. Because these
candle holders have the shape of cacti. Faces form voices first.

The mist mutes light. "Moods is energy." There is an alley calld Poplar St. Eptness is in his. Signals to the sphincter. Voice carries where one forgets others are not seen. The melting red wax soakd into the fibers of the rug. Our urn journal. Because the rooftops here are built flat & not for snow. Holding one's fingers at the tip of a match. Small dry ridges of an upper lip. Landings cannot escape the Z-form rungs of fire. Any old thing I can think of. Scurrying voices downstairs, hushd footsteps. The cat prefers to sit in the drizzle. Eyes rise raises days. Fasten faucets. Of listeners motion moves one in a crowd, lights beer, opens cigarette, follow others, settles silence till a ripple forms. Tart citrus drink. In the darkness of somber red tennies. Caraway bursts between my teeth. In a room begins stanza. The none too subtle smell of the kitty box. A specific withinness relation demands but calls size ambition. Alfalfa sprouts in a brown jar. How attend force? The smell of hops as a child. The is this road. All green sedans were the enemy. Not this. A kanga-roo boppo. Nervous energy stops into the night, excess people rain at sunset, emerge. Oolong is how long? A quick with the Chinese waiter dishes. Dawn is inconsolable. Up that what will later wonder brought. The smoke of that ship afire joind with the low dark clouds from wch rain fell. The chairs of noise in chairs. Constant trickle from my left nostril. Is a conductor glass? I cld have been a cobbler. Never shade center precisely lamp. One sentence I dreamt of, but later forgot. By ear jaw begins. Old mattress on that rooftop will mean sunbathers later. Habit up to alter street tears. Something only recently known, such as the dark side of the moon. Oregano is daily & dillweed information. In place of a sentence. Neck means listen at certain angle. Am I about? A way of rolling class up indicates sleeves. These green lines can never again be blank. On one bite down you cannot tooth. Interest is narcotic. This brings what to that? Many little tricks to move it along. Not this. Don't count on it. Can you finger a length by the tell of their writer? Even a skeleton is a sign of life. Opaque steams window. This marks a new year. Smells: wet smoke or pine wood. The crossd eyes/of the bearded lady/makes it impossible/for me to really see her. Above library windows painters on a scaffold brush yellow-green. Something in his coat pocket weighs him down. The vocabulary of these cars are traffic. I dream of writing in a grotesque notebook. Up into fog's cloud soakd fire's smoke. The small habits of children extend themselves with age, stooping old men & women. In an exchange elevator clerks chatter. Two cats not permitted to touch, because one has leukemia, play through a glass door. Idle around in television, mill camera jocks station windbreakers. The tyranny of these words is their history, uses over wch we have had no say. Any electrical built of city wires. An old bear rug sits on the deck in the rain. It's a tourist if it carries a map. It wants directions to Chinatown. The glare one sees in the eyes of woman, registerd as hostility, as she emerges from a restroom in a public place, particular vulnerability. The politics of his poetry = don't even ask. The stone piece of paper is a new man. Barbiturate life. The stem uniform town of the mining houses. That fern's fragile future. A typewriter is what you do with prose. An 'eye' dropper, by wch to insert liquid vitamin into gagging throat of sick cat. My jack name is hammer. Because mice & moss are the only things alive in that alley. Store's trapdoor in sidewalk opens to reveal basement steel. Wax wick of an unlit candle. Kites whip in the fish noon breeze. After several sleepless nights the clarity of the world increases. Who how we are we are. My truce with objects. Sit in sun, drink beer at a bus stop from a can in a sack. Hard as raisins in cereal. Smoke encircles cigar head. In Kansas, what is the equivalent of foghorns? Shade on one ear, the other in sun. As tho there were an invisible clamp on the tooth about to crack it. Fading stores of appliance signs. Tall sturdy avocado plant. No negamos credito—red white blue plastic flags on radio antennas (antennae) in a used car lot. My mouth is a wound. Is this vocabulary a formal? More layers in some parts than in others. An afternoon of lexemes. I write when I rise. What then? Heavy carding. Muffler fenders roar, black Volkswagens without a past. Mallarmé comes to mind. Women must bend their arms, holding handbags. An arc of flame shot through the chromosphere. Egg carton juts from shopping bag. Treaty concerning the root canal. Red old newspaper truck. These simply are day's devices. The beer of champagnes. Smokd edam. Out ekes meaning. Saturn's rings move at different speeds. Ball pin lizard. All is not neato keeno. The mark-up of mornings. Words like a filter. The fingers curl halfway in sleep. This small valley calld the Mission. Heights specific. Big skydance of the gulls in rain. A point words to a word. They have nothing left to ask you & you have nothing left to say. Knotted the gut of muscle. This what then? Haunt consequences as craft to predictability. Rich lush thick bush. Letters to stand make for thot. Green of the sun prismd down. From the bay that red segment of the air is squares. Plaster elephant rearing head. Words in air thrust against the entropic body. Its eyes were specifically human. As if to universe the sentences in state. Cat's anxiety while food is readied. Laundromat—rotating grind of the inevitable dryers, the loud bad ventilation. Horsehead nebula. This was the weather without winter. Why these words here & not others? Each frame hinged inexactly to its door. Sirens echo far from here. Wood prettier than gray paint someone must have thought "plain." Flatness of words can be infinite. Consequences quickly narrow choice, one gets to the down. Mission bells on rainy Sunday. Backwards walking Jerry new to the straight. Padding about in kung fu slippers. Illusional gestalt fails to abolish collage. What grownups refer to as poplin jackets, kids call derbies. Are these not samples? Early afternoon, time to get up. Ruling hard as the edges of a hedged class garden. Mother's voice redistributed by electronics collects at my ear Tuesday lunch will be fine processd luncheon meats atop man-naise spread across sliced insides of a Kaiser roll thin lips that we share black coffee & a strong sense of solitude precondition to knowing self, strange face always backwards in the mirror. Bristling this. This bathroom is the wrong blue. Just how to wear my trousers long never have learnd. We sat in the park & read. What salt paint does to house air wind. Old bear rug lays in the rain. Antique shutters, chandelier windows. No grey as true as sky today. A mineral habit out of water. Candelabra cadabra. Dime chip. Mind's music a dull buzz. He times socks as others do purchases. Wire basket to hold garlic. Box crushd cigar. Bourgeois decor not aimd at use. Of top-loading washers row chartreuse. In a far room I hear Peg cough. Heat with no summer. Towels just jammd into their rack. At the medium of each theater edge lies. Jets describe invisible lines in the sky. Waves redder got stick in the micro-era of lip. For what reason always something like a mute over mouths of pipes jutting from gravel or shingle roofs / rooves, keeping smoke & gas from just going straight up? First tootsie-rolls, then milk bottles disappeard. Words in head in hand. Were fashion pants then in draw-string? Like vultures, gulls circld a schoolyard. Freak mountains causd unexpected airplanes to meet storms. Now we live in Kit's house. Others about their wash as they do what you learn. Regular procedures for thot. I found the delta missing myself. Inches forward. The linoleum came up to the asphalt, right? Within clouds clouds occur. As if they had just been people wore their hair swimming. Life wld be richer if we had more moons. By the time you seemd to be the in the middle all conversation arrivd. How learn the nature of one's own work? Conflict punctuates the limit of words. Tanklike, the garbage truck slowly pushes forward thru the alley. Lawns all grow imperceptibly quicker to had begun. Night seemd too short. Easily more dogs were provokd. Sun's own glare above that of the bay. Even hieroglyphics began to look like newspaper headlines. A few sentences each day. Each day to climb to the house the steps it was more difficult. Wage war with bare hands. The sound of drums had begun to sound like the rhythm of primitive consonants. The circular sweep of the second hand. Intolerable was the vowels of whimper. Red eye. The constant salsa was neighbors. Cat's tongue dips into the rain water. The street took to you. Anchovy smell of testicles tongue tip of fingers touch as cock telescopes into hardness. Chance of thun-dershowers white-grey light. The shadow in the window watches me. Staind glass bangle dangling in the wind. Each sentence in a different room sinus clog inexplicable mouth blis-ter design problem not solvd hanging yellow rug "the long way." Covering furniture act of class affiliation tv is a gray-blue lamp. Weather alters the body cough. Biology of the ceramic dog. Defenestrator's lump in gutter. Paint-fleckd red tennies. Morning's head fails to clear windows rattling beans in a gourd house lightning cat's plaint a man she causd to let go & run had threatend to slash shirt-sleeves in the rain try to remember maybe it will all fall down houses with flat rooves & no sense of snow small black mouse. Nervous words hurt to piss is not a toy gas bill eyes heavy in soft sockets takes all one has to let light drift in weightless like rain. Head in face or other direction. Shadows cover words it writes delayd mechanism red light on green page yields gray. All his casual silence covers migraine torque. Interviewer clowns bull performer. Tentative title stuff. One window sees into another face on wall stares in third direction. Calistoga water bottle. Puffy flesh layer of fat. What the positions you prefer says of you head up straight ahead. Spine is essential & formal, hands small & wide fingers, nails that fail to stretch very far around. My shadow on the off-white wall is writing. Slippery elm throat lozenge. Cat chooses to sit atop flat old brown paper bag. Fine pharmaceuticals since blah blah. Utter filth verb noun someone to clean up mouse parts cat puke. His eyes burnd right into his skull smell of tobacco in hair & shirt. Modular stool drop. By now familiar territory. Need to make do. Prisms' little rainbows sway on wall till clouds loom up. Nothing to do with the previous thing. Active ingredients. Quien sabbath? Words edge up to align with probable meanings. Anything cld be describd in the orderly progress of consonants, thermal sock, dates in a baggy, sesame seeds in old plastic margarine container. Wake up empty-headed, contemplating progenitor. Cloud of breath bursts into open, cold air from mouth. 'Dead' of winter like 'rock' of ages. These words in the place of many others. Hand shakes slight tremor to streak the page. Echo of aircraft fills the clear sky. Hates speech but trappt by thot. Achieving the status of typical. Sirens surge toward some urgent thing. Water tower atop Potrero Hill shines in early light. The gush of nearby traffic. A jigsaw of infinite combination & no determinate shape. Stand on the deck for the sake of it. She sticks her tongue out, all those buds. Pigeon pecks its way thru Poplar Alley. Little tuft of cat blows on the deck. In a world where clotheslines continue. Strands of wire top peeling fences, long wooden back steps sag, houses jammd against each other. 747 right over my head. Sliding door slips shut with a pop. Cardboard boxes slump after rain. Teeth grind the morsel. The head is nervous & concernd to watch the hang-glider nosedive parallel to the cliff face before catching the air. Not quite rare cloths cover the couch. Brings back driftwood wrappt in a kerchief. Always ajar closet door. Once we sought solid thought. Candles angle inexactly atop mock cactus candelabra, flames' shadows flicker. Bird calls in the fridge. Marinated red snapper smells smokd, one-half baked potato afloat in sour cream, the salad will not keep. Ice plants will not burn, are not ice. Flat sun in a round sky. Brownfeet lopes curiously up to a receptive setter. I saw my shadow write this. Simple sentences settle facts. Ripe black pitted olives behind the round wall of that can. Anyone can feel nail's stretch over broad back of the finger. Rain falls sideways. Alphonse & Sylvie. Garbage truck the alley's width. Red bench gives way. Spin prisms hung in window & sit back. All tendencies to the modern slump with desire. Arms crossd over breasts, she walks naked into the bathroom. Grapefruit peeld, eaten as an orange. C's hatred of women taken as fear of himself. That color wld arrange itself into a wheel. All tables, chairs, couches draped in printed cloth. Sun shapeless in the morning haze, blue backpack leaning against the kitchen wall, empty envelope left upon the wood table. Whose name is Sunshine & never wears shoes. All one's life is not a poem but a life. Red flowers fade to black. Big brown jars filld with seeds & flour. That hillside is calld Holly Park but this in front of me is a bran muffin & a recipe for sorrel soup, haze vapors, cat favors its paw as the head turns skyward & orange juice pours in, Clark rattles on en español, rhubarb juts fresh from the damp earth, the sun never quite in sky's center means brunch on the east edge of town. What wld be the perfect sentence? Reads one only for the language used, discarding the rest. Jigsaw puzzle, red telephone, shoes, the Saturday paper, scatterd on livingroom floor. As if each word were a cut, shaping a solid block of meaning. Sky blue tape measure, dusty guitar. Each event marks an operation. Writing on a full stomach is not the same. Blissd. Blood blister on the lower lid signs decay. She runs ahead of the boy, turning at the corner, shouting, "C'mon, slowpoke." Toy gun sounds like tiny siren pulse. Keep spices in old 'pop' bottles. The man in the window works at a desk. Embarrasses you to hear too personal a conversation. Suzy Chapstick. SM porn—she inserts a candle. She's not even crazy, she doesn't have an excuse. His idea is their voices. Smoke stops at the ceiling. Leaves loom. By her hair can you tell who she sleeps with? In words letters keep showing up. This is a balk. So on. You have to make it last just to see it at all. He's way back there in the head. Fills a glass jar with cookies. In the theater heads bob. That face I see over shoulders. Some people who never face east or west. Steam heat drains head out. Hey grey—can I borrow your piece till tomorrow? Siopold! Weight of the intestines. Big T little l ingot with an i. Wire basket gathers garlic. So we climbd the three flights of stairs. Stars rose in the patternd sky. Thru the filter coffee filld the cup. Off to a fast start. At the end of the escalator a vision of household furnishings. Yet the spider plant is brown at the edges. Both bowls need to be washd. Even on the day they move I can hear them shouting. You cld hear the wind at the garbage cans. Small military jets shook the sky. She wrappt the tacky terrycloth robe about her. Thunderbird bottles at the base of the flagpole. Green handled broom with a yellow brush. Words hung flat on the tongue. A class of events that are simultaneous forms a space. Pill floats in water down the throat. Sitting in the doorway of the liquor store, drinking up. Think of salads as dessert. The cat sat in a Euclidean threespace. Dreams index fear. Each sentence points to the next. This motion tends to its own completion. What in the body is not the body, between organs. Cat's head rears with a start, O canopener. In the forest of the house. Horsehead nebula looks more like a bent thumb. But this is what followd. Wld male hustlers look as scroungy if they had a pimp? Bald man at the bar smiles, motions to you. Music to savage the soothing beast. What pops out. Not proposd as a line of thot, but what emerges of a mosaic of layers. More weather coming. Feet your oud. As the candle drips, layers build on the tables. See above mocks form below. Bedrest dictum flickering heart contra naturam if to party to moonset cops on the front porch tapping glass pane on the door, yet cat sleeps beneath the car at the curb. Kite in the shape of an elephant shades the light. Red wagon in the pit of the airshaft turns to rust. Eye focuses in the middle of words, just left of center. Time it takes to shoot thru. As spellings spell the eye. Content is a four-space. Trenchcoat on a hanger from a nail in the door. On the outside of the window the underside of an ant zigs & wiggles in a futile search. Fly sleeps in curtain's folds. The sound of a trowel smoothing cement. Engine revs up. To be a garbage man in the rain. Water in a pot boiling for coffee fogs windows. They still have clotheslines here & she yanks undies in from the rain. Pop of backfire scatters pigeons out eaves of old hotels. T shirt styles football jersey. Eats butterd smokd sea bass. Afraid of rain. Each is its own piece. The space of ice. Eyes translate the visible to head. Sure to have gaind 5 lbs. Square of sun falls on couch & rug. Cat in the wrapping paper plays. Dull roar in the sky says air traffic. Once white tennies. A free bottle in front of me. Black flies shine blue on a red-brown dog stool. Language comes to hand. Feeding ginger cookies to mallards. Pots pans dishes for a fraction of a second tumbling down sound drumroll beyond wch silence where song shld follow. One nostril clouded, the other serene. Her talking-to-the-cat tone. Some Sundays the afternoon is a kind of morning. If Mitchum is Marlowe. Whose name means lakes. My memory at the mercy of all these days. Will I have time to think this sentence out? Brewer's yeast in fish cat goo. Words warp twists thot where new idea begins. Just one day showd up. Putting off doing taxes. White-grey Kentucky walker, sweet face for a horse. Samoyed mixd with afghan, not what you might expect. Something has been eating that leaf. Lushhead. In Chomsky, generative means you cld create an American military base in the mid-east & call it a state. A buzz in the string as you plunk it. Context constitutes. Harmonicum. Blotchy nose. What then? A ground of puddles splashing back. In the sky clouds come & go. Let's start from scratch, she said, meaning scabs. Old porridge cakes on the glass wall of the bowl. In love, but not in sync. Cat will follow open tin of tuna about the room. I can no longer imagine painting. Disembodied voices using colord plastic boxes, calld telephones, to negotiate their lives. Until it blossomd (prematurely) I had not seen the plum tree in that yard. This pen leaves a thinner line. Thin lines in leaves demand our respect. How that cloud sponges the sun's light. Wire cart to drag to the market. Shelling heedless prawns with our fingers. Cat laps up rainwater from saucer. Four out of five cosmic rays from outer space are mu-mesons. A barrel of bottles spills into a dumpster. White-orange rock with veins of green. Many shades of blue in the sky. Gull raises wings & the wind lifts it up. Looking in the window I see my kitchen, but my reflection also & the world where it sits. Enjoys bashing spiders. We never fully unpackd & live that way months after. I can hear 'them' buzzing the prospective tenants in. Onionskin wall perfects communication of salsa. Sentence after sentence. Language is memory not image. 3 dogs sit in the back of the pickup, motoring thru the park. Hay in a horsechip. Writing across the light a prism casts. Words pose time's direction. Sound of metal cooling & contracting in the water heater. Smokelike puffs of cloud. By their window, the smell of burnt toast. Days it takes, as if awaking, getting well again to forget the constant attention to the body, weak, puffy, too warm. Rapid banter of Spanish. Buggy coleus dying alone on the back porch. I was the only one at that reading who still wore a beard. Telephond at work by poets, for an instant he forgets who he is. Tv antennas as scarecrows for rooftops. Bird whistles chur the still air. Then one day the cat doesn't show up for dinner. Some books read themselves in front of you, while you merely listen. Hair converts to grease at whim. Today the grey sky seems shapeless. Alleyway behind houses jammd together, gesture who intention is no longer rememberd, now reservd for the garbage truck. Pleasant foreign music spills from the storefront, enclosing the social club of San Salvador. Ali in his own eyes saw defeat. Redbackd brick building wch, each morning out the window, stares back. Sliding door won't revolve. Keep expecting the turmoil to ease up. Pressing the pen right into the paper. Anna moves to Boston. Above yet within the grove of trees atop the green hill jut telephone microwave transmitters. Baby in a backpack already is a kind of hang-glider. Ant in my salt shaker is doomd. We too will rust, coffee cans on a rooftop. Shld pentip drag a hair, words smear into shadow. Not sposed to rain, tho it looks it. TV: when pygmies down a bull elephant, they immediately cut off the tail. Even to consider the inanimate object is to project one's presence into it. Writing from exhaustion. Writing by moonlight. What begins as perception transforms itself into language. Night sounds from the back deck. In the city there is always traffic. That light crossing the dark sky is an airplane. Soft glow of streetlamps half lights the sky just above the rooftops. Across the alley I hear someone washing metal dishes. The hospital shines in the dark. Dogs bark. At what moment do we cease to be a couple. Someone on the next block is whistling for an animal. Bus passes. Some planes do sound just like in the movies. Sentences strobe life— continual sequence of data frozen into words, then fading before the next one. Not this. What then? You never see more than a fraction. What we hold in common is our imperfectness. An engine turns over. Will my cat return? The next sentence might be the next morning or even days later. Drip candles create a mess. Waiting for the bowels to move. This refrigerator is the lion of our kitchen. Terminal strategies of the tooth. In the salt ocean air of the boardwalk, only the arcade is open after dark. Meat of the banana. Sun's rays in the haze is fire powder. Pure perfect fog. His whole left side crumpld in spasms, phenothiazine reaction, we helpd him into the overhead fluorescent candy pastel glare of the emergency room, up to the dull eyes of the triage nurse. Gouging into a bowl of Familia. Words of others in my own mouth warp lips. That fear of artists for their own kind. Of is meant. That sentences wld connect is leap of fate. Real opposable thumb calld larynx, throat without a tale. Trowel by the cat box. Unknowable events of Tuesday last. Urine is sterile.

Each word picks a topic. Little lines of hands' back intercon-
nect, canals. Fine blond hair spouts. Out from cuticles nails
extend. Above wch a helicopter slides by, blending the air. In
your eyes I see all this & the limit beyond wch you don't know
me. Together, sun & haze flatten terraces of small houses. From
the palm fingers look shorter. Tweezers dredge flesh for splin-
ters. Spanish radio music full blast in the alley. Swish of broom
stroke. Some days wake not groggy, but dizzy, room continually
about to swirl. Stare at the page, walk around, sit down, stare at
the page again. I don't want to rook you. Simultaneity of nonco-
incident events is not open to direct inspection. The syntag-
matic at first seems to be a plane in wch these words occur in a
specified order. Later we see the bumps, curves, indentations.
Ellipses appear as point masses, into wch words might vanish
but over wch thot might leap. All I determine is the sequence.
These things exist in this region. This is an orange is a typical
sentence. All language quotes thot. Sentences are occasional in
the strict sense. This is a cloud chamber. No, this is what might
exist only within one. Thot strippt to gesture. Neon arrow.
Reading, one is suddenly aware that one has been 'drifting,'
thinking, one's eyes continuing their methodical across &
down, preoccupied completely by something, anything, other
than the text. Not hungover, but sobering, as one wakes up.
Micro fish. Only reading old newspapers does one hear the
'voice' in that language. One half of head cloggd with goop. The
eye without its images. Storm braids wind-chimes. "Eraserhead
saved my life," said the woman with blue hair. Sometimes
perhaps as if. Clouds too part of the planet. Flying over snow,
ocean's edge at a distance. California undisturbd by sun.
Fuselage shivers in turbulent air. Cities squard into meadows.
What if the last person to see me alive isn't born yet? In the ICN
babies plug into monitors like batteries. Cloud scoops hover in
the ocean air. Mucus pressurizes the skull. Plane begins to nose
downward. Wittgenstein's ears pop, a proof. Hello, La Jolla. Use
seat bottom cushion for flotation. You bet! Not to confuse the
literature of solitude with the solitude of literature. Flying later
that night saw webs of townlights shimmer in the dark. The

bank of the arroyo falls in on her, changing poetry. Coffee is a hard drug. Lose for a day your hearing in one ear. Dream of playing hardball catch in the street. Write standing up. Night clarity. Woman calls, sez she has the cat, will bring it over, never shows up. Behind shades shadows cast lives.

This house, my home, merely postpones movement. Pistols hence. A zoo coughs he coughs. Falls tart. Rain in the airshaft shifts light, no it doesn't. Thru the building, dim corridor residence hotel, the shadow went, silently checking each door to see if it was lockd. Dialectic is the ecological response to catastrophe / intervention, we're the only species that requires it. Circadia. An orderly distribution of rain on the window, more dense towards the bottom. Dawn patches begin to cloud up between the pre-blue show. Drops connect, convert to streams. Truce tart. Language extends memory's limits. Seam colored cleaners. Always wires & pipes extending up sides of houses. Awe enables apples. Pink tail of a white kite. The dog extends & a paw sits. Fever is the other inhabiting the body. A grunt aground a crag of cruises crowed. From the tip of rabbit ears grey feather dangles. A writing-crew way of wrecking. Your brain doesn't just happen to you. Eight buy gum crowns. String of bells hangs from a dis-used hinge. Call that one in an egg nog, call it art lived abstraction, it. I sat in the ghetto of the bus. Amid puffs & bursts of the audience whoops droplets of bombs plummeting over the destroyer, then rise cheers, antiaircraft fire & gull-jet swoop. Small men in long cars wear hats. When I saw, I lookd again, the museum guard was holding onto an old lollipop. Garage doors on rollers. Logic to the sand & qwik. Afterwards, rows of empty garbage cans with their lids off. New smell of toxic paint. My teeth crunchd into the caviar. Lots the poem P. Dead coleus in a clay pot. Proposd speech blur as roar. Inner organs swell with food, press on one another. Not this. Gelatin caps melt in the mouth. Chicken beef in almond hot sauce. More to Mephistopheles than a red acrylic tail. An inn dented swerve. Each word has its own arc. We run into a new multi-colored Lewis in knit cap. First chewy dissolve of a gum stick. Moody plea unaskd. A concordance of faucets. Richness categorizes Larry by saxmen of tone. The eyes of children clear in head. Thumbable pose. Education, a valve reading Off. Flame im means able. Voice on train intercom mutters into static. Legs all sleep tuckd in the cats. Lizards rip bug heads, chew skull & swallow. What the other imagines each means. Sightless as the golden mole. Day man billeted. Axioms in direct condition leading to identical facts. Space post of deep cards. Paint brush flute. Nor either that. The head slowly in its own way. "Here where I am fine & that's I am." Salted rice cakes. Calld cumulus council issue. What is a serious question? He wants color at all times without clothes. Better have a topic sentence. Upside from the mock ceiling a chandelier table lamp hangs down. Words as if they are. Objects of words I have not photographs for. Dry spots & dead ones. Scription. The psychology of glad wrap. Old dried flowers in a cup. Apron tied to the handle of the refrigerator door. Ward 4 planarians inch. Last night's roast chicken still caked on the knife. Several types of one quark. "Glad" is a registerd trademark of Union Carbide Corporation. Finger lady eats. Sphincter permission. The idea type that has a face. Plastic bottle of Woolite beneath the bathroom sink. True feathers pink. At times conscious of the strobe of sensation. Is this how the desert came to be painted? Water heater in the linen closet. This is me to tmesis. The heartbreak of sore eye is his. Back bought books burgld. Scop. This is but not this. Merely scars upon a page. Cinders & ciphers. The thin lips & cleft chin that ripples thru the family. Coaster is roller knot. Reading Steve Katz in the library means there is nothing to do but wait. Charlie calls the ivy creeping. Donald & his nephews arrive at a cavernous still pond precisely at the earth's center. Blood in the lava. Pigeons sleep in the plum tree. Bear with the cat face. Newsprint stare of a Korean gangster. Blood in the larva. Medium sliced mango chutney. Each new blank ridge the valley above another page. Telephone just waiting to ring. Wld what water be was. The orbit of ideas. Behind the sculpture hides a tiny piano. Brain's a jellyfish trappt in a skull. The hand of my reading dance. So-calld bed clothes. No stone touch reality. Eyes wrinkle. Whistle bone. Where the "püd" inserted her claws. Not a goy will understand amulet. I call this game employment. The sisters & all brothers never met. A row of perfectly-formd circles meaning learns to write. All interpretation resents socio-subjects. Perhaps nowhere so close as on the bus, no body 'at home.' Cld I wld barely write? The absence of chairs in a gallery. Row shrink. Anger's engine. All brown doors green along one white wall. Known as the animal that invented the hat. You hassle them out as the one what makes to pick. These I will weave in later. Lesions illude. Boxer silhouette barber sign. Red blue skateboard wheels. Leaving suspends the rage. Crisp dish. Waves of behavior. One sees all the cardboard in the streets. Halter top, brown shoulder. Dame nuts. Red dot by the number means a surrender. Out in heads, uniform individuate. Bodies brace bus lurch, strain in neutral faces. Was that last week weak? One eye on either side of the nose. Familiar eyes translate sounding, inject reading staring you back. Doesn't even know he's confusd. Not easy. Moments in store window reflection, no means of figuring who that is. Nor each. Laughter up the air shaft. A square pie. Guitar leans against the wall. Here I think. Words are the line's pulse. Fly butter ochre atop the concrete cream. Any morning is after. Wind screen banging gray doors in dawn. The radical discontinuity of thot. Footfalls to the porch on the back stairs. For a second the sun glistens in the still-wet ink. Om pog New York, NY. Nose prints on a bus window. Pi demons might row technic. Chair & a couch in a kangaroo's pouch. Thot will not will not replay stop. Civilization leading to the 2-ply tissue. New mode inserts. Rose lightbulb. By a bowl of bowl of plums flowers. This is my world. Lens kinda sigh. Gonna. Pulls long red ear from scarf. & then went down to the shops. What then? Man mit a name for drying dishes. Not wind what it touches one hears but. Cat's head curld into paw naps. Each radical is charged. "You always alter everything." Together being letters. The poetry of power return. Spinning phone dial, spinning back. Beach of blue mud. First kite means fish-born. She climbd up the side of the cliffs, wearing high-heel black boots, carrying in one hand a bag of potato chips. So not. I think of & write fo. Exactly not. Hippo down, druggd, suffocates on her own organs, too heavy in the body. Sewn air is. A word between word & wood I heard. First means son born. Know when not to work. Photon. Grey film on the bottom of an ashtray. To be dare simple. Any analytic sentence is a synthetic one still packd. Milk melon of Asia. Bumps that grow on an old man's ear. Mute traces hand moves thot's leaves. Those instants when the letters of words fail to cohere. Particles of how. Simultaneity of events at a distance may be determind only relative to an observer within a specified inertial frame. In the sun slowly in the bay window prisms hang spinning. Songs of certain birds I've heard all my life, but whose names I do not know. Ya milk of knees am. Each day one pushes oneself into the events of the world. Gives a spaniel grunt. A gone to Boston, a new life, but a green banded agate to wear on my finger. Eggs tend. One thinks what one believes. Page crossd my rainbow. Spring swells my nostrils. Weft warp, horizontal vertical. First the first letter, then the word's length, then consonants in the middle. An old beer bottle dying in yelloworange flowers. Can you see the seams in the sky? Axe ekes. Adz. Sun's neck on the warm of my neck. Red-eye drunks by the fountain at dawn. Kit wanders in the dark, millions powerless about the airport. That gut of anger calld wage labor. Window's page marks not the drawn edge, the light's line patch between to form a shadow soft wedge. Hartz mountain. Seep dent. Many dreams stir the sleep. No modern thing a such post. Words first in a row of all. A freak eye was one's needle. Layer of empty wallets at the bottom of airshaft, from when the women had rolld the tricks. Who by erasure writes one. Cats pace the quiet deck. Plough pages the plunders. Finger swole & itchd, bitten by a spider. Fly in blue sun shines light. A clear hot day returns me to my childhood in an instant. Structure any cloth or fabric. One who proceeds by statement presumes the future existence of things to say. Writing it as who will see writing. Plastic baggies hanging on a clothesline. As reed read red. No one suggests words hold the paper together. Distant Tahoe summers triggerd whoops of sudden recall in the 50s children laughter. Scratches on my arm point to a tale. Do Ron he bad. Imagines the mind as whirling rolodex. Two engine no rime. Buckets of water out a 3rd story window. What then? Not this. I vacated at the long end of a stand. Moon cycle on the sky dome: what rises as lower left sets last. This is another sentence. Space is the same in all directions. Eight clear threes together hold beer in plastic. Budgies chirrup sweet. Thin wind. Second day of spring the rains return. Two identical friends of mine in very different tennies. Holding on not to love but its image. Life seen all thru a speculum. That jolt of other in anyone's eyes. Atop a small can of Dutchboy paint a larger one. A description of my writing that I do not recognize. The panda's lap. Reducible crucible. Formal socks present a problem. It all mushes together. Trotter to he fuck. Odor of burnt figs. Wrong paper rubbd becomes sand shark way. Pushing brain cells thru the hoop. The green side of the brown door is far. Irish sez 'h' with an 'h.' Antlers entangld in christmas decorations. Webs in the head, thru wch waking. Sun direct in set. Spiral of my formal self flushd in john. Cacti guised as candelabra's disc. Tongue tip against clitoris spark. Get mean with a tar fiddle. An oval imposed on the face of a penny. Margin types its own form. Each sentence is a test. Like eye of the thing shapes. Hair of my eyebrows appeard to droop. The bed of sociology clothes. Nothing in my digestion had broken those soybeans down. "Staring like all those penises don't." Feather visage—she wears an oatmeal mask. But to do nothing doing. In any transition of an isolated system from equilibrium state to equilibrium state, the entropy cannot decrease. The tar street of the heavy-heater in the breath. Movieness. A gentle jackhammer's far insistence. Stepping outside, cups his hands around a match, head (cigarette in lips) tipping down slightly towards it. In do tow the joe goo. Pen in the sun hot when pickd up. Wind child I gauged earth's spin thought. What's the structure here, as if. Unseen in petals eaten by the holes. What is like what is said? Two ceremonial chances echoed, cannons to count each out. Earlier sentences, our old friends. Slomo mojo soho dobro. Hypnotic, white foam of the boat's wake. Tan the face but the legs lookd Japanese. No self without other. Stuff tough rough cough. Fragments of sun

shimmer on the water. Cowboy shouts into a public man hat in
Levi cutoffs & a telephone. The large glass mug, if left on the
stove touching by accident the dark iron frying pan drying over
a low blue flame, eventually must crack. Once here start found.
Powercruiser ploughs the bay. Features heat haze erases.
Remembering not to swallow while brushing my teeth.
Foreman hollers at roofer. Just tilt forward. Quails scamper kid-
like. Boxy look to thinks. Store from a too-small sun a dime
visor. Sometimes even these words cannot recreate their own
lucidity of only a few moments earlier. What information is it
does. Writing of death's others, means mirror is fading out.
Words dry into letters cake. A druggd man can only trudge. Of
the shadow of life wires in daily phone effect. The lid pulld back
by one hand, the edge of the eye briefly touches an outstretchd
finger of the other, releasing a small synthetic membrane dedi-
cated to sight. Arch middle worm heart. Many also own a
second collection of books in a far city calld home. Chewing
nature she said, "Gum." Small dark bottles of spices. On dog
plops couch. The achievement of a work is to propose new prob-
lems. House I see a jetliner fly behind. The privacy of the deaf.
Struggle us ray only fines bruise. I saw the figure 5 in gold. Cuts
motorboat path in white bay. To in as which. Herd have.
Revolting door. Cold punctuates head life. At what point is this
piece its own history? One one, not one two too. As for. Atop
small pole grey phone transformer. This the. Buffs &/or grind.
One word a small slice, like a papercut, in the unity of silence.
Paste ideas a form. Sea's hull, the geodesic serpent. Ward for
false spring back. Divide my friends into groups according to
how much rent they pay. Order of the order. Caged birds whis-
tle. Pipe atop types of rooftops. Reluctant wakefulness of the
body. Rockefeller phlegm like money has. This week the cat
sleeps on that chair. Mole's in way way. The sun loses shape &
the sky goes gray. Imagine these people mean all cars. Albino
dalmatian. Proof rusting brush. Visitation Valley. Wind open
over bottle whistled. Cat nudges book in wch I write. Ion on
billd. Ahead of the storm a breeze kicks up. Modern wave,
siren's multiple lengths. Child I was is here also hidden. To have

figured the sides of sailor into the spikes of phone poles. Do you stay or do you say wch way is this day to be made at sea so mad at me as can be or not? Cigaret crushd in the clover filters. The line's a fine spine. Only a term now to wch I give the memory "blister." Sealing sea lions. Tar pulleys on a roof lift. Letters, words more crowded in spots, jammd, clusterd, evend out thru print's filter. Prop a position of stairs. Ab scene as in cessd. Remember learning you can write? Each new page is a promise. Whore frost. Bleeding into books. Sun shines before it dries for a second in the ink. Any group that calls itself "children" is dangerous. People impenetrable to cats. Flame is a liquid. One grass bends in all this direction. Sky pulses day & night. Pet mutant rump. We are far now from where we were. Words of my shadow over these hand. Perhaps we cannot find our way out. Tell ball paddles bat. A new plan for the living room. Not my sirens to wch house I hope roar. Tall dry stalks in the rural ghetto garden. Tether. A limit she places on her willingness to feel. Each scar leaves a word. Where we were we wore war wear. Ocean's what is the porpoise? The car abrupts into the vertical of the phone pole, glass will not dissolve in blood. Trees anger one shaking sees. Visceral wail of children denied. Dno tich sin teger. Cat launches at fly. Atop a bruisd yellow dish containing four wooden, rotting pears, the kitchen table. Morning clatter of neighbors, a backdoor bangs idly in a soft breeze. Calm be plex. Awkwardness of song against the grain of speech. Milk shredded in a bowl of wheat afloat. Congas, mouth harp, accordion, mi corazon. Plastic diner tiny sore. The red phone is silent. Not getting the other side means reaching close. Harvest of the universal man. Gary Moore's sarcasm, Henry Morgan's limp, Bill Cullen's noxious laugh, Betty White's dull glare, Allen Ludden's slick, Jack Narz' name, Gale Storm's crewcut. Kites in the window form a shade. Such as any term stilts moniker. Hum of jets not liner, but pulsing, echoes add in. Teaches what just each is—politry. Pigeons in the park do bark. Equals form intrinsic periplum. How terrifying those heavens were. Camera one to rapt backer. Years ago, saw/heard Merwin at Berkeley, party after—Robin's house, M's sullen loner number—what lasts. Once in the teapot red flowers wilt. Letters: numbers. Roughly quick moves wave. Rooms in America always hum. Changes timed. Row ahead big blossom of hair (the flower we wear), thick, curld, dense, dark, billowing, blots the screen. Beyond fennel on an old chair I stood out. Frenetic: some words possess general content only. What then? What makes ears ring? Look like the moon halves in the bay cantaloupe. Storm clouds / my skull. Habit oral constant. As he reads, all the poets scribble in notebooks. A slant south lines paw. Tugging pants on, keys in pocket scrape my leg. Mill pepper. Drinking coffee too fast, heat esophagus. North youth in Chinese beach parks. Time is, time's not what you stop. A certain exhaustion bred by precision. It's the social function of clichés something something to tears. O'Hare airport bartender's broad girth. Old sound, some body's taking a leak. Of olive bottles. What I thot was / not of use further / turns out to be. Stroke pens. People go to work, expecting rain. Not this. Each new page is a thrill. Sounds house the mark. All calls cause. & of thumb held at an angle by an arrangement of two fingers. Marsh ruby, i.e., grapefruit. Sunbathers & pigeons sweep over sleepers. He don't want no / methadone no more. The elders too often mistake the deterioration of the young for condescension. Poor old tired comma. Into about under of under bit a bit into part under of a bit into like. Political terms, like women. Tone of the fountain in the plaza, cool constant kielbasa in a cafe. Wires above barely noticed. Bread dry grass crumbs. Woman running this way in the distance gradually turns out to be a slender female child. Citrus juggler on a unicycle circulates. The fastest, fattest crap you ever saw. Groans shutter, rattle stairs. Nothing like drinking to remind one, perception is discontinuous. A certain gape expression defining uncomprehending tourists. His throat cut in the fight, his small green bottle broken & no stores still open, he found a parkd car to crawl into, sleeping in his blood till the clinic opend. The cathedral tower form crosses twenty-one, bell two. World a tide pool on a larger scale. This steel presence drums by the rhythm of flattend. Popping an unopend fuchsia blossom between fingertips. Friends neck with three stiffs. Kids pounding caps with rocks on the sun hot concrete, sniff snaps of sulphur. Red pigeon's "feet." Art chairs alter spines in a too deliberate sun. Between wars is ceaseless grass. I took the tortilla to church next day. Intestine of walrus parka. Systems idle to watch a fire. Grow your own voice distant. Large dogs paced about the rooves. So robe uncut blue-calld dragon. Here the sun has set but off the windows of homes on that far hill it shines back in our faces. Warm trenchcoat weather wearer. Bakery alive with hot dough odor in the middle of the night. Beads of sweat gradually 'greasd' brow. Tying my shoe, trying not to fall over. Rents differ down. Recurrent dreams in wch a holocaust has recently occurrd. Urinal smell of wintergreen. The sound of water before it boils. Vast dawn. Any one step cld cause the vertebrae to disassemble. The far storm of a hard summer after a things edge. Here at night the heat's just right. Monoclinic. Her brother, the firefly, bids me good day. Untended gulls asleep atop motorboats. A red band of sky barely visible along the east horizon at dusk. In my direction her cld see I walking. Periodically we fall back into our bodies. Back to Twenty Languages I came again. Clay pots await plants. Hand this long call. They sit on the fire escape sipping beer. Smokestack galvanizd. Jets built in the image of a shark. Porn cop. Red letters on a brown halftone. This stance gathers. No one knows exactly how to read it. His bull wrestled like short sleeves. Then the mauve rises slightly & one sees the first blue meaning night. Ship forklifts across a yard. Any verb inappropriate to the noun attracts mosquitoes. Coming in by ladder. In what ways are grey days less real? Neon et al. Old iron barbecue filld with rainwater & rust. With their jets define the sky. In small poems one's work is merely sliced into facets. Faded on a line between bass antennae hung a twin flag. Bright eyes peer thru the cartoon dark. Familiar talk focus party voices. I can feel the weight of my face. Call mocking of gulls shrill hawking. Incensd, in sentence. Once or fart. Lines insert false time. Black bugs in the air like helicopters afloat. One does as one, waiting to see limits extend. This Kit grins watching. A 'thing' calld use. Behind swimmer the breakwater gathers. In eyes/one sees/out again. Rough deck. Cricket between tea & thunder. Without approaching, it appears to get closer. She has morning in her eyes. Hear sea friends read him. Steve sez "Yr grammar is fuckd." Why city life "chooses" crip. I see Peg behind the glass door, moving silently about the kitchen. Bumbles. Tracing over old letters, for emphasis. Water on the jogger's edge. Impossible to write this "in lines." Tweezd each letter. Lone ant wanders the shower wall. The syntax of nostalgia wch is essence. Faucets also beneath the sink. (S) figure 55. Each wedge in a stone of air. The slender eucalyptus-shaped leaves of the small banana. Lines cross words, propose a counterbalance "against the grain" of the syntagmatic. Tho one arrives no footsteps approach. Then one evening the stomach simply refuses to work. Once these terraced hills houses. Stuck, they stretch & strain in the trap calld the roach motel. Charles dear Bruce ah. I had to set it down for two weeks, to see if I believed it. Any commuter vacantness of a campus on a weekend. My first real meal in days. Is name a trade kleenex? After years with Peg, so little settld. Just what makes who questions a month? You can smell computer application of gestalt theory in the name Exxon. Make it make it. To want to survive the body is the highest form of denial. Rat scampers with mange. Slowly learning the language of plants. Unpoppt kernels at cup's bottom. I'm not writing down your inner life. The history of social skirts. Depth perception is a temporal construct, brain adjusts information of the eyes. Mega-tive. My grandfather's walk's slight wobble, "always a sailor" grandmother said, tho he'd been a soldier loading ammo onto taxis in Paris, wch then drove to the front. Wind against these words. Dark halls angled awkwardly, at either end small bulb's yellow glow, cords thru transoms & over sprinklers, radios on in each room, the floor john behind the elevator, this latter being out of order, the odor of rat shit just behind thin walls. Concentrate stare listen. He collapsd & died right there on the street corner. Keeps me in skin. An old man who likes to wear an electric guitar wherever he goes. Out the way new stretches shoot. She steppd out of the doorway & askd us, "Are you boys up for dating today?" Having no age Jack botherd his friends. When your mouth collapses you'll deny speech. Star. Some shine alternately red & green. This hall Smith call. Enough smegma under the foreskin for an oreo. Strap so elastic glasses don't slip. Each time one writes—invent these letters' shapes anew. Nowhere in the middle of meaning to assign blue ball all. At exit permit person in front to clear barrier before inserting ticket. It's speech if listen. No, Lyn, wrong, tranquility is not a condition of mind & tranquil the body, but each an aspect of tone at the interface of both. Hill high city side. A ball of gas in the gut as focus. Shadows lightly writing. Target zones will lead to a better snake. Fill these furrowd lines. Bedbug morning, silverfish afternoon. Flow err. It's the body's party tells all. Any semibetter literate stands under it. In the history of ideas each term is suspect. Rain makes lawn bow hose's shower. Sinuses bulge, then drain. Blades dig into my grass back. Technological noise of a sleeping house. Stretch all these directions in lines. M stands not behind his work, but to one side. In the one to two large tropics each dozen animal requires acres to survive. A kidney machine for Peter Pan. Functions each finger. Dehydrated parsley flakes. Into peat mulch settles. You dream most just before you wake. Brains burn. Words badly inkd argue: this was not inevitable. In a latte corner over rummer players card fingers, saucers in cigarettes. 'Ambulance' spelld backwards on the front hood. Fern & will beneath nasturtium. Words glide into place. To read without Jerome, was it first moving lips? Perceptual equipment is limited really. How think to spell the Dutch? Cheap black pens with fine fluid points. Cloud fills the way pages gather. You cannot hear the argument. Drill nose, find hair. At any instant one-third of the audience is caught in a trance. Watch children to enter gamblers. These words just flow by (phone poles from a moving vehicle). He I was said his grin pen just sitting there poisd to grant permission in air. Specific number, the abstract mode of particularity. That anxiousness filld the full moon room. Head cold like swimming in chlorine. Deep in Stan from peace writes the calligraphic. The idea of a literature is the idea of a market. A glass bejeweld by a tall wood walking stick doorknob. Patience will make any man dangerous. Call stage to whisper cats. All in a day's angle. Eyes in the familiarity of a beggar. Splicing Enslin to Tatlin, echo Tzara. One cute choice x'd. Morning's matter. Odor of acrid cigarette. Latent manifest by its absence. Scab artichokes, Jerusalem potatoes, Canadian grapes. Sixty pages in a notebook. Curtain skirt. Some sentences seek error. Beavers glance pall down. Extrinsic music. Snail prongd forehead. Blips of clarity in daily life. Nightie campd on a couch in the light blue. A kettle stitch to bind signatures. Nobody empty shell home. Life proposd as jars of ground garlic. What then? Hah! Words digest. Dawn hot with summer's heat. In embeddedness with bed. Components of a fly's back. At that record's stillness end. Hot, hard, heard. Rain mountstorm Sutro. Telephones in the distance. A not laxative. The territoriality of social work. I hear off faucets. Gas articulates the interior (proprioception?). One into the irrevocable steps. This is my work. Form forth from tides edge crabs pool. The body is a balance. Two irreducible we quarreld between languages wch. Once I resented lesbians their knowledge wch I cld never share. Bufflehead duck. Didactics is a line to the point. Nothing wore his glasses more, wading into the sea surf. By 'once' I mean a stretch of time long past. Refuse commonly personal cannery death workers. Subterranean activity, bubbling in the gut. Surrounded an air sail craft carrier by boats. Gravity of the line will come to the bottom of the page. Hear change pull in jeans pocket on. This is the distri-bution of junctions in the epithelium of the small intestine. The nude clothed solitude of a person on the one beach. Hangover causes cavities to throb. Snap pits pend. Literature does not lead men astray. Referential lettuce but film obscure, deliberately concerning being sweet whippd by sentence in a calld lust. Talking quickly, each word given equal weight. An with 'E' whisky. Needlepoint according to Jennifer Bartlett. Sunset are in that true period between colors & dark. Fooling myself. Of ants writing alterd by letters. Science, although reas-suring, cannot deny people suffer. The sun on the far side of the bay was still up. Inappropriate adjectives in constant use exert pressure of the normal. I ran into the Savoy at an old school pal.

People talking fast, like they want to get off the phone. Rewriting reads this. Barry calls it fractal. Butch above the beadles. Selection & combination. Adjust as the pink sun sets in the east sky light. If I try lines, it just degenerates into aesthetics. Lurching muni forward bus. Watches were not common until about 1880. The flat hills go grey then &. Horrified to see what I've made of this life. Elbow print on news. Legs always falling asleep. The edge in Erica's wit. Woodsy be wld. The shock of a new page. Asymmetrical is an profit structure. This will not look the same in print. Hum boiling in a water. I feel a fever in my jaw. Red moon as it rises full. Refuse to concede your limit. Several visible storms were across at once small the valley. The gallery system will trivialize anything. East dusk at the rainbow horizon is a magenta blue green pink. Simulated leather 'director's' chair. Scribble. The point where perception goes general: when it does, it all goes at once. The porn of democracy. The kind of pens that got handed out in grammar school. The six world in braille dots. The noise on the street after the show lets out. Heat days the clear sky as hazes pass. Sucking sound of a kitchen sink, suds & the debris of veggies & rice. Cat's chimes turnd toy wind. Cautious imitators of their teachers seek tenure. Cool extravagant heat in a climate elicits sudden behavior. Rainbows on the taut surfaces of small bubbles of boiling water settling thru Yemen Mocha grounds in a black filter over a green-gray cup atop the white stove in the light of morning sun. Distant indicates blur gray of rain detail. A = A + 1, one being context. As neighborhood from downtown emerges into area the passengers of character change buses. Sun on my neck. All blank page promise is. Pair of taxis. Dark old man in a cheap jet suit & black fast-food sunglasses eating a dark burger at a stand under a fedora. All of history containd in the concept of different colord inks. The freaky lady, her grim man, their crazy daughter, her silent sons. Please pass the tuna fish sandwiches. Chin stains mustard. WB: "What seems paradoxical about everything that is justly calld beautiful is the fact that it appears." To do this crazy. The whine of an electric saw. The import powder odor of an inevitable bath outlet. The space was the last letter of the alphabet to be invented. In the vacant discarded pile of a lot of an old clothes weeds. Boys quietly carrying skateboards uphill. The blue floor bolted into these tile stools. Only the relationship between signifier & signifier can engender the relationship between signified & signified. Any verb noun trails. Action is a text. Was that my template? Words in blue ink struck out in black. Rum nor storms. Plumber's leaks, the ebb & flow of investment capital, the war on inflation, war is a contagion, the fight against cancer, Jimmy Carter wins congressional skirmish, his courtship of the American people, the romance of the economy. The tacky guitar is blue. Foreign policy is a language, language is like a quarry. Frag in the mirror meant table. M1 is the total of private demand. You are inside now. Target zones will lead to a better snake. The thyme of sighs. No metaphor better than another. Catch up catsup. Call this movie "Deep Grammar." In four fours shun a fact. Peg moves across the street. Writing weighting. Whatever it is you're doing in that big book. Idea do eye the ferry. Like flags tatterd in the wind. Tail in water turnd up ducks. She means he's mean. Appearances scar tiny. The parties of strangers are pure behavior. Blow sand about in the feathers. The sky clear & the head too. Low bomber swoops over borate roofs. Pistons go "pfug, pfug" in the engine. Nose brushing under tip of a finger, his gesture is back. What you call a unit of windchimes. Giggle throat jury at porns. Curtains knotted together to let in sun. Fart cauliflower. Persian sounds. This not cancels this. Coke turns the cartilage of the nose hard & fragile as glass. Of the glass curve in the windshield's crack. Hungover, but not so you'd notice it, the world slightly out of shape, events with no sense of sequence. You ouija wld? Cat thinks abt jumping into my lap as I write. Fox-hunting hound masters bag. People who honk horns to signal friends in the middle of the night. Just a doe beyond the rim stands clearing's still. The patience to write in spite of a toothache. Blue mate in a pot. Life distilld to notation? Contact dissolves soft can. The point at wch words jettison meaning. The italics of shadow passes. This body more than a vehicle. Wrought wrote havoc home. Bright red laces in new black tennies. Waits for the dark blue light but brown shoes in a suit to change. Woman found hanging from a fire escape. Have to not ought. Dark C-shaped hair sharply defind on the white rim of the bathroom sink. Low morning houses in a Victorian fog. Astronauts are simply a developd mode of truck-driver—you can tell by the quality of their CB. A club in each it calld the town bar. Mi amigo, the bald, cherubic nightshade. Waiting for the old woman on the bench, her bus dozes. First simple metaphors, then mix them, then those wch lay at the periphery of the domain (e.g., ships passing in the night for the romance between the U.S. & the OPEC cartel), then mix them & cast into passive constructions until what emerges is a discourse seemingly neutral & descriptive. This s separates 6ix. A man trying to rouse his friend by shouting outside their window. Mark milk crates to park off a place in the plastic street. Young man sitting cross-leggd on the curb talking intensely to his cigarette. We with in were. But if policy is a language, action is trappd in the linearity of the syntagmatic. Your catch I drift. Bob Dylan & George Lakoff born on the same day. All are some language words. Cessna flies into the glare of the sun. A pine summer stillness in the warm trees. The rippling white lines you see at the bottom of swimming pools are caustics. Many most several. The incense of hot tar in the morning air. Black teeth pops crackd between pepper. That leap thru an inertial block just to get up in the morning. Jots. The shame of Cozy Dolan. Of a long green avocado plant stalk. Not all slang sticks: Smith hurls defi at McAdoo, won't withdraw. Is as is as is as. Normd against October scores. Dog falls open where sun sleeps thru the window. Avocado, shrimp & sprout pizza, with a steam beer on the side. Dry sounds chewing cereal. A large tannd man in red swimtrunks pulling his laun-dry home in a toy wagon in the subdued light of dusk. Juicing carrots into the pusher. Collapsing the distinction between competence & performance. Effected affects. Taste of chablis in my throat when I wake. Sloping narrow Chinese streets. Did you sleep good? This enhancement drugs pleasure. Who says words are their letters? Tourists sit hunchd in a doorway as I pass. The last day in May. Room red city of the humus. Alphonse punches Sylvie out. Brick step smoldering on a cigarette. Asparagus fern needs water. Comb to back dried hair. Monarch of the dailies. Gawkery. Nixon was hardly the problem. Amid _ human herd. Cartoon elves, dancing in the sink for Ajax. Ash see a long I gray-white later. At wch time a newspaper announcement of promotion termination will be made. Who just set George up. Lunch with Curtis, dinner with Bob & Francie, Chuck & Rae (later Carla & John drop over). Of tar stain around the wet wch. Writing is our workplace. Hammer-head lost in the old rusty dust. His voice shows concern. Some find body. Lemon-grass in the eggs. Write into the binding, righting. The mushroom people only want you to join them. With red summer noses. A good index of character in the shoes you wear. Line from an angle nylon clothespins. Duck barks like a dog. Nips ton. Signs strung with signs, each word a xmas tree of winking connotations. Waver. Hammermill Graphicopy. Gingy candor. In eyes see their focus. Day bore empty schooldesks in our inkwells. The line exists only in relations of before & after. All this not carving this. Sun shines on a bank of galvanized shingles. Foreskin infected by bacteria under friend. The jolt wch is always a new roommate. & under vest shirt. Fog burnd off more quickly than I expected. Chest feel beads of sweat I roll down. Rushd, troubled tones. Broken green glass grass. Here fog is an early sign of summer. My window reflection in store across street. Endless whimper & whine of a pup in yard down the alley. One was this example. Her collections of everything provided an excellent ecology for the production of roaches. Desk if I make it is a lap. Left Joanna's stag fern hanging in the kitchen entrance. Each block on the bark starts to dog. Large pages have their zones. Alley moves west as sun shadows shift. Tendency to tell too much. Can consonants count? A small man with a small beard. Eye passers this by. Red onions a burgundy really. Hark. I hear glass doors slide & slam. Where poor money go to spend people. This sense of in-the-middle. Not this. Tilting the page in order to get at it. Membrance. Long Japanese knife calld a hocho. Hedge the words or wedge the bet. What I see in the scene of "A."

Explanation as mother sez "All that's there is to it." Gently typos scar the text, light touch of the other. Spin cloth. Where does your work enter life as daily practice? Smudge on world reshapes a lens. To vote is to abdicate your personal authority. Notions derive debt. Representation deprives democracy of its aura. Storefront sounds of butcher paper & windows coverd with buzzsaw hammer. But Sartre's anarchism is explicit: such is the subtext. Epic acid meets draftboard. Not the same person who began the poem. Thus bond gossips. Gulls bark. Quake shall not another these survive houses. Imagine language a picture of the world suddenly begun to melt. Parkd dog in truck whines left. Them shoes is for sportin'. Cat thinking feed. Floral design of a tile floor. French syrup over maple toast Vermont. Chico-san. All fence leans in wood direction. Give your hair extra body. Add these curlicues up. Brain is a bulb at one end of the spinal cord. No rough edges this brain. Brains in a plate in a place to eat. Card post weather. Threads in the towel begin to slip & snap. Siren markd by tragic. Why are pencils yellow? Newspaper midnight man on after bus asleep over falling cross-words. A series of needles into the root of what remain of the tooth. Fucks that flail to die. Why not talk loudly to oneself walking down the street? Today I feel. Ten years since Bobby got his. Ivy creeping, dandelions charlie. More solo now, sense peace. Cocoa smell of seashore butter. Sound's afterimage when fridge shuts off. Sea desert sight-see. You can tell when a hammer is outdoors. Kibbles. This house lacks crackers. & congas punctuate the park radios. A controld burn on Bernal Hill, white-orange smoke engulfs homes. At black clover bee nibbles. Marxism without a party is like _____. Bands around doorknob of elastic. Wind blows calendar pages to mark time's advance. & today's large letters sloppy. The only thread I cld find was floss. Surface missile shoots thru oceans. Trying to write on liquid paper. All fire sirens in directions. Fathers gather. Form slices art fiber. How much do they know they know? Cow congas & bells. Jaw still sore but the infection receding. Paramind bolic. Connotations denote. Old beachd rowboat in red sand. Halicki one-hits the Expos. Up its cat. Last wisp of fog on Bernal Hill. Wake in sleep stung clover. The courage to eat breakfast. Sixty set Harley at down. Jillian drops over. Shrouded woman sits in the old sun. Col. Mustard in the conservatory with the wrench. Think impossible not to not. Drink what you've been missing. Different amid musics. Morning wake to aching bladder. Not narcissism is ample. Gargling induces the need to spit. Bees bend on the flower swing stalks way. Up early to fight infection. Not straight do go toes. The low sun eliminates detail, landscape reduced to shadow & shimmer. Flap bird wings furiously, then soar. Jesse-cat mews to be let back in the apartment. Weigh after anchor words. On the east slope of the valley the sun seemd to have yet to rise. For dragonfly wings. Normally I'd be asleep at this hour. Spicy. Grenier's poems study balance. Thin tan white band of flesh across her back. Solitude of the dawn hour. Men see boot. Potholders (boppos) on nails along a white wall. Old palm kids bottle with fronds. All-purpose soy sauce. Missile is a molester. Tall boys are shy. Kids at the height of swings leaping from arc. Run out of honey. Cld all not cause sun to come up? Date stampd on milk carton. False arrest moves the test. Days to simply cross the page. Food wld good. I hear Fred stir. No clear bullhorn tone but words. An epoch of sporadic pre-party formations. All equal heads are. Gradually traffic brings the volume of day up. Wears all scout scarves. New way to use Roach Motel is to hit them with it. Yolk out of shell drips. Scarf as a verb. Red blue kite high in the lone air. Sleep is a puzzle. In Federales eat Mexico. Stare at page, waiting for words to form. Stuff all this flat. Each letter the focus for not one sound, but many. Overtells. Rancid transit. Jacket book. If he goes down, if he takes a turn, that is, if the system slows to where the pulse breaks off. Fresh production of strange needs is all. Court rules for a fish. Slide jet & dragon collide, appear to fly by. To the traind bare eye, each star pulses two colors. Woman's whites pale as her nurse face. This is a submission. For a lone brief instant the rainbow in the sky turnd into a cloud. I have found myself laughing. Sun lit the full lung, breast strokes the water's surface, beneath wch I swam. Propulsion generates balance.

Later there was no second cloud left there at all. Bitter cucumber. Assembling her constitution. Blue shoes (don't make it). Carrying her hand in her sandals, she walkd. As the oven cools, one hears stove's metal contract. Room moon lit light. Sweet function. Eye hearing foghorns lie awake. 25 years ago yesterday, the state burnd the Rosenbergs: yes, we get the message. No ump pook beware rubbish. Tengo dos Dos Equis. Not sky is without its night changes. Sat, sipping bourbon, in a small bar on Bernal, listening to her speak casually of growing up in the southern hemisphere. The middle words differ in. Gland piano. One wakes with the taste. Ghetto Lenny. Thread rope wire. An old fellow walking haltingly, pushing his own wheelchair as it holds him up. These fleas jump around like words. A baseball team named the Pigs. No green church was surrounded by longer white scaffolding. An accent the blend of Britain & Brooklyn. The indoor air of a soupy pool. White mail. & watches pass traffic. Tender lesson in the Tenderloin. Lady busdriver's friend rides along. Life constituted of tiny particulars. Left lane left turn. Winos slump on a stoop, pushing the bottle back & forth. I quiet poetry. Trimming a balloon. Not standing writing simple. Five shits in two days, each progressively bigger, until you wonder where it's coming from. Glare burns off morning's fog. You remember the page. Arms his infant like a dog. Pachuco tattoo on the back of his hand, blue-green on the muscle between thumb & forefinger. I like to watch them write coffee houses in poems. Godzilla sky. One spine walks straight. In an alley he hunkers down & opens a can of Kal-Kan with a small knife. Universal smoking joint. Warpd wood. Bend sun toward each sentence. Say please. The fatigue of clarity. O ambientes! Renderd proposition of wind delicate by hat. Facing pages. Tufts of swift fog. Birds in the pet shop died in the fire, but they saved the pups. Away, I recognizd her year blocks later. The limit of performance to audience ratio. Eros bows. A mote of dust gets in under eye's lid. Sleep your remember. Recently I rid myself of books I'll not read again. All of a single cat condensed into a glance of religion. Is Mickey Mouse black? Out drawing self, it sketches this. A message of marriage from friends in Rollinsville. Bare error. Further notice. Weather this nostalgia fills. The ache of syntax. Not this. Rinsing sight's orb. Military silver zipping by two small jets. I hear neighbors sorting keys on the porch. Tho something very much like it does, does not occur in nature, save the sentence as writing. One bird in the whole sky. Hoped eyes lies were not you. People who smile with only half of their faces. A border set my sunglasses forth. No theater more elaborate than seduction. Cargo-container containing cyclone flatbeds beyond a fence. Circular stains on a stove top. Scratches a pen with a badly chippt tip. The fridge comes on. Fog over hilltops spilld to the west. Fork spears leaf of romaine. Read earth's core as wld spelunkers toward their hot descent. This package is sold by weight not by volume. Sun's one center at bay shines directly on spot. Shoe's stitching starts to rend. A whole "pay" becomes other, unvoiced realm of speech. Telephone spiderweb over hilltop. Get mind to hand or add tongue to eye. Plunging from my house into the daily circus. Ear word shuffle pricks. Many moments on any page. Sees man-horse. Life is rapid, Ovid. In store's big door sleep dog. Xod Konja, knight's move. Clouds are heard above planes. Five Fridays in June. True ablutions require waking. Duane is 30. West of London. When I first see & hear the traffic of an unfamiliar neighborhood, I realize we live in outer space. They will sit beside me rather than stand on the bus. Up at dawn in an empty flat. Fish paper wraps wax stick. One can see the distortion in the world. Did I think what just? The after taste of olive oil lingers. & into in under an of into by. Vulnerability, if you think about it, is total. Baby straws. The vibes of an all-night donut shop. Not this. Needing to run, to sweat last night's poisons from the body. Toward writing is the stain in the page. Needing something cohesive in the stomach. Umbrella bobbing, neck goes over spine like shoulders. The characteristic quality of any item made for sale. Cld get anything in there. Solitudinous. Hot chocolate Mexican. Remembering the alphabet as if it had a logic. Blue chalk. The sun wakes you, not directly, but by its first insistence at a new angle, until you remember, hearing the steady breathing of one next to you, this is not your usual place. Cork to protect kids, where once door's latch was. She wears rings from around the world. John waiting, to use the milling people. Sirens echo in the valley. Lights whoosh up with a furnace. Morning on a used car lot, all motors idling. In the drizzle above the American an old Victorian whips. I am the destinator. Sight writing ceases down. At a loud thump I whirl around, to see a woman lying sprawld & crushd on Mission Street as a car speeds off. Never regardless of how much a red glass of wine you drink, wch empties. At first she's still, lying in the gutter, then her body heaves convulsively & she begins shaking. Blue eye skies. Everyone on the bus rushd to the left side to see, then to the rear as it pulld away. Grass smells like cut my body. Arches have no deltas. Forms plat a sure form. Banana with an "r." Paint outdoor tabletops of a crackd cafe sun-red. First summer sunburn stretches forehead's skin tight over skull. To catch the light run against the bus. Harder to think on a cloudy day. Or wood swirls in a glade of letters. Messages of the inner organs. Writing writing. Team flakes. Icy mutt stares at my wistful cappuccino. At the age of 23 'Pero' (the pen) arrives in London & is greeted at the door by Krupskaya. Dots of heads in air of hair. Cardboard tube at the end of a roll of two-ply. One red boxer was green, the other on the screen. You can feel the presence of a microwave oven with your heart & lungs. This forth calls not floss. A berth of boats. All the kept psychology in. An R in a circle dots the 'i,' Marigold bathroom tissue. Be-boppin' boffo be boppin'. Ache in legs after running is muscles' acids. Wood sinks into ink pulp. Garage sail. Light hydro. A world without a theory of genre is unthinkable. Sally toot in us. Mohawk & Skyhorse go free. Ear any crafty glyph the word twists. Passport out of hell, red J over swastika. Err. Fluoride is a byproduct of the aluminum smelting process. Foot cross bare linoleum. The instant in running the lungs open up, air blossoms in chest. No place but the gutter got dogs left to shit. The secret 'turns out' to be the existence of a secret. Ungents rove. Keep talking. All that billboard behind structure. Man walking briskly down the street, hands at his side clenchd into fists. Indirect late of light afternoon. If body's a delta, conflux of rivers, heart is sea & sky. Whole thought occurs in the body. (Years later) A day of rain the middle of June. Without prose for whom context is not. In the lobby of a Tenderloin hotel, old sailor sleeps in the shadows. Fear markets the governplace. Her hair, a verb. Power the poor mantis of the end stop. A clatter, signaling a tape cassette turning over. Did not the second week of September, 1752, exist? A point is not a part, wch is a line dividing hair. Ash tips white cigar. What I think. This was information of a kind. Footsteps on the rear stairs. Kites far from places. Sitting with notebook in lap, awaiting words. A word on the page that might be a spill. Sheets wrap around alley clothesline. Hue's color depends on eye's clothing. Not all clouds burn off, but those wch remain look sculpted. Gradual penmanship of decay. A guy who insists I'm Geoff Young even after I've told him I'm not. Gull shop shin. Windchime's shells wound together. No body leaves one options. A month after moving in, still unpacking plates. Bought nerds. Family is the world's false buffer. Never forgetting teeth means bad for a second. Design on the mug visible to the drinker only when held in right hand. Down sails in the anchord bay. Day's banter is a form of barter. Language ebbs, drifts. In Quartz Hearts I hear hats settle where heads sit, over necks. Between glides islands a chopper. So many names end in n. One sleeps in write. Landscape on a polyester shirt. Gulls after romping huskies in the surf. Chatter of wind chimes. A single infected hangover settled into a bourbon bad tooth. The desire to extend self to others never quits. Dangle instamatics against belly, Bob. Bikers gun iron ponies over pavement. The nausea of presence calls the past forth. Sez ash-fault, or bitchament for bitumen. Run twiggy kids ahead towhead men, portly wives. Epoxy for the mug's handle fails to set. An instant is each occasion. People who resent you reading their t-shirts. Wax cola cup flat in paper. We dream numbers in arabic. Moonburn. Familiar whistle of nameless bird. Green gray & lavender pigeon's neck shimmers. A neighborhood where people tie gauze curtains into simple knots to admit sun. Amphitheater of the angels. Three tufts of cotton alone in deep blue sky. Chilidog bearing children purchase skateboards. Morning breeze blows my hair about. Pine fog in the tea garden's trees. Each neighborhood has its characteristic size of dog. Neck sits if pigeon contracts. If only we knew how the future hides in the present. Catching Trotsky with tarantulas. Voice a voice blown returning as May. Beyond whitecaps watching the breakwater. The years it takes to make a new town your home. Storks raisd bills gulping adders. Robin on the light pole questions me. Charter bob boats. As the old ones die, the responsibility we feel expands. Gum fever left in the nostrils, in the jaw. Firecrackers burst in the morning air. Quickest are the lowest clouds. Remember to feed the plants. Walking of the bipolarity. An exhaustion in my mother's voice. Black boat's tug smoke. I can almost feel my teeth dissolve. Hang clamp like on head over. The body always burning its fat. Up wing current lifted the gull out to ride it. Cat lucky not to have caught that bee. They reject her because she's leaving. Soft hushing hum of water in pipes means faucets turn elsewhere in this once-large house. It's trite when she said you see it. Not noon yet. Nothing at 10 I didn't know here. Voices in the alley in Spanish. Eyeball flies. An insistent hammer. Needlessly to have reachd complicated wld have both their lives out. Posing as All-American Boy. Cake urinal deodorant. Letting the engine warm up. Dull pain was never a pulsing that went away. Wish I had some O.J. A loud is not speech reading. Squeak in clothesline's pulley. Large stood the old, empty house. A laugh that edges hysteria. Down people imagine sitting. Rubs sun lotion on her nose. I don't write recalling it later. Orlando's in the slammer now. Glass water never the color of its own. Symmetry of a cobweb. Up listen I smells smoke. Room placed by lamp's shape. Hear the fact of radios, but not what they play. Chewd into the discarded apple of life. Yellow plums the size of olives. The destroyd tigers. My reflection in the window. Blimp over the city floats. Tv antennas rock in the wind. Fire smolders in the cigarette in the tray. Avocados nearly black. Mid-twilight, the instant street lights go on. Bicycle chaind to a drain pipe. Over flowing chocolate beer melted down into the throat. An electric guitar somewhere in the distance. Gum in the fevers. I smell burning ants. Indoor plant moves. If only the pages are patient. Diminution as writing first of an idea. Hunchd on the porch steps, scribbling. The lens of his glasses stoppt at concentration. Turn to page 71. Quickly as we unpackd as we cld. I am hardly who began this, tho it defines me. Bowl's apples meet curves. I mean defies me. Each reading & stealing other's work. Church bells mark noon. Never nether, neither tether teething. Language, the universal equivalent. Time chronic. What I began one year & five days ago. Pepper dimensions shakers partake of. One blue house on a hill of white. Tends theming. Girl latches squeaky gate. Laguna code. Pipes jut out of stucco. Made fact is a thing. That sneeze has to be Alan. Many shoes on few feet. The shock of seeing this typed up. Hours ideas pass. Each accent is radical. Mounties guard harbors. Fireboat a water spider. Golden anger raises a wall. But the gate swings open. Ice brown bottle under plant. A long day of words markd. These gestures in the thought of place. Pins in my sleeping feet. Where the talk taken went. Churchbells phase out of sync. Blare we transistors from our own stoop? White butterfly about my head. The former cogitation of recall was difficult to ease. She's feeling her lack of sleep. New flaws sought order in my own brother. End, tho determind, is arbitrary. Left in the bathroom of the rainforest. A wonderful thought that got away. I write on the side to crouch on the walk. This is July. Letters are more than we know down to write. A child's easy expression of grief. Rats this long with big hairy dicks. Rotting ladder on the deck. The almost-red leaves of the Japanese plum. Scratch, scratch. Let the world select the words. Like eats a machine. Later clouds are whiter. By graffiti is day. Small planes thread a still sky. Peg's credit. Clusters of fireworks as we near the 4th. Gin wch tonic what. Watermelon fever. A shadow, like words, stains a page on the cross. An accordian on the radio. Drip all little faucets. Book in the sun is hot to touch. Long distance object constancy & the phone call. So after three years we split & I seek a new mode of being daily in the world. Is to light language as. Wearing one of several vests. To sit one last time in this yard years later. Certain terms tend to bunch. I had sailor in foot's grave one. Lonely for a hula hoop. Wordy as tho you ever understood. Shadows of thought. Eyes dilated your anticipation. I see the East Bay. An ant cld pick your fingers up without it crushing. Spontaneous combustion. In the plastic old dish sat blue soap slivers. Phone calls me back into the house. In the clouds is the sky. Separate faucets for hot & cold is barbaric. Back gums die. Whatever happend to Chiclets? In the twilight a high airplane somewhere heading. David Bromige learns to drive. Fingers always, in the doorknob of the vicinity, print. Demand each day is a new life. Kerouac's comma for the distaste. Sit in a schooldesk near my bed. Slow the lift of any launch. Putting rice cakes in a toaster. Middle if we had learnd for to write words from the instance. Today language comes spilling out. Many towards several. Grandfather's helmet hangs from the wall. Proprioception of muscle-tone is calld awareness. I hear Fred at the dishes. Cut. Four times what I read at the Grand Piano. We are always from this case of our suffering selves. By afternoon the fireworks escalate to civil war. But whether the plural dillweeds at dusk were rhetorical was deter-mind by what it meant to sit soberly in the term. Just words seeking forever. Up the wooden sides of these houses ladders ran. Fiction's first task was narrative & its second the syntag-matic. Appreciatively kneaded the furniture cats. Bottle of india ink props the window open. Sky seemd to smear up in the clouds. A line drive down the third base line. The prosody of their argument because of its distance & the intervening sound had the traffic of rain. What you think of whenever you hear a toilet flush. An airliner threaded itself between the silhouette of the clouds. Letters pressd into the drainpipe read BTP. Only twilight is the true light. Dust on the neck of my one guitar. Now the orange snail stalks the cat. Your message here. These lives were as simple as our terms. Long, curling yellow-brown stool light enough to float. Ambi to valent. Sugarless gum with a metallic taste. Carried his tundra across the piano. Words that stare back at you. In cha-cha Himalaya. A book in the pocket bends, words warp. When the bridge on the bled of his sufficient was pressure, it nose. The clock of our liberties, however, cannot be turnd back to 1868. Each height colord according to its cloud. Mosquito bite in the palm of my right hand. Houses alongside purpose with no visible pipes. Archd neck of a fork. Side was that out. We sat in the car talking, double-parkd in the dark night, not to one another but scripts each had determind was needed. Nude helicopters hovering above the bathers. Two weeks later the shell of the burnd-out hotel still smells like charcoal. Consternation & cauliflower. Can you tell when a siren is on the telly? A whistle with a bird toy. Video flame. Eye & my cat stares me in the wonders. We hammerd a nail thru his penis. It was music of a type. I had yet to learn how to read her signals. But a note clung to each psychology. Morning is nausea. Memories were no easier with the morning lessend. Many die for their half-apprehended politics. Suddenly, as the clouds turnd a golden blue, the lowest sky took on a deep glow. Firecracker sets the infant bawling. Then letters were easier. Wondering wch neighbor might have syrup to spare. But it was like being around anger, waiting for the grandmother to reveal itself. Car pulls in front & honks its horn. Entropy was its hour. Hot coffee makes me sweat. Strings in the homey distance of firecrackers. An urge to get on with the next page. Each location identifiable as to dog & pitch. No mail today. Garbage cans dragging neighbors out to the street. Paint flecks dot window's pane. Wld they eat together this last time? Mom sez 'Windchimes give me a migraine.' As was it tho "the sky" was a fire. Old fishermen who wear knit caps even in the hottest weather. Tops liked to wander about the roof cats. Porcelain goose sits in the window. Always over is nearly it. My Oly growing warm & flat in the sun. It is a disagreement with wch to sentimentalize. Baseball on radio. Our distances dissipate at shorter days each voice. Ferlinghetti sips a beer & stares at Twenty Languages. Random burst of conversation calld giggles. Freighter rotting in dry dock. Night gathers as the tribe falls. Overhearing the conversation of two realtors who meet in a bar. Also tops walks along fence cat. A gull pulling fish from a plastic bag. Cousins are closer birds than you think. You need 11 men doing volume to stay even. This was a poetry of series calld disengagements. People standing in a motorboat as it pulls away from Mission Rock. One enters the village as into a form. People staring silently at the bay. The first surrender is that of law. Trying to imagine what I mean. The chief in the cap is calld yachting one. I used to live in a complex better'n that. Catch cld marry a chill here & one. Working from storyboards. The drink will eventually join the ice. Strauss Trunnion Bascule Bridge. These were new chews on wch to toy on. Larry's sax to David's whistle. His clearest moment was his special writing & wld not long last. Astral Glade, Austral Glen. When the last night falls in the light, clouds die. Tugs in the shadows of China Basin. I hear the dog dog (collar caller?), not the dog. The day after a game of baseball, bones & bruises speak out at every step. When you see it, it gets harder to invent. Chicken's fat congeald in the pan. From the basketball came the dribbling of a kitchen sound. Some need to stare at the tape recorder just to listen. The juices sat in the pan of its own turkey. Morning, a limit. You think one of those shirts, but never wear it to own. Cats dark under alley stairs. What is the water in a drainpipe of the sound? Something square wrappd in a green napkin droppd & forgotten in the street. Sentences I write. Elephants before peppers. Beyond the white city these rumble houses simple with decay. Dog refuses to give up the frisbee. It is bush in the darks. A man with bad teeth reads others smiles. Common heads have become place above our upturnd blimps. Leaning over these pages. Being less afraid of a woman if it is being walkd by a big dog is sexism. A black-n-white pulls up the narrow alley—then backs out again. Just riding the effort entaild a massive bus. To be done with a writing is to lose it. The sequence of messages in the eaves is intended as a pigeon. Zen only works if you're exhausted, Phil says. Some of the finest Donald Duck t-shirt in our time has been written in poetry. A paint-chippt yellow chair. We call this parallel. I believe in sentences but not as speech. Knowing fourth period the seventh distinctness means lunch & the ninth grade. Nutmeg sprinkled over hot acorn squash. Saab story. Breeze bends the olive tree. Light sonnets by guitar. This is not the order in wch these were written. My spoon informs a long frappe. In baseball, the feel of a clean hit extends back up the batter's arms & into the shoulders. Industries echo. Any page might take an hour or weeks. It's a rich, young black salon too full of slender women. A Martian boulder by the name of Big Joe. It's not then. The shock of being here with you. Go silently proceed the players. Her name really was Krishna. The leather spaniel leaps up into the chair. Morning coffee's aftertaste. That you be specific is less correct than that you be important. Bees swarmd around the pop bottle's open mouth. Children resist mother, pounding on logic's shoulder. How do other books fit into my work? What then? I live deep in this forest. Fit this is a nick. I hear Fred typing in his room. The burn settles lightly over the sun shirt. In print, my words have moved far from me. We will spell how it was rememberd with difficulty. That transitional time, at the end of a 3-year relation. Oversaw intersections film each crane. Muscles hemorrhage from all that running. When none come back later, it of you's the same. I have a friend (you'd recognize the name) I'm certain is doomd to suicide. In Minnesota that there's imagination surpasses the pelicans. Each paragraph has three basic phases & sentences of two types. It is a square four children call game. On the chicken, big hunks of garlic. A numb sort of feeling as prelude to pleasantness. This work reminds me of Mario Merz. A pillar center not at the rotunda of the inexplicable. Mid-arc, the volley ball hovers over the web of the net. As you go while composing your own poem, you continue thinking you read this. Gringo scrotum. The light flickerd blue. Probability theory tells us there are unlikely to be more than five intermediaries between yourself & any other individual in the U.S. It was a chair that for species had gazed in one hind with its books raisd into another, sitting into centuries. Pocket notebook disintegrates as it fills. Explord some unwhere fore to here. Roaches starve in the glue of these little boxtraps. It ruled thus that we had declared into a specific payoff with unenterd unknowns, whose game wld be happend, tho secret. Some dishes need washing. Drops hung in the tree like birds of water. Writing lets me penetrate you. Mask become a simile. A man in a sleeping bag atop a mattress on the roof across the alley in the foggy dawn wakes with a start, then recalls perhaps why he is out of doors. Under the door was a tree with an over-pass in its trunk. I see words on the other side of this paper, but am unable to make them out. An intense couple at the next zodiac sat in low voices, arguing the role of love in the table. A cup of coffee—for the thrill of caffeine. Vibes way in the ground gave back to a ukelele. Together, we read these words with one set of eyes. Where perhaps it was some morning. The act of jotting these marks on paper organizes the whole of my life. Assumptions these were false. An argument where correctness & logic does one no good, because it's love. Be was this bop. Our house swayd gentle in the earthquake. His accents converted into eyebrow signs. Daniel Buren changes stripes. Phones sigh a sax. This is my memo pad. It was room again for the debris to move around the time, gathering in the busboy. Night-bloom-ing jasmine. A psychotic was to dispute what was there. Lemon-grass in scrambld eggs. Foul catch was this reason you cld drive a line in the territory. Sesame-onion bread. & that did what mean? A day of feignd illness stolen from wage labor. Not this. Traffic management of the syntagmatic. What then? Our age begins with Pound. Music rang above the telephones. Voices muffled thru the neighboring walls. A waiter named the page Crystal. Uneven grays light the sky. It wld be modern soon. My voice is all treble. Will prevented from office for running be you? A little radio I never use. This Chinese half was only one step from the cookie of a fortune. Fine arts of far planets. The slender letters will one time be straight, then later they will slant. Brown glass jars of beans & grains on a white shelf. Have to cancel you. News is an insult. Broccoli has to steam her. Wch words are weeds in a field of thot. An angle falls at the rain. Veins I see in my palm. This brings to our sequence an attention of 'A's. Not to worry. He or he later will already has change this. After socialism, there will be featherless chickens. The kind of sleeping person who brings his cafe with him into the bag. Objectively Pabloist. The dogs in their banishment mill at the door. This prism fails to trap light. She has a morbid fear of buses, I said. These words are bruises I make on the page. Why don't you say he sit down? That odor of mould particular to oranges. Was this in the middle? Song of the carpet sweeper. If the nursing woman sits opposite you at the manual, this is a table, but will you know it? The waking bird shakes its wings & feathers. Rose are what hips? Simple as a lash in the eye. Even the time in our poisons are druggd. My view of this valley from my deck. One of each is a subject as well as the context. About 150 typed pages. Space traces the travel across self. A pebble is always broken, always whole. There was no one in the conversation not listening to one another's room. The red spotlight just blew up in her arms. But if you think cruelly, May is the carefullest month. A film or crust over the kitchen floor. Acid with smack mixing speed with strychnine. A shipping container for caskets turns up on Langton Street. This is how we came to resume writing, that we might free ourselves of literature. The pulsing beep of a garbage truck backing up. Storms heavd about in the boat. Alphonse & Sylvie move out. Home pedalld the children. A sneeze brings him to his knees. A turning page was blanker, revealing a calmer time. Always an accent hidden in the voice. Dry was the day I left night, it (it) raind all the weather. Charles Dodgson's fondness for little girls. As he wrote he cld feel the pages on the damp dawn chill. A sudden round of sneezing. The house surrounded morning. A simple modest cold. Her trip left solitude immersed in him. What is poetry? The red cyclamen bloomd in its way. Magazines & books came free in the mail. Are these solutions not? We go small time now. Music nor I am writing. You make my toes hurt. We will look back on rain splatterd windows thru autumn soon. The sentence pauses long enough to rear its adder head up with a hiss in your direction, before settling back into the mottled camouflage of its words. It was like trying to word the mind wch had somehow slippd your find. An honest record skips. Each street had a symbolism that was shaped in the uniformity of submerged trees. I am Joe's kidney. You cld see Lewis on his coyotes, shouting at his porch. Performance piece: on a 5 buck dare my father sinks his hand into a vat of hot tar. In every telephone there were rooms. An audible marks the quarterback's despair. Day gradually steamd into night. Toothless man in a tweed cap, from wch a pigeon feather sticks. How before the new view soon bobbd into world. Anything might come next. The damp on the sitting steps finally soakd in.This is a weather report. Why remind it was important his shoelaces matchd himself? The violence of charm. To these almost too far apart bridges seemd instant. Is thot a thing? One never exactly saw a clothesline pulld tight. Explosive technology road. Chirp's jade. Revenge of the cloud. He thot of hands as television antennas reach out. The stillness in the laundromat when all of the machines stop. They of here was there a place where north grew right out of the ground. Small metal hoop that holds a lamp-shade's calld a harp. So mail wld be no today there. We ate lunch at a riverside inn in Benicia, where the water still smells of salt. Nor spelling in any predictability. Weeping willows filld the town square. Jazz of the bay filld foghorns. Delta towns of houses on levees & a boat dock in every tree-shaded yard. Cars of the whoosh. John Harryman sat in my lap. Round the leaves of nameless bushes. The relativity of a fixd position is its own advantage. Not this. The dust of day, disgusting in the way it coats our sinus, is in us. What then? Old urine (inexplicably) clouds. The compost dying back into the tomato plant. "Investigates" means anything you do. Uneasy cats between a truce. Pig out on my familia. More cartoons seemd news than the accurate. Faces of astronauts painted on a plate. Long miss-ing the greenhouse edge, I sit on a foundation & wrote of these down. The terms are more complex than the thought. Was there vines, berry & dillweed? In video, the spectrum of color is reduced to types. East coverd the it fence, nearly pulling ivy down. Airplanes swim thru the night sky like sharks with flashing lights. Shot rock thru a pile of poppies. In baseball, each ankle serves a different function. Twitching at the door, the landlord stood in anger. Think of the act of writing as a sitting, minimal dance. If it revolves, even the referential word will have a revolution. She returnd to find 3 small birds, confused, exhausted & hopelessly trappd in her studio, & they willingly let her touch them. This is role memory. The idea of kids as an audience. This is what skin does to your coffee. If this notebook were lost. The waterfall becomes a skylight when it rains. My body a slab like a huge bar of soap. & we sat around this laughing table, smoking the kitchen pipe. The warp of the line in the loom. These words write pen's shadow also. A Maurice Sendak kind of morning. Breaking at a scrape I cannot limit. Rational behavior takes too long to explain. The wing of bird rustles. Transcribing tapes, one realizes 3 voices are always speaking. We cockroach playd with an albino for awhile. He uses imagination to filter the daily. Scissors cutting the sound of yarn. Teens speak of nostalgia. This vacation is like a passage. Dream again of the Corn Palace. This enclosed mind will fade from my porch-on-stilts. Aftertaste of cannd soup. Was this the center of the tunnel that led circuitously to the earth? This language rejects imagination as a gesture. Had chest discoverd they buried on a lockd literature? Well, you know, it's always like that. Legs rubbed up against their cat. Between poems, beer tabs pop open. Closely see & you will look the lens on this scratch. In any game among adults, only one knows the rules. Cldn't they? Words loom up smoke-like from under the carbon ribbon. Ex-distances tended. Now you're in a book again. The Salton patch on the sea was the grey horizon. Accidently bumping the map, then watching it swing back & forth on the wall. The hand before them was their own shadow. Sung prose. Is this ocotillo? Cosmic remake of North by Northwest calld Close Encounters. These functions meet a chair. Ash-fault. Solving problems, as tho life walkd that. Ah yes words. So some discovers to do who is writing the writing. Now, the kung fu schools are starting to go broke. & these pointers are less a connective than a direction in that style. I find my friends smoking dope more lately, a quiet desperation in the air. The sink rises as the sun winds. He & I built this town. Here the red-orange pool is like the swimmers & an ocean wears caps. Beginning to write a note to David just as he opens the door. In the forgotten garden slants a shovel. At a certain angle this pen won't write. This was nearly the thing of the bottom then. That artists are full of shit doesn't change the art. But the stop problem was you cld not. What I'd like (right now) is a vitamizer. So you escapd it. An old man talking to his shoe. Only night wld for once hold if still. Everybody knows just exactly what's wrong. The feel of new flesh against your sox, new shorts. A long bus ride across the city on a halfmuggy, clouded day. Corner remains in only one yard of the light. A natural is anyone doing what an unnatural wld do with perception & taste, without knowing it. In these trees the cultural is a blight. Speech is easy & talk difficult. & there will be a windowless new tomorrow in a basement job. People who insist it's immoral to have political thoughts. Finding less you often phone your friends. It goes into a pocket pad in snatches, then is honed & set into a fixd context in a journal, then is typed & later typeset. For just an eyelash all this much seems a big ingrown. One's distance from anything proposd as a relation. You can hear the here from cannons. This, guy walks barefoot thru the streets with an old gray blanket drawn about his shoulders. Gutters are beginning to leave the clogs. Mr. Dynamite's Glasshouse of Players is a barbershop. We are at the middle edge or the either. One cld almost feel the tear when he wrenchd himself free of his previous life. Barely amid withdrawn bustle & the burning light, the buses diffusing off people of day's glances, awake yet on their labor to the way. One reads a room as a map of the 3-dimensional kind. Thus time crossd another still path. My taste is with the messier writers. Sullenly the law of the shadow in these eight trees grew in the school. People who own art galleries like to imagine they dress well, but casually. His natural appearing trimmd had the attribute of beard. Michael or Sean for example. So he murdered her works "not without cause" quickly & she read his wife. Writing—an eruption from the continuity of silence. This was is this. A hotel in wch only the winos aren't lethal. As if it was the shadow that built its cast. Sweating after a hot shower. Codes adhere to the traffic of cars. Coke sign that is the announcement of the corner grocer. No groves colonizd this bird. You understand this, but not as I meant it. Was time there yet? What about Creeley's politics? In the substantial chatter more distance appeard. These words signal an aesthetic code. Shld you not eclipse into the stare. We call him chronic. Pets mean nothing to the mirrors. Zimbabwe: class struggle in the guise of race war. Where is this Curtis works? Slamming the door to make it shut properly. All but difference makes the time. We were both conscious of talking around her boyfriend. I very nearly was determind, & I had to become invisible. The purpose of this writing is your arrival to read it. Deep in these streets we stroll conversation. Day begins at midnight, when images are shadows & figures suggestions. Here I am no less a turista, stranger. Bullshit, sez Larry, sitting on the deck with his alto. Three stand naked in a one-piece suit. What is language but a series of delays? The sentiments list the saxophones. On a cold night steam spits & whistles up from the gutter. This cat is the meow's. I see the expression in Tom's eyes as he lights the fuse of the firecracker. A new moment. My reflection simultaneously in three facets of a tavern mirror. A sound particular to the break of balls in a game of pool. A week away from work. David whistles the sextet from Lucia. Rear porches lack ostentation. Furniture company's ornate sign—green star on a round red emblem, green rays shooting forth, all above white vertical letters of 'starlight.'the bus that never comes. The appeal to the actual. Discrete marks a utility company makes on the sidewalk locates buried lines. Delicate structure of ankles & knees. As she pulld the sweater over her head, the horse bolted & threw her. Think of pen as a scalpel. The thought of what America wld be like if Ezra Pound had a wide circulation, well, it troubles my sleep. Digital, what alarms us cannot clock the ache of not sleeping in. A bundle of black plastic bags of trash in front of a downtown office highrise. The barber's comb inevitably rakes your ears. I will look back on these days & know them to have been hard times. Bob, writing, gently chews on his lower lip. This is the end seen from another angle. The explanation of a rash. All shoelaces droop at the knot. Pinching the flower off the coleus. Using stomach muscles to force the burp. Slick funk. She speaks happily of her new lover & I sit there in silence. The syllables in a face. Rings coverd in thread hanging from the bottom of the windowshade. As Benny reads aloud, I write whatever comes into my head. Basilica means where the pope comes if. The one person you know in this room is not the one you want to talk to. This plant's characteristic is how it mimics others. My stomach no longer adjusts for booze. The sound of helicopters hidden in the fog. Sentence number 6190. Gilbert Kalish & Paul Zukofsky on the stereo. Kirby calls in the middle of the night. Realism can only reinforce oppression—no art is representational. Squinting at the page as I write it. Having run already two miles this morning I was caught with the impulse never to stop. If only a record cld turn itself over. Bertolt Brecht was just a guy. Mole appears on the scrotal wall. The ache of thighs after a 3 mile run. Everyone stops to see wch house the ambulance pulls up at. typos are the mark of the other on the body of the text. These words summon literature. Family is the petrified forest. Sleeping with the performing arts. An accident causing stains to streak the page, S forms a blur. Hinges harbor thought's fibre. Sausages & baked beans in the men's club atmosphere of Hoffman's Grill, across the street from where Warren Harding died. The gutting of St. Marks. What do you mean, "can't find the music?" It's the army of toys. Form follows fiction. Just who's that kid's assignd adult? They had to be art students, because they dressd too well to be artists. The winter sun shines on a shelld Italian building, a dirt road & a dead German. Semiology of the garment district. Playing 'first set' blues. I wldn't. The film of a basketball approaches the real hoop. Your eyes prove this writing. Weaving from the rooves & leaning back porches of each house, the web of wires gather at the phone pole. People huddle around stoves in their bathrobes. Glade of squirrels, orange monarchs, turkey vultures. Windmills that have lost their blades. Possible behavior. Baja Baja. An odor specific to porn shops. Suddenly, amid houses, five acres of sweet corn. We sit in our skin, bones in a sack. Imagine London hills & arroyos. Teeth pushd heavily together as he listens. These sentences are my friends. Towns south of Oakland still strange to me after 3 decades. Standing in a field of cattle who stare intently as I write this. Myself wld just like a glass of water. There are no simple statements: everything has to be modified (I didn't say that). No one yet has solvd the problem of after the revolution. Squirrels of Sunol scram as we near. Orange cones in a pattern over asphalt—men working. What they see is what you get. A long day of art. Eucalyptus riddled by woodpecker. Or cattle scatter as we approach to regather & watch warily from the ridge top. Teeth jammd into gums like foxtails in a cuff. Sourcream not pancakes. Irby quotes Olson: tourism begins with Sherman. Shit just spills from the cow. These words I've left behind no longer constitute my voice. Aztec Buddhist thot. Cows turn & stare. These too neat lawns! The second of August, 1978. I explained the vista. World is round by hearsay. Each face a page on wch life scores a text (truism). All these squirrels mean fewer foxes in the hills this year. These roots crowded in a clay pot. You never know who reads anybody, 'less they talk about it. Here the sun never rises over water. Aw hell yes. I was listening a lot this last spring. Soap bar's design fades quickly. Grunt. Doorknobs are one form, faucets another, yet the function is not without its similarities. Target's pattern on the towel. The patter of little thought. The design of spelling. Small birds shake the peach tree. Rolling over, half-asleep in the dark, the soft, subtle odor of her hair. Stages of light that become the dawn. We share a peach, wch is our breakfast. Words must never belong to these faces I see crossing downtown streets. Homes made of warehouses or an old garage. What it means for an artist to go beyond their national context. Theater is the face. I scar, she says, easily, because of the amount of pigment in my skin. I there is here another. Wreck of the body. Grey-blue eyes behind long lashes, a mouth whose roundness does not quite extend to its corners. Downtown, one must block one's sense of context surrounding motion. Smell of peaches fills the kitchen. The head heads home. This heat is lost between the floorboards. Pain in a pin. The sentence is to language as a park to nature. The exhaustion of the week. Sitting, & suddenly the chair's not there. Men who shout their way thru supper. Walking thru a house at night with the lights off, you notice its slant more. Mother in a modest Dolly Parton hairdo. We danced at the Dreamland Ballroom. You can hear scratching in the walls. I run to flush liquor's corrosives from my body. Bruises on my spine. When you're single, women throw energy at you just to check the response. All news lies. A ring around the world I'll make. As the poppd foul ball descends on the crowd, it gathers, rises almost, to greet the falling orb. Something Bill Parsons droppd at Hiroshima. A round, red-rimmd wooden bingo chip lay among the dead dry plum leaves in the gutter. This is calld warming-down. The pope dies. The cloud flowers thru the telescopic lens. Flesh simply drops from bone. The shortstop pedalling back, his glovd hand shielding upturnd eyes from the sun. Flags in the civic center plaza flap in the breeze. An old woman gathers aluminum cans from the public bins of trash, dragging an old shopping cart along as she walks. I know another who goes around with a television strappt to her chest. One never writes lines, but a line, always some particular kind. I lookd up from my duties at the sink, mint odor of toothpaste deep in my throat & nose, to see her reading my green pocket notebook, smiling at lines she herself had said. Blankets, slept on, leave their folds & texture indented in the body. Ted defers to Robert, any Robert. Lock doctor. Evil defined as the one who is casual about being late. You never see light in these windows directly. Wide blue eyes open & for a second stare at me, nothing in them aware yet, then shut, breathing settles back into sleep. Natural animals of history. The faces of dead politicians grinning from the pages of an old Life. One makes marks in secret even these. Helicopter, first sound of day. Jill sighs in sleep, breathes deeply. Brain a small stone in cup of skull. The old Philippine men dress up / to shoot pool at Palace Billiards. Flameproofing cleaners & laun-dry. Sweat spills from me at the smallest excuse. I sit after breakfast of granola & plums, after coffee, imagining my life. Burning fog. What small trace here encodes the aesthetic? Her distance from her own world is what frightens me. An old man in a tweed cap pulls himself by the handbars down the aisle of the bus. A neighbor returns a typewriter. The orange cat's paws promise size. Thinking of doing. Someone calld Douglas.

Someone calld Douglas over. He was killd by someone calld Douglas over in Oakland. Gulping milk straight from an open carton (then crushing it as one might a beer can). It's hard to believe that the time has come to leave & think of what the morning's bringing. Eros in the resonance of the bat that's gotten 'good wood' on the ball. A wedding more Irish than Catholic. Next day, ache in legs' muscles tells atrophy is not total yet. Unlike clover, crabgrass does not go flat under one's step, but pushes to one side or the other. Sky caps on a break milling around together, sullen with good reason. The odor of unseen dog poop here in the grass. How basically simple these letters are. On a handmade box a mattress makes a bed, next to a card table, makes a room beside a wall of simple sheetrock, studio empty after the performance, makes a house on a quiet street. The mortician's inevitable obesity. Ted Berrigan's short fingers. The wind in the palms picks up. Writing long messages on toilet paper & saving the roll for a party. There are robins in the peach tree, ulalu. I dive back into third base head first, the baseman tumbling over me. Dublinese: I was glad to see the back of that pope. New York: what I'm doing on the page is just trying to amuse myself while I write. Do I dare to shit a peach? An old rowboat in the sand intended as a toy. Is that a bus coming? A butterfly works its way thru the clover. When I say myself I don't mean you. A truck backing slowly into a loading dock. In America the corporations feel compelld to present a good face. This hangover makes of waking a pilgrim's progress. He dined later on. Suddenly a new-model maroon Caddy drives up the park trail. What a word is before the ink dries. Beyond the palms, the sound of dogs at war. Rhymes of passion. A dozen blackbirds patrol the high grass. Why people fold their clothes before leaving the laundromat. The wind fills his shirt as he reaches back to pull it on. The emptiness of a blue sky. One kid picks another up & literally throws him from the boat. Trying to look nonchalant, walking down the street with a hammer in your hand. Your function here is collaboration. I will just stay here to make a point. There are three colors in the world, wch one did you choose? Fate, doom, nostalgia & death.

The little fellow's whinjing again. It was later than he'd expected when he got back home, but still he calld her only to discover that she'd already left, so that he cldn't tell if she'd waited & he'd faild, or if she'd forgotten their agreement altogether. I watch a white copter cross between towers of the bridge. Vida holds the Dodgers to a mere 12 runs. The question was whether to walk up the small hill—it was only 4 blocks—or to wait for the bus. I've seen so many old people glad to be dying. The distractions of conversation. Rock music is the television of the young. Sipping from a bottle of carbonated water. You've got to be careful, since almost no relationship will survive an abortion. Old white stoves at the entrance of an appliance shop. The way cops stand behind a suspect, one always in the blind spot. The new day is gray to the eye. I've little patience for the thing "made up" (true or false). How many limp or hobble as they go down the street? People who let their decisions happen to them. When I heard Rae was moving I wanted to cry. People in their morning trances on the bus to work. From the hilltop you cld see the entire city, or at least the downtown, wch was what Everyone meant when they thought of it (grey & white verticals tightly packd, sharp pins of light— the sun's reflection in a thousand windows), although it was not a hilltop at all, merely the highest point in Dolores Park. Just sittin' in the car, lettin' the motor run. I sees that little dog blocks from his house, a genuine sense of territory. A secret calendar on wch his seasons are markd by the time spent (after years) with each serious lover. Just when he'd decided to stop writing, get up & leave, several ideas occurrd to him at once. We stare into the blue-red "counter-glow" of the east sky at night. I introduce Gillian to Jillianne. Leaving the theater into the warm night, I choose to walk home to extend the solitude transferrd to my body by the film itself. In a space of days/faces fade/into phases of/who one is. Urinals are constructed so that men need never confront one another, sideway glances down. She wants that flat, simple / expressionless stare / which shows no fear / in old photographs. Walking slowly past a 24th St. bar that night, I see a boy, maybe 5, dressd in formal Mexican attire, blue embroiderd felt sombrero large for his head, atop the bar's counter itself, singing & dancing a song. Versions return/ typed by the lightest ribbon. In Mr. Klein by Joseph Losey, the station at the Metro is introduced by the camera's gaze on dry branches, a black bough. All the world's / in one word / caught. Grey kitten chases its tail in the field of my lap or climbs lightly up my trouser leg (even as a baby, its claws razor sharp). The green glare of fly's wings crawling in the sun over brick red kitten shit. Walking the cow thru the flour. Can you make out the outline of your parents' nightmare? A whole night of behavior. A young man sitting on a suitcase on the curb in front of Greyhound, reading a map. Hours later, the taste of fresh dental work. Between customers, the lady plays solitaire in the ticketbooth of the porn theater. One word in each sentence is the hinge. Poker is a field of games. Positivism of the piano. Pots hanging on a line of nails on the kitchen walls. The twisted, foreshortend arms of the retarded man. I of course saw none of this. Way to go, Sam. We ride slowly up in the dark freight elevator to get to Barrett's loft at night. My self-image is not spacey. Waterbed animation. No body wanted for a hangover the next morning. Nightshade & I ate pancake specials at the no-name cafe. The use of a storyboard to block out thought superimposes its own form in the matter. This room never gets any larger. A watch is a snake coild to your wrist. Seven miles to the pound. I'm a very transient girl, she said. Musicians who feel a jam is the ultimate mode. No organ is eye's equal. Dances like a puppet. This is my work. When the water temperature got too cool the internal parasites multiplied quickly surrounding the small blue-body, red-fin samurai fighting fish with a white gauze that killd it. Sopraninos unite! These are simple sentences. Music in search of a cave. Rough hair of a guinea pig. Blake's realism. The cement truck totalld Duane's Chevy. What they shared was not the sex, but the need for an intimate language. Imagine Norwegian. Did I say that? If war is chess, then policy at least is poker. A species whose sense of form is in the shoulders. The world of nouns in motion. Moon's enough light to write by. Conscious of leaving the toilet seat up as a specifically male trait. Drugs change the superstructure, not the base. Now we're in the neighborhood of this sentence. Saxophones & washboards. What does Bruce Andrews think of Douglas Woolf? Sometimes you see the age in language by erosion. All civilization is in the spine. When I smoke dope verbs decline. You cld see where they had to reconstruct part of that brick wall, but you don't know why. She sits in the bath, sipping tea. There are 20 musicians in the room right now, playing as I write this. In the well-lit latino cafe I see a short red-haird woman massaging the shoulders of the motorcycle cop. Tribes of horn. Cotton in their ears (continental airs (cotton underwears)). SPEAK UP! Ground floor loft scenes. Language is eyes. Man with a 9-string armadillo. Just the idea of glasses. The cold, damp metallic surface resting against the fleshy tip of my nose as I drink the beer. My descriptions of you always fail. The acoustics of any corner. This can be understood different ways. It is wonderful to see names in a work. Larry says, "You must be some kind of maniac." Holes in the ceiling where stovepipes went. Until they get loose, get into the rhythm, dancing to them remains theater. But this is not the order in wch I wrote this. Most music is bad percussion. Surprised at what different lives we had as children. The reality level of the news is zero. Always one woman (seldom more) in a loft jam. When all verbs are nouns. I judge people by what they do with their walls. Not description: quoting. Certain knocks at the door as identifiable as voices (inscribing the option not to answer). The way editors come on at you. Do fish dance? Poetry is the theft of language. Guinea pigs whistle. What I want in words is the pleasure of a fact, how I notice those peaches rotting in the dust out the open back door of her studio on a hot, breezy August afternoon, the two of us just chatting (low voices) on the large bed in cool shadows, but it dissolves, eludes, no word to capture humidity's essence, the smell of wet hair, background music of invisible "birdies," no facts at all but that of words, scratches in a note-book. A stillness precedes thunder. Ambiguity digs. In ma-&-pa stores, one clerk just holds the gun. All these personalities are tuned. Equal librium. I get the needle arm caught in my shirt sleeve & drag it across the shakuhachi record before I realize what's happening. All the books I buy but never get around to reading. Everybody at the movies talking to themselves. Architectural music. Occasion is a hopeless term. A work that goes on all night, musicians coming & going, regrouping, sitting in, sitting out. White beard blossoms under blue Dodger cap, his skin that brown oily hardness from sleeping out of doors. I just put these words together. Dance without music. At this hour of the night all you hear are the low-riders, squealing their cars around corners. She rejects the nationalism of context. A good work is read before it's written. I do not remember learning that you pull the cord to ring the bell for the bus to halt at the next stop. Our first art is playpen & sandbox. A discursive topology of energy. An algebra of the occasion. Two sentences I didn't use. A resistance in the body to using telephone directories. Coming to respect more each day those people I know who are capable of quick farewells, clean transitions between one situation & the next, who can shut the door & turn to face their suddenly empty apartment with no trace of despair, confusion, loss. In the middle of a story a character sits down, lights a pipe, puffs, leans forward into the glow of the lamp & begins another. Flan is a kind of custard. If one were to go deaf in middle-life, wld one cease to think the sound of words? I'd say you have an eye for the humble. MNT bowels give out. Small blue cup with a gray-green handle. What are these weeds in body's garden? K calls from Squaw Valley, talking of sandstorms & an isolate (prefabricated) city. Words don't mean, they tattle. The yellow bus, passing, fills the window. Let's imagine the coast. These words construct an object you hold in your hands. Milk softens the cereal. In the conception French of the world physical, objects focus attributes. Red-headed lovers (are there any others?). A list of axioms & observations. To remember, in love, the important term is the specific—jealousy the demand of attention in an absent moment. Uncle Rebus. Toweling off. One's first idea of style is excess. A new driver boards the bus & adjusts his seat. After laundry, the ritual reconstitution of the bed. After coffee I always sweat. "There's a burnout," she said, house on Elsie Street gutted by fire, heat's permanent shadow on the wood. A blimp in the sky drifts by. I stare straight into faces faded in the glass (store or bus window), but never am I seen. In writing, the primary quality of any object is its name. These scars hint at aspects she no longer reveals to just anyone. The refusal of the stomach. Auto with a whack cracks the tail-light's glass (red plastic). Bittermelons green in a cardboard box, atop an upended orange crate on the sidewalk by the storefront door. Days convert to hours, leaving a residue of surplus value. What I love most about a perform-ance piece is to watch the preparation. The architecture of bill-boards, fire escapes, back stairs (culture of the not seen). I sit in the morning sun, sipping coffee, popping knuckles, whispering these words out loud as I jot them down. I'd know my mother's voice anywhere. Whether the willow-shaded streets of a strange town, or the initial seduction of a new affair, the revelation of another body's particulars, one's capacity in the face of the new to pay attention has no limit. One sees storms cloud the simple penmanship of these pages, as shadows or turbulence. There is the yellow chair. Holding the cat like an infant, I open its jaws & drop the orange pill past the tongue, stroking the fur on its throat until it swallows. Summer came later in '78. Shah Gives Hua Royal Welcome (tight security). Vanilla Envelope. Form exists only in the particular. The flickering fluorescent light makes my eyes hurt. Dialect equals humidity. Notice how I trust aphorisms. Just getting off a bus—crossing thresholds always puzzles me. Anything is possible—but discontinuous. An old man who cldn't tell the difference between Greek & English. Fish don't swim upside down. Dents from teeth in the No. 2 pencil's yellow body. Gallery hours. Thick rubber bands versus thin ones. Near midnight, I pass under the window of a small office in the industrial district, its lights still on, & hear the sound of a typewriter. I only think language is like this. He has ideas but thinks of them as sentiments. Laying out & pasting up, days are wasted at a rapid pace. Little knots in my beard thru wch my comb rips. People at the corner market talk poli-tics, but ain't never 'public language.' Each day our eyes sink further into the skull. A blindspot I call Father. The fact that it makes no sense isn't even gonna slow him down. Because the keyboard on wch I type at work is not the same as the one in my home I own I make mistakes each night. Flour pour. I see him scrambling in his own head, looking for that sense of balance. Stupid about cars—I only hear one noise when the engine runs. Television's lie is the continuity. The newspapers want to know why I don't write in lines. I imagine walking thru the streets of lower Buffalo one not-yet muggy summer morning, looking for an apartment in Allentown, bitter toward my lover at that moment, resenting my life. People like their hand resting against their face. This sentence soakd up too much whisky last night. Hippie capitalism's the worst kind. On my desk the crush'd spider's body stains the file folder. Traipse. Since I was a child I've had an idea of the particular—shoelaces, faucets. My grandmother's eyes no longer register my face. Hard ass poets. At night the literal electricity of a main street is so clear I can hear it. Terrible people who wiggle their legs all the time. Now do this. Without repetition is no form. Threadbare red wool shirt. Think of a kayak as a shaped canvas. Stifling a cough at a public occasion. The whirrs & chucks of the pinball machine clicking itself back to zero, the free game. At this busstop, the people with picket signs get off & others with tennis racquets get on. Another spiral memo pad dissolving in my pocket. Several shades of grey in any sidewalk. As the camera's flash goes off his shadow is cast for an instant along the white wall. Everyone's got an idea about the belt they wear. The universe situated between a & the. A town in California somewhere, calld Solvang. The dog tied to a parking meter by the door of the bar. A blur in sentence's where the word slippd. Bright blue wad of chewing gum on the walk. Milking stools & card tables. Thus thus. Simply writing it plural makes it abstract. The kind of cheap pop you know will spin foul on its first bounce. Narrativity. Some of us just thrash around in our private lives, never solving anything. Some days shoes will never stay tied. Somehow, in mid-September in the subway, the strong Xmasy smell of a pine tree. A paragraph I cld write for the rest of my life. Even in Chinese the sarcastic banter of highschool kids is specific. Ripples in the image thru an old window. I play Eddie Cantor on the jukebox. I'm content to eat a salad. We stand naked in the open doorway & watch the rain. A star on the shoe means it's Converse. This is not some story. The gray mouse tries to climb the pole to the nightingales & their seed. Today it remains morning until nightfall. Winter chaos in the wind-chimes. In this photo the ocean looks just like the desert. I spring into the milling flock of pigeons wch leap into flight. Underfunded. A touch of tahini for Mother Cabrini. Flat light & sharp shadows on the objects of a tabletop (camera, tortilla, half a tomato, the poems of Alan Davies, the shine of cups) after the first light rain. One sees in the face of sleepers all the strain in their lives. The water is boiling. I step into the cafe to write but am immediately beseiged by old friend D., his act at long last having totally collapsd in on itself & nobody else to tell it to. Bad art of rich students got up as punk. Since when? The steam of coffee & smoke of cigarettes, blue-white in the rainy morn-ing's shadowd light. Remember to never let the coleus flower. Sharing the bath. All my friends are perfectionists & it gives our crowd its taut pitch. The white pages make up only a third of the phone book. He won't stick up for what he believes, but that's part of it too. Just to be with another person involves a tremendous jolt. Boppos hang on nails on the wall. All my writ-ing is concernd with the quality of light. Carla says that, in Steve's work, the line is any act of completion & that what makes it work is how it will be at a different level almost every time. Words achieve critical mass. Bob speaks of the jungle of letters. I think now of going into the rain. Must of thought. We simply stood in the middle of the hot tub & kissd. Palm trees & plums. Streetlamps flicker before they come on. A damp heat softens tissue. I stood on a street corner & began reading aloud. In the glare of dawn people sit in their cars, letting the engines rev in garages or at curbside, everywhere the hum & small blue plumes of carbon exhaust among the trees that front these white stucco houses. Ethereal: eat the real. Iteration alters. Paraworthies. Putting the words back where you found them.

3 variables in any shadow. Sweat spills & my pulse flares after a good run. She dreamt of an opening at the top of the baby's skull, inside of wch she saw waterbugs all curld up. The koalas are falling. Danger: contains oil of mustard. Steaming black bitumen just pourd into the carpark. Each clear dawn is utopia. Inja—land of elefants & tygers. At dusk, lights glow with a glare. Wind winding clothes on a line. In the distance (possibly the office of the auto repairshop not open on Sunday morning) a telephone rings & rings unanswerd. The higher the bench, the hotter the sauna. The instant the wheel of the bus touches it, the cardboard carton bursts with a pop. Raindrops on a pane slide together & down. Poppies bloom at dawn. The weight of the asparagus fern's branches has become too great. She said she heard this poem on the radio & liked it. Different tints for different prints. Even in public we recognize each other's need for privacy (seldom talks to strangers on the bus). The blue in the full moon in the dawn sky. After you've done it, it's done & one can't go back, experience is not something you visit. Cat sniffs the steam at the rim of the coffee mug. Just to go to the mailbox is to change worlds. So many women fear their bodies. One last day as an ethnographer. Fear of being put to sleep. She brought the old woman some pills she'd been saving for 15 years & orange juice & sugar so she cld swallow them, then sat outside with her family after all had said their goodbyes & just waited. Not collage as form, but in form. How many frames per sentence? Two mornings later, my throat's still raw. All you Leos need to have it stroked. Single sheets of newspaper blow across the lawn. The descent into winter thus far has been gentle. She carries her clothes to the laundromat in a pillowcase. Fire on Mt. Sutro. Here follow french puns. Apple juice serenade. A guy I last saw in the max yard at Folsom. Time's many. Sucking the last beer from the can. The meaning here is not delayd. Jeanne D'Arc BBQ. Waterbuglike armord cars. Moos on the tenor, moans on the alto. Tongue pokes idly at catgut lacing in my jaw. A drummer's wrists. I call that a mongoose pipe. The most political thing you can do is face the language. A course in applied writing. Homeboy. At the end of his wrist, where normally a

hand wld be. He speaks his mind. The feathers in the chande-
lier. Day sleeper. Tolstoy has Melnick's nose. Sets shells on the
sill, to couch the light. So this wld be a period in his life, brack-
eted by what a notebook might hold, whole months in quota-
tion. Amid all these drums & horns, the pianist plays only to
himself. The names, for example, of cabs: Checker, Universal,
Veteran's, Yellow, Arrow, Rose (colors blue & white), Luxor,
DeSoto, City. Shadows of wasps hover on the sun-lit kitchen
wall. Acrid smell of cat farts. What did this use to be?
Helicopters fill the dawn air. Bebop on the upright, some
tympanist on conga, clarinet in the corner, sticks on a 2nd,
smaller conga straight from a marching band, our music
builds. The Imam & his beads. Kit sez of Carla, "you're keeping
the story form alive." In wheels Larry. Summer weather at the
edge of October. A plastic green worm with wheels & a saddle.
The joking chatter of the men who shine shoes in the john at
the Greyhound depot. Black rolls of tarpaper on a slope of roof.
A horn's only a bird in your palm. The odor of dust of erasers.
The man in the front of the bus keeps shooting at us with his
fingers. Cat's nose nudges the book as I try to read these poems
of Lee Harwood. Some changes are in effect. It's all hard time,
straight time, short time. That Japanese couple is speaking
French. Let's taco on down Mission. All shifters mark the discur-
sive. Ears in the air don't hear it there. Call me Uncle Pockets. At
any dance or jam, there's always one hippie fighting his angel.
Imaginary tongue on a non-existent tooth. Dusk, the hottest
day of the year, in the city, the intelligible world. Ted turns his
head from the flame as he lights his cigarette. Bodies burning
in the trees of a quiet San Diego street. The Vatican secretary
of state enterd the pope's chambers with a small, silver ritual
hammer with wch he tappd the late pontiff lightly three times
on the head, asking, "Albino, Albino, are you dead?" then, there
being no response, removing the papal ring from John Paul's
finger &, with this same hammer, smashing it. Attention's
intention's tension. Dork means washerwoman in Polish. Fat
plastic wheels have transformd the modern tricycle. Yellow-
brown buttery phlegm clots in the back of throat. One guy in

the band just sits there, drinking from a bottle. Morning sun bursts orange, then fades into yellowwhite. Old refrigerators on the sidewalk in front of a store. Whenever that door opens, street voices enter. All of the tags in the back of all of the shirts, blouses, sweaters, jackets in the world. Any description condensd marks art's place. Instead of ant worts I saw brat guts.

What makes this the last paragraph? Was it the turn's tide to turn then? My body digests jaw's stitching. Not this. Ice tongs attachd to my head. Retracing my dark in the steps. If you ever navigated on the weary canal. Downward press momentum out. Cymbalic. Civic men sleep on the old center lawn. A greater glare when the sun sets, in windows or off a crane on a highrise rooftop. Several lips on his tiny uppercut. Early to bed, early to rise, makes you a wage slave in the bosses' eyes. Row a pole of flags without poles. Deaf from Mexico. Was this more confusing a new time? All these drivers were pilots over in Nam. Washers wade. Waiting at a truckstop breakfast cafe for her to arrive. Two yankees out late. A ring & string of twine hanging from the shade swings in the breeze. A pulp bruisd into a sugary banana. Backing the Pontiac out of the garage, grandfather crushes the dog. Disproportionately high up off the motel floor, the bed rooms are large. The bus is a great leveler. Glands for different hands different. Honey odor of commercial detergent. Small plastic arches of a golden white fork that ends in a handle. Squares of a larger billboard image pulld skyward by a crane— word 'lager' hangs over my head. These are the mornings of metaphysic. Two boys in cords & sweaters on their way to school, their sister stooping to tie her shoe, calling after, "Hey, wait for me." Sing force self to one it. For no reason visible to me, the woman in the plastic & metal bench seat in front of me on the No. 14 bus turns around & starts shouting in Tagalog. Many & one. Uniform green pellets feed the rabbit. Crayons & small cigars between the distinction. Henry's large, furry, orange paw stretches thru the narrow opening at the front door. Toy is a shit. No, baby, I'm not here, only these words are. Vest lessons are croations. In the beak of the wooden duck descending from the stage ceiling, the magic word of the day.

This journal fading red into black. On the weekend they shut the escalators down at the bus station. Blue sweater forgotten on a red chair. This driver just sort of aims the bus—lurches in jolts. A weapon is shit. Baby's babble scrambles syllables, but the prosody speaks joy. Into read reading. Is you is or ain't you ain't. Is morning the magician? I sometimes carry my ass around on my shoulders. Residue of drain netted sink's watercress. What is love but paying attention? Cafes take in the brunch. Sentences occur in speech only as the attributes of an educated class. Of fog between hill slices. She plays the highhat with her eyes shut. This takes people as behavior. Searching the wanteds for 'philosopher, part-time.' Never dry completely hands. I love rubber chicken. Fly the coffee beside a cup. The sun sets in the windows, thru them. Pet it be with new wood blew. On a hot day, woman who delivers the mail makes more mistakes. Autumn in Cullowhee, snow in the park. Going downtown, just as Everyone's going the other way. Light was. You can see the hammers hit the wires when he plays. This sweater penetrates wind. Donner is a party or pass. Wanted not not is not-not wanted. Any store "under new management" is not the same. This often hill on wch I sit so. Animated conversation on a bus across the bay. Kitsums. 118 ridges on a dime's edge, 119 to the quarter. Words smear these hands. Wind kicks up. Than what? Plays the piano the way I type. A little occasion here, as befits the cloudy. Parakeets shrieking behind a green lace curtain in an open window as I jog by at dawn. What formembers brain regrets body. Words scar the blank page. An old baseball in a bicycle cap, pushing a man up the slope. Marimbas at the heart of this music. Knot this this. A canvas shoulderbag gone black with age. It was the tenth month, October, meaning eight. I wrote that a year ago, two paragraphs. Duty off officer. A scudding percussion. Some wrote me body. Hair cut from my beard flecks the basin's porcelain slopes. Self given one two it. A closet for the water heater, wch just sits there. This light is a pilot. "No," I say to the man who asks, "Is that your diary?" "it's a book." Bra sees thru blouse strap. In Puerto Rico, 85% of the people qualify for food stamps. All good sleep approaches writing. Consonants drum in the throat. Sky time catches laps. Confident that she misunderstands his work. You almost know you think it. A chaos of context. See these cans. Like the color code of a Mexican city. We changed to have record the fail. Arranges his books according to their size & color. Town roads around find. One sees where the muck of the rain dried on the window. Two forms number & the next highest two. The constant accompaniment of her bracelets. Shade in the flower fades. Well I do see color. Dull gas heats one. Hear the hoses. Gray deep cirrus roils. All dressd in blue. Was it he? Tongue's a sharp pink against brown-blue flesh. Even the waves weave free. Children are always falling under the wheels of wagons, carriages, trains in Reznikoff's poetry. To wear it seemd a bracelet copper. Bob calls to ask if there are commas. In under of at of about to into under to by—in within to out in under of which whereas of what—above without in under of into under by of about by out out. Echoes in ears' arches. Was I written? This sentence, strategically placed. Library mesh wire windows. Every sentence is representational or citational. Only plants liked large him. Echoes in the flute rend the note full. Palm bent the wind. Little dog yaps at the garbage truck's hydraulic wheeze. A flag of pale rows without flags. Carla wld write Little dog yaps, the garbage truck's hydraulic wheeze. Distance where the red set has yet to sun in the hills. The duals of the antiprisms are trapezohedra. Dance this. Hot farts! Gathers as one grows elbow folds at the older in flesh. Soprano's conical where clarinet's cylindrical & wood. Orange month rhymes with with chimney. Gulping soup so fast that the empty bowl continues to steam. Lights darken as city appears. Where the cat by accident dug in its claw the tip of my finger began to swell. This point is a blade pen. The trill of the tricycle bell. Pyro replies wore technics. The flute doesn't have any business. I light this call flower. What Fred calls the gasoline aftertaste of Brie. Tampons a pink box by the blue toilet filld with sky. Dental disturbance. The only solitude of the dog. Dried grounds of coffee down the side of the cup. End by the blender on the fridge a table. Suddenly I am as if rejected. The sun looks my

shoulder over. Those levis hang on him like slacks. Red tail
sweep free around the night lights way. Imitation citrus flavord
dietary artificially sweetend carbonated beverage. This mew of
the hinge shuts as I door it. Foulmouth. Air mapping room's
windows flies against bang. A music wholly of local gestures.
Here am I now alone? The small dark corridors behind &
beneath apartment houses, crowded with garbage cans, wreckd
bicycles, old doors. 5 cooks at the coffee cafe. A misplaced sprin-
kler soaks the walk. Counting the sky in the airplanes.
Sheetrock is lovely. Writings hand. Another think coming. New
history always repeats itself in this way. A young Asian woman
walks past the laundromat window carrying a bottle of (bright)
orange soda. Solo sax. True consonants are static. This ungain-
liness of language angles the the. Shaking chocolate atop
steamd milk in a glass mug. Rewords recently have been moved.
A young blond Anglo man walks past the laundromat's steamy
window carrying a bottle of (bright) cherry soda. Half-flushing
formd shit. I am an example of grammar. A door on hooks on
towels. The furnishd rooms of hell are crampd with beds too big
for solitude, half-sized refrigerators toppt with hot plates &
views that peer thru bars of fire escapes at the glare & bustle of
the small, all-night grocer's sad unending celebration. Not this!
Twine ties a foam mat up into a roll. Rocky groups of piles out.
The mushrooms had taken over. False all these starts. Rova: the
gears of four horns mesh. Tassled green yellow room, never
used, hang from the high shade (over a lamp) of the ceiling.
Junior Gilliam's deep sleep. To & then the ships went down.
Shaped canvas, a frame of mind. Order is not an accidental
chance. Lately I've been reading paragraphs. K as if with a
chamomile. When I sit on the hardwood floor with my back
against the wall & my legs straight out, I love to notice the
muscles around my knees stretch. Orange cigar's instant is for a
tip. Some sounds you feel. Design is boiling by mistaken water.
At night as I sleep a part of me hears the doorknob turning &
turning. Hvphenaterialscleroticity. Hands sweat in the
kitchen's rubber gloves. Augur fits. Name that tuna! Net clear-
ings. Pipes run along the beam wch supports the ceiling. Pay a

man at a one-legged phone. Zithers offer either order. Wall hung on the abalone. Simple forms with rich textures. Aid first stuff of bandage kind. The shock of a new haircut. In trombone slides. A pair of white nurse shoes, lacking laces, abandond on the sidewalk. Out of one I don't know it's only how many. A room smelling of old baseballs. Water sips cigar smoke. When the grain of memory is regret. They's who? Banana's ideal for holding sticks of incense. Calls Peg. At concerts I often sit near a wall, one ear turnd directly to the music, that I might hear the acoustics. Studies brain in the American. These dudes sing beery r&b on the bus on their way to the night shift. Be evidence who holds truth of what self. Over the sign's list announcing cappuccino, au lait, mocha, espresso, doubles & iced cappuccinos, these words in red: no regular coffee. Meticulous weather these days seems the. His assets in cassettes. Chairs asleep on cats. Four trashd-out newspaper racks in a cement block. The inverse architecture of order in the forest is plants. Everything's akimbo. Water in a mineral bubbles glass. Sweat on a drummer's arms. In the machine we have a perfect pistol. A shadow crosses the half-moon of my Olympia's letter e. Unable to pen blue night from black late at tell. "I see you went to Berkeley," the interviewer said, "have you ever been arrested?" Thus the further from scotch broth we get, the larger it reeks, looming of home & roast beef. Tubas of the forest. Each place is a new mark. The heat of the gum against your tongue. The tundra is this. Braxton wears a towel like a scarf, over the shoulder of the baggy green cardigan. Guffaws, chortles. Beeps of a computerized cash register. That is the garbage of a roar truck. A formula written without operational signs is indivisible. This being again begun beginning was. "I want to talk to you about that second Louie." It is not crumbs to find your trail here without the easy of way. Feudalism of the soloist. Plastic old green water containd in a trashcan bath. Two-syllable world. You don't pinch the hold so much as pen it. Beneath it I saw white. For orange with cloves an incense stick. Some musicians collaborate, others associate. Literature carries some sentences within it. Striped workshirt with the sleeves

rolld up. How in those round he draind the 50's. All that long
spine. My pejorative the name. Unconsciouslv, she pushes the
bangs from in front of blue eyes. For boogie quest sing. Left to
write. How does mill steel one? He's got an odd idea of cigars, to
call them 'smoking pencils.' Shadows depth cast cause. I feel
the drum's concussion in my throat. Although this music was
new to us, we understood it to be noise. One senses gravity at all
times. Gold under arch delights, we gorged to hearts. Shadows
shift when the sun sets. Hours that takes for shit until edge &
ass are warm on the porcelain of the now numb seat legs. Porch
is full of wood worms. Room whispers in the next. Dave Holland
'strumming' the bass with his thumb. The blind library in the
woman. Fact is a metaphor. Seams one scene. I am always look-
ing at your work, stealing from it & using it in a hundred ways
even tho a lot of the time I can't read it & basically don't know
what you're doing. Not this is thought. Half of the hammer
'head' is its claw. When was the army in he? Tone scarfs. As if
the sun had turnd to thing, chunks detaching once at all, limb
from limb, dropping like some other existence into the cold
charcoal sea, but now light was like coming into language. Too
close, fire engine's siren stops. Point but not page pulls the ink.
Insert spacing between short notes & a sax will prove percus-
sive. Such choice, tho not by solitude, proved good. As Kit reads
aloud, I hear a child whisper to his father. Grill griddle burger's
brick. Can you hear me by the window? Each page the morning
mounted him. Thought's hinge at a period shuts. Molo polo,
ponius ponies. Writing simply erases a certain blankness on the
page. Or the strings razor was a bow drawn over the bough. No
solo for a tuba. Agh slaps palm brow. All the time. This was the
stones of probation. A choice to make statements break in the.
Rust side at sea city. One afternoon my grandfather came home,
saying he'd seen my father in front of a liquor store on Solano
Avenue, fighting with the clerk. Tea cups rust. No memory for
titles. All glue. Is that a sentence or just an idea? The self means
the house in the rented dream. Lavatory cleanliness of an auto
showroom. Noon after blue clouds breaking patches late into
up. The stiff sound of paper bags. That wch is draws straight

blood forward. When, standing, Bev's face bends forward into the lamp light, to read the poem set flat atop the piano, the bulb's glare shines on her glasses & for an instant we glimpse our own rapt faces. Spice hater. Improv echoes epic. A roll-top copy of a perfect desk. Can use light to alter time. Gathers around the pigeons writing. The violence of the flute. The this was day to be. The weight of the hat on my head. Uranus line leads to this. Soft & fast. A woman in her shades raises a blue nightgown. The fan turns slowly on its stand. Send nuns us. Categorizes shirts by pocket numbers. Write these words from me as I fade them. A fly lands atop Kit's finger & promptly takes a nap. Blue fork chippt upon a silver plate. I'll quote anybody. Lovers wondering whether they & they or they & he ever were. Stares straight into the bell of his sax. Sleeping, I saw pillows back in the Buick's bag. No two batting stances are alike. After the ice's gone, continue to drink the melting bourbon. Torque it. The refrigerator of companionship's hum. Dawn in public. An odor in the nostalgia of Melba toast. One word, then another. Beginning is this I not again begin? She sits with her hands wrappt about her midsection, as if for protection. Force in contradiction expresses the coherence of a desire. The meaning is evident & gives no clues. Coffee shaker's mug tall as salt. One always hears ice in a bar. Chance will never throw the dice of an abolish. Just an ornament they wear about their necks, calld a saxophone. Orange dented fender's Opel. Carla: boundaries mark the time spent looking for boundaries. We were not ringing for the phone to wait. Brisk & steady. Day groan. She remembers not the dream but the dream journal. Electricity rattles with fridge. I wants that music. Spain on the falls brain rainly on the main. A religion of bacteria. Mary Hall & Carolyn Korkegian. The tone of the bounce of an empty aluminum beer can. Back on windowtips fingers door smudges forming. These works, words, wait on a closure they attempt to put off. I voiced the name but cld not recognize it. Shopkeeper in front of his store, hosing down the walk. Glass-gold leaf reads x-sign on the ray. The way a huge hand will lift the small cup up, daintily. This is the alphabet of economies. My poems are pyramids that begin at the tip. Stir of sound beginning to first roommates. Heads are just gourds (rattles, flutes). Imagine the butter in wch possible worlds are knives. Slavish to the spelling. Yellow room into the sky comes to gray. Knowing when I'm rude. Matinee. Towel atop the piano for the quartet to fetch, to blot the hot night sweat. Once each ash tree shall soon be page. Professionalism means calling the telly a monitor. Lines ebb on a word. This state keeps its top court upstairs at the library. Flaking off the tatterd leather chipping jacket. His shadow on the floor cld be taken for a chair, arms arms. Time weaving the spare in one's world. The logic of the piano. Who wears a sweat pants woman? In certain faces strain centers at the eyes, in others the mouth. Running bakers in the form of salt shacks. All possible meanings obtain. Pseudoantiprotodetestimonialistically. I long for the end of the individual in the act of writing. An empty roar of jets in sky. The chance of the sax to just enter in. Don't cat on sneeze. This sentence is just as you find it. These laws are the flaw. Bulging, round, black-tinted windows of a camper on the back of a pickup. Worn Frye people by predictable boots. On the table the hammer swallows its shadow. On the writing can. Prosody signals context. Old holders & dark pot. Going to a coffeehouse to read a book is for me one sign of depression. Here is why this. At first this grass seems very mild, then you have to sit down. By bridges ridges. All senses wch can discern information at a distance are located on the head. Strunk & she talks white. Hunkerd down, playing his tenor on its stand. See butter blade streaks knife. Not one word in the constitution mentions art. Tissue pushes thumb over crumpld ass. That's funny, that plane's dusting crops where there ain't no crops. This that bus coming back way. Honing myself toward a solitude I'll never accept. The page to a surgeon. A civilization based on imitation leather. Tongue of cat's surface rough. I love watching streets. Going to having be. Breastrokes. Ing go beens. People who confuse lumpen with left. Only the table atop an ashtray. Little rips on the screen of an old film print. Clutter atop the seeds, spices, oils of sideboard. Around the bright white flower's core is a halo of orange against the rustdark background & I imagine this maskd welder high above the street some kind of bee sipping a pollen of pure heat. I so do it do so. Clone for a day. You lickers gander. Record / record / record // attack / attack / attack. Many time is the. The computer's down. Pedestrians scamper in across the sun. At the end of each poem, he grunts. Days break. Pianogate. Sentence out each stake. Wld it hold in the world? The loom of peoples shadow in their windows. He's doing his homework. This 5 call corners. The telephone's easier because you're actually talking. Of the senses in the ream. Maybe you shld stop here. Knot this this. No /moking. Inch crush dark: obey. A closed quote speaks to its period. Bounced planet ball into the panda. Do you revise? Frontal tickles caffein lobes. Everybody praises ignorance. Board filld with cup cups. Loving your labials. Bamboo light in the dawn curtains. Anything you know is only echo. Aliens from visible planets are perfectly other. Cambridge mass. This Tuesday is. You can't imagine smell. Name of Tamal in the half place of a bad name in a false place. Needlessly she inserts Occam's razor. Squeak's faucet. After dinner, coffee & wine to hone your attention. With childd engine difficulty a morning turns over. Bill Owen's photo of Reagan on the telly beside the well-trimmd yule-tide tree, neat pyramid of wrappt gifts is, 1978, a cheap shot. Road was on the eye this coverd. Your basic jazz tuba. Blue Wednesday before the day. The function of this form is to contain the reading within the sentence. "(trash) ray." Black rubber covers hammer's metal handle. & L letters a name before M. Writing too moves by strokes. Track or yellow caterpillar. Even voices are different outdoors. A big dream of trucks. Proprioception extended leads to the sax. Ash fills the tray up. Sometimes I write only that part of the sentence wch concerns me. What can be calld is only recalld. Because they can play it, jazz musicians know each other's work better than do poets. Instant waking is in each I am. This bus after sunset: night of the living dead. Room a chair in a green cream. Themes pass like clouds shadow. Then cross & down across a. Already in October in cardboard, a christmas wreath in a window of the Thor Hotel. That is the end of the sentence. Firefall of sparks amid I-beams. At once to him thru long rough years, gruff with tender intimacy was her tone. It changes nothing. Rocking thus the memory of chairs. Indian summer's Indian summer. Each top begun at the letter. He loves green shirts. Day after day the white. How isolate red tomatoes? Not this. Rubber cement. What then? Roaches walk the wall. Bull spittles as pit snarls. The phone awkwardly sitting on its cord. A coleus in the cat. Lyn reads in stocking feet, one tapping syllables out. I saw my clear burgundy end filling vial at needle's blood. What Bev calls the ammonia odor of old Brie. Coma clumsy. Consciousness comes into being at the site of a memory trace. Rent liquid deter. His poems are written in thick mauve felt-pen loops on the backs of old out-of-date leaflets. Old palm. Try our tasty teriyaki. Bores ed the ing trip. Anyone is always somebody. Involuntary right of the eye seizures. Book holder made of a match roach. Two virgins fumbling in their mutual terror. The ordinary displacement of careful objects. The book of meaning. Look whose way I sought a face of never this she glimpsed. The firestorm of last night's liquor still flickers in the body, smouldering in the tissue of muscles that refuse to pull taut. Footsteps heel on high below the sidewalk. All gone Quinn. Each day write free. Each sentence according to its number of changes. What Carolinas be to mean in the its. Scribbling in total darkness, just hoping the letters will be deci-pherable later. Between seven & thirteen my counters fingerd. Newer music stands tend to be very skeletal. Here was a pigeon without cities. Poetry readings (as we know them) only began 30 years ago. Any contrary is a positive light seen in a symbol. She's lonely in some way I can't solve. She bearded to scratch his want. Sentimental weakness for the awkward sentence. & to each nameable shape a specific, complex cloud. The mismatchd forks of the poor (my own). No writing to this end. The shyness of the cat as it takes a nap. Let sky pie. For anything less than murder we only jail the lumpen. The boil of noise as it waters. That's bad Brie. Filld rise with sun factory. Ezra sleeps in the windowseat. To be rules are made. My content is non-admitted phenomena. Scraping leaving paper tracks. The season of

Chinese jumprope. Three of the drinking cups. Watching passively, disinterestedly, incapable of action, as the fork slips from between my fingers, bounds off my shirt, lap, the edge of the chair & onto the tile of the kitchen floor. & cut montage of forkclock to timelift. Who's got the power to enforce spelling? Feam stalls. That was a case of not seeing the word "tho." This tracing all. No ear closer than Bob's. Pills in swallow, forgetting how to mouth. Straight thru to the end. 'Back' in the yard (3 (wooden (rain-warpd))) chairs. Characters in the novel in the text. When an. A single strand from a bedraggld broom. Was verb a fence? When you look at the sentence later you see only the commas. To try imagind words. Letters falling like digits. Wld will was be. Odd that it's important to leave a certain x unsaid. That scratch. Here the local order got skewd. A fence is. Paint on the metal worn away. 3 polis in each max word meant. Wear your coat overall 3. Three thusdom. So one's work has a constant flaw & that we call personality. Mind in the gape mines. Certain people who prefer poetry in translation have some idea of an other. As what I have imagind it is always to do this on a rolltop desk. This poem's got 19 lines. Possum that to the tell. It's normal that men fart when they piss. In verb is France. Wit is the soul of brevity. My 3 people. Boh! (?) Stove top coffee spilld on the ground. As the cement hardens & numb-ness wanes, warm sensation throbs, swarming about the polishd presence of something new, foreign, become a part of my mouth. Pants is in an herb. In the film lnvaders from Mars you can tell the mutants by a mark on the back of their necks. On the rug bare snap cat. Sullenly last summer. Football plus puss fuss none. His language keeps dissolving into his voice. Take a mouth open, say deep breath Ah. Morning edition's Ax-Rape Victim's Own Story replaced mid-afternoon by dismissal of Head Coach. Third sea as in fan. Haze of smog stains the noon sky. Hued on the far side hill haze gray the bay. Irony is anyone's last possession. Sit she sees how. Bags & bottles. Foot rush of up stairs steps. Ears' hair words waver. O picturd to my pose. Larry, snow scapes. Bathetic. No anesthetic for a collapsd lung, but at least you can take the scissors. Because wanting to get to the page next. As he leans across the counter, one foot encased in a black canvas tennis shoe rests lightly atop the other. That is the middle in a not middle yet. Even the phonebook's got "Survival Guide." Who last porch slept on our night? He speaks his present with the past tense. The mock-air underground of the conditiond coolness. The banality, it all coheres. The small johns between the popcorn distinction & the pimps. Here is everything wrong done perfectly. Colours alter pages of the hour. You convey, you convey. Cannot wrote I believe this. Deserted means they left. Spitting stove sizzles on the grease top. Today's paper, already lining a green plastic trash can. Matricularity. He sez what his poems aren't. Vary weirds. Smell is the most nostalgic of the senses. P (r (oof)). She went away to be a penis. Sharks swam past sand. His reading felt like MSG. Argues order augurs ardor. What do you mean, pole tomato? An end of idea's land. Rough equivalance. & lens an ideal. Repetition disperses particularity. Polar lunch. She loves her language too much. Cat watching the dream. Had to have had. Groove a center around eternal records. 183 sentences in 15 days. Finally until day one. Untitled. Seven for city & tunnel its hills. Words in the head left for dead. The brain does all the back work. Each room anchord by the location of its sockets. Low light. Rumpld look—of an old phonebook. Ripe soma. Taped in a store window, signs fade. Import eyes, desert rock soar attribute too ovenly prow out the thine. The morning mind's first moments —just remembering wch lights to switch on. The wakefulness of resistance. All faces at a reading (but one) turnd in the same direction. Rod wetter. Each period trails behind. View of the spatial mystery. Coming home in the dark. We on the sea saw sails. It's a black dream made into a vehicle. The morning of tricks. Brie was Fonda in Klute. The line of product stoppage. The leisure of the theory class. Wet or wrote. A lady in a green soup. Elects a translicity voice. Who here is missing? Wait, reader. Big swaths of painted paper. Bawa go cong. He is a unit of meaning as a writer. Pulls at her tongue softly with his foreskin. Any statement in the mouth of a person is explaind. But depend for what comes thru you. Cave painting in Marin

County. Wide ruder. Hard to think of words in scrawl as object. Face it call dog. Lately I've been checking my body to see if it's there. Flat at one end of the boogie, harpsichord at the other. I have not yet escaped the orbit of jealousy. Some know all blame difference. I have to make a sound just to clear my throat. T many lines hang from a shirt. Cork's hollow whoop pulld from its green bottle. A door's jar. It's nice to have one pain. Advene the conjourning. Psychosomatic emphysema. Thru modern windows the dentist of the machinery I glimpse. You can see thru the burgundy to the reversd letters of words on the bottom of the plastic glass. In the room light dawn gleams in the dust of the air. Without a beard, a man's chin is just a wound. Pharoah on my bills. Meaning drains quickly. Sentence edges must be hard. This yard on the schoolground (asphalt carvd by the white paint borders of invisible games) set aside for smaller children. Lights shade the throw lamp. The joy of a new book, unexpected, from your favorite writer. On many porches sleep dogs. The more memory involvd in the writing, the longer the sentence. Palific Pacisades. I can hear workmen up on scaffolds, painting the outer wall of my house. Martian eyes adjusting to our air. He said she said I said he said. Light between lines write green. A model of life is my opaque projector. Few seats are not worn in the chair. After this woman I've been talking with casu-ally gets off the bus & it starts the slow pull away from the curb, she comes running after, tapping the window where I sit, yelling out her number. Cups waxd in beer. You never know another body until the instant, clothes off, you do. Sensation to kill the tequila. Naming the beasts, the inflections. Moon's nine noon rise. Stepping on a fuchsia blossom & hearing it pop. A glass floats in the worm. This is a sorry buy. Awnings must make some one. The museum of pushing & shoving. & the bleachd worm is dead. No things but in relations! Home from the thick bus on a printout, squinting art work. The song of stucco chipping. One's whistle diesel hears. Bourgeois reader, you initiate here your own destruction. Heavy on my way in a dawn bus to meet Taggart on fog. Stunnd at these political murders, she & I just walkd off the job, bought a bouquet of roses & in silence went to City Hall to place these flowers on its steps. It is impossible to explain nature in blue eyes. Lit neon (letters reversd on a window's reflection): Burritos To Go. Sienna smoking. She skippd on ahead down the street & turnd to look back, laughing, big grin, just to find what I'd seem like at that distance. Sentences shrink gradually. We build to suit. One lunch, meaning middle, ideogram or China. Cyanide spray in the mouths of babes. Fossils often occur as words. Cardigans curdle. & suddenly the testor's hospital smell of corridor in a familiar balsa wood. Nobody "turns" 30. Twice you never write the same letter in the 'O' way. Guyana, how did I let this sick thing in a far place focus all the out-to-lunch rage in my life? Fall my nose seen as a water. Block-long one-story industrial space. Half the honking, double-parked world in cars for the rest. Libraries rebind paperback books. This needs & feels. Whenever in a circle of friends two become lovers, the remainder pose a gauntlet of humor. I pop my pleasure for knuckles. For an instant the look in your eyes goes wild. Cary Washington on the face of George Grant. There's "mint" again. Jack signal hammers day. My Theory of Devo. On the blue sunset skin of the telly faces light thru a dim window at watchers of. Reading is always an act of war (between classes, over consciousness). Thot moves where many words went before. Leo Ryan's face was shot off. Took the bus on his shoes off once. Simple things done clearly. This art was for the model. The beautiful woman I sit next to on the bus begins to speak to me. Denoter detains denotation. An auditorium of winos giving blood. As clouds think of specific. Just who are you, other person? Eyes enlarged his glasses. Poetry is changing & no one's in control. To edge that, he sat on a chair's note. Briefly the cat stirs from its curl of sleep to see who passes thru the room. How up I was off counter, up pick bag for an instant, unable to put change back in remember pocket. Small prose graphic. Insects are the letters of shells. Your consciousness is first of all the consciousness of your class, & this is never more clear than in the sudden flowering of the emotions, the waves of anger that on occasion sweep 'inexplicably' thru you, flash floods of being. That this reads the miss is not pointable. Beer yellows your mind. Few drunks of milk are completely glass. Ageism of the word kid. This (this not) not nor (not-not) not that. All final gestures lie. A small dog leaping up the asymmetry of steps. Each body compromised into its chair. Tire's flown. Little rivulets of drool. I often say what I am in the middle of forgetting. The opposite of any primary color is the combine of the remaining two. Sun on the crystal refracts the window. As we enter this room all three men there are holding hot wet tea bags above their cups. Of dizzy at the top I get a new page. Empiricism stops at the infield's edge. Her horizontal rising. A tin vat of poisond purple Kool-Aid. A good attention exhausts reading. Negotiating getting to know you. In the start it norths to set. The odor of ants burning in the sun's light, focusd to a weapon by a magnifying lens. Many mumble on the steps aloud, sitting the Bible library. He says three words & I see he's an idealist & disregard him forever. A basic is the most flat salt condition. The book as I read it dissolves. Steam billows out of the processd sewers. King/Cleveland Sousaphone fingerchart stapled to, peeling from, the music room wall. Gong shares out of touchd ploughs may be playd without being. Bob's brain was blown out of his head, spattering the blue NBC minicam. Rapidly in the sky trail the jet diffuses. Poetry is not a thing but a relationship between people, translated thru things (calld poems, wch themselves do not exist save as aspects of commodities, things we might exchange, books, magazines). Pave the raincoat means. The sound. Cross out some puzzle words. The spray of a tennis ball bounding down the rainy street. Red bluest red contain within the trace. The anorexic's sad smile. Livers, stains & founts. If the fly is just walking, something is wrong. Nostril left in limitless ooze. A key on a nail on the wall. A lawn forms those weeds. This freezer's full of film. First morning each stale taste in cigarette of. What is your ISBN? Fingernails mean culture can be clippt. Rain shushes traffic. On the ash of instant words turn to writing. His voice is in his face. Between my clouds you can count the ears. If we talk of ex-lovers, it means that we're testing. Metazoans tried. Cardboard sign in the window: UPS. Warnings often attempt to drink us.

Once they've counted the dead & questiond the survivors, there's nothing left to do, no further story, but they can't set it down, they lack a sense of closure. East meaning passes to west. Cats design laps. Facing this, I said East. My mind being what it is, I laughd. The true type of the length depends on the size. Pedagogical functions of theater under a single, dim, soft-focusd spot. First he puts the chalk in, then he checks to tire if they nickeld the see. He's got an Asian thing. Caps of scraps, bottle & gum. Contempt or rare he is. Store next door neck. O rare is his contempt. By of that under to the of then of into not not. Reality is nothing more than the subjective penetration of daily activity. The weeper street. Thru his blue sweater I see his red shirt. Beaver made fedora by Stetson. Table damp always under the saucer. As system pours into the caffein. Curlicues of intent. Morning mourning. Before I was tall enough to look into the kitchen sink, I thought adults hid things there. Names without plants for them. Systematic rule-governd violations of convention. No idiogloss, no isogloss. No punctuation wld wear you out. Seaweed curld around the jellied chopsticks. Blender buzz of small scooter. Broken or lurid. His ears are forward, almost on his jaw. Beef adore abide states & hermit. Poetry is lung museum. The body was a garden. None of your words belong to you. The invariant plane of a characterization curve. Days of the week equal to the fingers on one hand. The fill's fly roomd by buzz. This story was over before you even heard of it. Tilting the clear glass sky cupward. The clumsy balance of chairs. Yoko. Mercator's weird lens. & pointing a three-space to vector. I feel a duty to write about lumber yards. Tear what words out. Personality breaks down quickly under stress. Is em (thought)bedded? Giving a hoot. Pro-crow mag none filed. All these guys just loitering in the aisles of a 25¢ peep-show arcade. Being equals things. The (near) distance at wch your eyes, dark brown, fill my field of vision without giving up their focus. Coins in the Chinese center of holes. Them's just ears there 'neath that hair. The dog's definition of legitimate. The sexual bond is not seald until you've each been in the other's bed. He I see watches me in spite of that white cane. At night, as I carry the garbage down three flights of back stairs thru the shadows of alley light, stray cats burst into darkness. Aka. Words never adequate to joy. Between thick moist chopsticks to the edge of ginger lips rose open oysters. She used, she said, in regard to her strategy of contraception, "a little bit of everything." Writing is pacing. White faces death. 3 apron women wearing. Standing by the two caskets I realize how small they always seem. Rain solo of the piano. Moving together, slowly, our attention is total. Blue wood ashtray filld with glass matches. She yawns awake & stretches. Three pipes out of wch a chimney sticks. Thorough, tho rough. Make it a note of. 5 good writers in one room over dinner, each in their private despair. These Toms at day house. For one instant the synthetic reality of this poem goes slack, jolting you back into the world from wch you've fled & wondering at the extent to wch this vicious ejection might have been deliberate, but this moment ain't it. All 9 elemental crystals are structures. Cretions. Atop an envelope to be sent, atop a green sweater upon a table in the room floors above my street, sun the two glasses. As she walks across the room I watch her, at first anticipating the sneeze, then stifling it. The back of her lean hand reveald, she rests on its tension. The drill of public works in the morning air & thru all these walls a muted disco. A crook-neckd squash plant the size of an egg. He don't mean Romany when he sez "gypsy." Each mask is a statement. Throwaway tabloid. Pickles papaya. For months on the job they (we) flirted, over lunch, at staff meetings, passing on the floor, so that when, finally, they (we) touchd, the rest followd immediately. Pull canvas over the shaped skull. This is an odd one. Photograph of your pregnant halloween mask, wearing only a friend. One hears the wind's cut. Dust down into the helicopter hovers. My mother, my house. In a far music I can hear room & a hammer. One always owns several magnifying glasses. With one spine hunches straight, the other sits forward. After a long afternoon of bed together, they took a slow walk down the hill from her house to his, feeling dazed, euphoric, dizzy. They seem jagged to walk with hurriedness. S.I.U., Brotherhood of the Sea. This scrawl scriptd. The sun prints. What is cyclamen to the

morning? Each sensed with no despair that this first moment
of their affair wld always be its simplest. The cord tip of a metal
ladder hangs from the ceiling from the window. So I one day
just decided to make this poem & in this way. The window is
dust on the lens. Now the telephone's just a penis. Please wait
for the chew. Drunken, he's apt to think this sentence
profound. Thicker inks of stroke. Rotting bodies started to burst
in the hot Guyana sun. The cheek means listen touching a
finger. Cardtables. His throat clears Tom. Firemen are guilty.
Twenty salt motor languages boat. The personal will not tran-
scend. Left a basketball lost in the ivy. Early morning waking
sighs. Holding the sphincter, releasing the bladder. Euphorians,
kick back! Like a beach exactly. To sit simply, containd in
another's quiet. No as to the degree of the one daze weak.
"Bedroom specialist" prefaced with any pronoun of gender.
People in that room mean shadows. I hear heavy feet. Dancing
the watch, not listening. I don't want 'good' language, but as it
occurs, heard clearly. What is not possible is possible in morn-
ing. Only silence truly echoes. Cloud makes deposit in the bank.
Carcinogens of the heart. The far houses rise high over the near
spires. Portrait of the thing as a young artist. Rise behind the
sun high. This isn't a room. We live curvd in an embedded
space. Loudspeaker at discount mart's door announces bargains
to sidewalk. 30 two times 2 to the fourth power doubld doubld.
First Wednesday in December, 1978. Per doubld haps. Louis
Zukofsky sees a horse. A word for museums. These kids want to
be bad actors. Pointing the north grain of this table. Cruelty is
syntax. Structural smoke of a dock belchd over the black fire.
Thick black brows, thin lips, front tooth pushd back a little,
throat focuses voice thru teeth clinchd softly, little man, lithe,
long fingers. Many believe aliens to be a finger form of nail life.
Is that like a boppo? A profile whose woman has no nose. Me &
this other creep. Otherwise weeks for a meticulous ashtray in
an unemptied house. Each senior slowly stands up & in turn
argues Roberts Rules of Order. Forest is the regret we leaving
full. This sentence is about to stop. Brush once your hair there.
Zukofsky smoking Kents. Is longer thinner? Moonlit, we stood

at the ocean's edge & you used the pier's railing as a ballet barre while I watchd, pointing the Little Dipper out in the dry December sky. My home bag is my book. I'm waiting for a bus, for the idea of buses. Can of oranges, bundles, strings in a banana net. Bear pen's black cap in teeth's grip to jot, standing at the coach stop. Mourning Tuesday. These upholsterd tropics. Hear night in Chinese gales. No association is free. Morgan scabs beer sip. Got to put 27 acres onto that plate. Meet her, miss her, face her. Just write it down & look at it. Each avocado follow his must. The tool & die maker's daughter. You don't light having this cigarette recalld. Peruvian coffee & a cigar from Honduras. The air in the line pulls tight. Little ears taste of wax. Lapis with sodalite switchd. You are in Baltimore & I want you here. The bus hurls kids at the sides of the bottle. Or the cigarette held (wedgd) between fore- & middle-finger at the innermost knuckle, filter cuppt into palm off wch a small blue-gray cloud curls & folds. Myrna Loy's nose scrunchd. Now are we in Peter's room-land? Bow blue tie. The keel of this household keeps his perspective. A new rise begins to moon. The peculiar crime of Ramon Mercader. El hazes eye. I squirt this ink for the same reason as the octopus. Treble in one line foretells trouble in the next. Motives to acts as champagne to a ship launch. A fountain constructs a crane. I live here. Thot kindld cool coffee. The conductor's use of his fingers. Was it not my page that shook but the hand? Doing homework assignd by a dream. Let the engine roll before starting the truck. Nobody just reads straight thru. State S.O.B. office bldg. In fairness to the body. Curtain drops the applause. Meaning clings to words like smoke to a sweater. This street pukes dried paint. Try & wring a content. The bike holds tightly onto her thighs. His ax-nose slic-ing the air, freckles cluster a spot, its peak. Age sheedy dray. Demons rate. To me yes too in general to. The difference between prose & mentality. Out of that sleeve stuck no arm. Sultry she says, meaning the weather, herself. The black tat-tood. Microphones make it official. Man likes still to wear his old hat hard. Some big truck out there. Back into the lederho-sen of the elf went the stomach of the clock. We went to sleep that night not yet fully lovers, only to wake into the act thereof. These words turn into strokes. I never jitney down. Keeps the stroller on the bus from rolling. Sometimes trashmen change their days. Others set certain offset sentences aside. The ring around the moon at midnight's big. Tan man in a suit. But the second time on the same day I misplaced that knit cap, I didn't even bother to go back & look. So dis real is proved ism. The only unit is the whole. Moving light in a red object slows waves toward the length. Point at wch smile generates dimples. Intra-chiropracticalamitousness. 'squitos zone offense. The bedcovers of disorder. Draw arrow to where word really goes. Of the books on a lean shelf. In the unconscious the path between contradictions is always a straight line. Lights wait for the pedestrian. Tensed anger might be a joy. With his hands forming the plaza, walks down fists. We live in a shoebox at the end of the stairs. Missd her heckle, dockd her jive. Dizzy with a big cigar. I see nostril in silent profile, shade moving rapidly, lips & jaw, underneath the half-drawn conversation. Hair's a sap, leaking slowly from the head. Once one who was isn't is. She claps loudly, as if to enforce it. Special is our language doom. Sheep eating pumpkins. Large furnishings for such a flat few. The conductor makes a fist. In the wall on a line hang pots, pans, skillets. Your face on the body of a girl in a tutu among a line of like pre-teens staring hopefully out from a yellowing photograph torn with an old care from the Baltimore Sun. Wasn't came as be was. Just to purchase a pack of gum seemd a triumph. Waterfall still of a photograph. He writes like this because he talks to many people. Into the lemon station backwards snakes hook-&-ladder. Ethics comes into play only when one of us is absent. Miss Scarlet in the library with the wrench. Conditions under wch a violin might be playd like a flute. Here was but here first. An east view at dusk lends little light. In what ledger is this a sense? A motorcycle jumping to conclusions. Crayola page sticks a streak. The difference in sex with an orgasmic woman. What is your morning of theory? Sentences caption intent. Among another is others. I turn the light on & the afternoon vanishes. Tamara O'Brien calls to ask me what I'm doing & one year later, two days ago, I meet her at her desk at Far West Labs. Rule-governd convention effacement. Like talking radios of radios to radios. Poetry's a process carried out together by groups of men & women. A profound guitar makes the lyrics banal. Each cup of coffee needs to be thought out. A head thru pelvis, line, spine. Your voice remixd in the light blue phone. A new beach like an empty page. Keyboards differ as to number & punctuation. Another invention each the word of once. This room is the consequence of bad politics in the metaphor of a triangle. The morning of message is morning. Now the fridge starts up. Waiting for sleep like rain. In the object minds symmetrate. Flies despise my eyes. That scratch. She wears high boots, long skirts & means you harm. Veil dark glasses serves as this. People struggle, groan, puff to reach the rear of the jostling bus. What then? A large blue swimming pool simply sits atop the ground in the backyard. This one surrounds (around) room. Neo-deco deja-vu. A thot were passd evidence. Bouts of liquor. Doors demand one another. Art is the only product whose sole function is to direct our gaze toward the producer. Chill a dawn. Hard edge hair cut. Windows vibes wall off echoes. Gazing at the cash register, I imagine the total tells the hour. Auto racer in a Pauline Oliveros jacket. Words in quotes float. Hidden gulls fly from wires strung. Highsmith: the dream dissolves by its own critique. Far back to road towns. Cat scoops its place out in the sand. This too & all this. Colds first appear as chills in my biceps. I face writing north. Each redundancy makes a forgetting. Bowels over lower bowls. Unstable table. Dog climbs the large steps. A bus in an elevator turnd on its side. Wall demonstrates peeling paper. Be specific. The page encoding. All her vision is peripheral. Read 'wyf' for 'wife.' The city began to objectify sluggishness. Packing the unsentence. The dude will take your air. Chair will if pushed topple. Only a child wld imagine any elder secure. Not I am embedded in a three-space. Exacto blade gouges thumbnail. Doors slam. You have to hold the book open for it to stay there. Number of crosses it rooms to take the day. The horror of the sonnet. Hugs come. I shuffle these words around before I put them down.

Tibetan in a Pauline Oliveros hat. In a checkbook any sum is provisional. Forward from the time flow pours of past. Ears predict the genetic invention of glasses. Women walk so every wch way I watch. Warm days in winter foretell trouble. Spoon onto linoleum drops. Thots drool into speech. Spilld gutter bleach somehow powderd in the left. Dad in the bathtub was his form. Sun strip sit set. The cord of syntax starts to smoke. Scraping a stick into dirt with words. Shards of childhood's family. Back taking taken steps. Night fades orange into morning's burst of glare. To show off rolld boots, jeans worn with cuffs. Vidience. By the bay of waste in that vast water flatlands aerate vats. Close your eyes to hear the logic. Rainy shadows cross the dawn windows in the light dark. Too cold to read. Because again one because one is because began again causd beginning in again once again is because one once begun again began causd beginning in again once again once. Gulping down warm cannd beer & bickering, this sad sack little construction gang takes a week to strip the old, outer, paint-chippt wall off, stapling up fuzz pink insulation & new red boards, but before they can finish or start to paint anew the boss splits with the money, leaving our house webbd in scaffolding, chilld in the rain. Even a tree bends to the large storm. Full moon behavior lasts 3 nights. No color with true holograms. My ear is a Sousa-phone. Rattle framework in their windows. Where the yapping dogs of literature teach. All purposes & extents. A mattress in flames in the middle of the freeway. The dark color of a tv in an otherwise light room. The choirmaster's children. How out having to walk to think. I get him to sign his book for me, so that, when he sees it among the used ones, he'll understand. Bird's flight in motion wastes no rain. Conceivd as black tape to block the story off in the paper, 3/32nds of an inch is fat & clumsy. Now to talk in words from mouth. The sort of man who smokes cigarettes held between thumb & forefinger. Peachy green to define round thus. A certain dull buzz signals the door open. Tulis—Tamal—Thermal—Thematic. Odd ease at intensity's center. Tuba City arrived from the card. That pain in your eyes near tears when you come I've learnd to know means joy. Her in down mucklucks. You in that pullover I bought for Christmas. Match dental book. Now I'm inside you. Fresh dung of new odor. These words give it away. Several of gyroscope kinds. The violence of the leap between any two sentences. Our roses are not Greek roses. The requirement of intersubjectivity is the existence of you. Word symmetry of the cross. Spindrift. Where the this lines the cross. Up these stairs in pairs. The shadow of a window stands in a neighbor. Screen doors are what you must go through to get to anything else. Impersonality shower of the motel. What you leave out versus what you forget. Sunday inserts in the paper advertisement. Not sufficiently objectified. Having faild to slap at its side as it pulls away, they catch the bus. When sentences breakdown. The inside of a small piece of torn skin on one's cheek. She was not able to decide if a sex change meant she wld be a man or a lesbian, so thot to try both. To leave a leaving vehicle run moving. Fred wanders in bedraggld & happy. An unclean window blurs rain. When boiling water spurts from the pot, the blue gas flame flashes orange. Parahypernoncalldsoeuclideantenspace. Hard hat area. Needles. Shadow comes to door. Now news the here. I concede my inability to starve (I hope). Her hair naked at the towel, to dry the window. Horns of the big trucks deep like ships at sea. An old, bent-over tam atop light purple Chinese lady. I leap on the M car on the hunch it will get me there quicker. The calculus of hurdy-gurdy. The only thing that will eat pig shit is a chicken. It's hot as the beach downtown, but at the Mojave a thick chill fogs all. His eyes opend wide to read the title of the book in my lap. In the wire wind phones sway. When FDR "passd on" it was too near Life's deadline for them to do their proper, usual, gaudy job. Drip tar in the mastodons pit trip. Feeling the pressure it takes to hold the pen all the way up to my shoulder. Toast of the aftertaste. All beginnings require entrance. In some men hardware stores browse the way. That violinist is chewing gum! The stain of wood shingles on the water. Storms at sea loose in the stomach. Ash shaped heart gathers tin tray. What if there are no songs of experience? As if they say the dead exist. Following a cup of hot chocolate with a mentholated cough-drop. Get infant's 'billy' lights eyes turnd shut before patchd on. Road signs in the sticks all full of bullet holes. A grown football between the legs of loose men. Conducting begins in the collar bone. Gestures these generators let. Speech on the shop floor more intimate than my parents. In the neutral storm of year's first light. Meat neck. A fresh glass of the ocean thrown into integrity quickly loses its water. O Snaggletooth, I see you. Who cld imagine that fat man lying beneath her? Oh, he's a terrible racist & smells of wine & I don't get the point of those half-finishd tattoos, but I like him. Shadow building on buildings. Magazine means ammo. Plastic lunch in a bag bag. I draw words—the way an impersonal nurse draws blood. Orange food means fast decor. Scarves' lives. Territory is stylistic. Sausagelike, dogstools glisten on the rainy walk. Accidental industrious orphan. Tetherball pole sunk in cement inside an old tire at the center of the policeman's paved patio. Cheap fluorescent glare of the light diner. Sleep on the couch. What the firehouse is burning. No poem here. Words up out of the house before to speak first hours of the day. Stereos clash up airwells. The swimming about sex means lines. Barrett, listening carefully, softly tugs his lower lip. Blink lights of the office phone on 'hold.' These sniveling social democrats even had the temerity to publicly polemicize against the call to smash the shah's blood-drenchd dictatorship as being mere 'wishful thinking.' Summer is more scarce in letters. Abigail asleep on the floor, old blue coat her blanket. This is winter. Fashion nation. Driving tennis is like much. Sign in late, check out early. Heat of the space throbber. No weather excites like the instant before rain. Whenever I sip away from my lips, up rush carbonation & air. When he asks for spare change, she takes all these coins & hurls them hard at the gutter. Eye pace. The annual Xmas eve family fire tragedy enunciated to perfection by the television clone. Spine of fire formd escape. How many people know the inside of their refrigerators? Once where plate was, food rests on a fork. These are how words get made now. Concept was that terminal. Alan sez he sees the steam rise up off my shoulders after a 3 mile run. When other apartments run in water you can tell. Marathon groceries. Dunk like the orgasmic slam. Tonight I dream I'm preparing a lecture on history, so spend hours in thotful, slow, luxuriant formation of sentences. Medicine cherry shines thru sun on a windowsill. Poetry in this land can only travel on the seald train. The wind in the cigar will continue to burn. On Christmas eve she calls me from her parents' house & we talk softly for an hour. All these elaborate streets with back porches not visible from the house. Taps his ash sizzling into nearly-empty dregs of cup's coffee. Trunkd. The juggler's eyes watching entropy gradually creep into his act. Strong window banging in a hinged breeze. Department of Leisure Services. All out of seven odor variables. Ghosts rustling make the sound of grandmother folding brown paper bags. Inner leaf of the red coleus. People stare into windows as if you can't see them. Into it we saw slomo try move. Report to security. Pelican seldom flies inland. Just as all our gestures are quotations, borrowings from friends, family, acquaintances, lovers, so too is our vocabulary. To shit sitting, pull shirt tail up. Endless arms of Robert Parish. On a yarmulka hangs door. There is no document of civilization wch is not also a document of barbarism. Flagpole depth against stucco gray has no cream. Round yon version. Nearby argument in a nonspecific flat. Think how often your eye stops, slips, bolts ahead as you read. The moon we broke. This 'state of emergency' in wch we live is not the exception. The pass of whooshing traffic. Teleology of the heliotrope. Go out in the cell & flicker heads. Old tatterd pink bedspread covering raked leaves piled in the back of a pickup. The sun comes out of the john & you are that much higher. This never means more than it says. Either time my Pound comes to be grandmother four ways out. The silence of the throng as it descends at dawn down stairs & escalators into the subway on its way (many ways) to work is felt as a general but private torment. A steaming bowl of small rice. Simply we lie, one by one, in bed together, until the world is only weather. I saw toes in that sandal countless. Chronic bourgeois. Beards, birds, boards. A bookstore calld Plasma. New totals reach same features, show sisters. Meads are net. The numbers of morning cradle light. Balloons of thot & speech crowd the room's wall in this comic. Kye zulus of the caw. Weak tea. All that cracks are puddles in the sidewalk's remains. These sentences 'sit'beside one another with no more connection than stories in the paper. On the sway masts bay. Can you smell soy sauce in the farts? Gippd cutter. Doubt occurs in the stomach & only later in the shoulders. A tall building radarlike atop each transmitter. Two commas around a word amid a string of them. Fred shouts at Ethan. The lone applauder in the filld auditorium. Recording guitar in the studio, play sitting down. Lumberjacky. Slowly the bike rider glides her motorcycle thru the streets. If there are things here you don't understand, there are going to be reasons for it (them). A bit trance. Vaseline Alley. Pen jars full of mustard. Short poems are politically correct. Weed salt in the sea foam. The achievement cancels the premises. Humming-birds look up to see phone on a pole. I can never figure out what eidetic is. The word less. Dumb sentence. Lore more. Often misreadings are better. Yacht's white wide wake. Puffy thot seeks white form. Rollers unroof loads of tar. At the end of my trope. The foot of his story. Syntax is a series of swivels on wch the words, gingerly, are lowerd. To the sky the west is flat. Trailing are beauties. A gum, the body recalls disease. At the head of each driveway, green plastic on gray galvanizd cans of trash await the scavengers' pickup. This is its own caption. Write this notebook down in a red. Their portable television just sits on the rug. Heavy slugbank beach on the foglike. The nausea of satisfaction at the end of a large cigar. Left a smudge of thumbprint at the grease, a margin. Carries her bourbon onto the bus into a plastic cup. All one bird flies in directions. I might hear anything you say. Language junk. Diversified bever-age. Phone car to make quick call stop. America will be open. Metric plastic ruler, orange alone one edge. At night the lit streets form an interior. Tampon & bay's water, floating on milk cartons. An emotion picture. Gulls of natural confusion. No more than 5 people anywhere will ever understand what you're saying. Not learning to does read stop. Waking into the act of your presence —all I'd ever need. Lawyer in a bowtie younger than I. A dream in wch I'm giving a talk for wch I've not prepared. Shouting pigeons at joggers. Odd threads & old crumbs glisten in the rug. One morning after another, landscapes rise in the shade. He began to complain of a backache & in a month he was dead. Former hype. O helvetica medium, helvetica bold. They pull roofers from the hangtop. Her hair here in the air above my head, as she lowers herself onto me, all about me, leaning forward & down then for the softest kiss, light brush of lip to lip. Sails await slack wind. Without visible cause, my cigar tilts out of the stone ashtray, rolling off the table & onto the tile floor, leaving its path of gray, powdery ash. What is a hook-&ladder than sadder? This sentence is not referential. What the C. Turner Joy befell? Watermelon sugar is Bolinas. How does the sordid ink spill? The average career in the NBA is just 6 years. Sit upon rooftops sipping clothes off beer on such days. What you do determines who you are. Tarward lift buckets of sky. A swivel wooden chair (invented by Thos. Jefferson) sits on its castors by the kitchen table. Scales up & reed down. Revolving dork. Scab read. Shaped like an ancient flower. Is the false antiphonal fox? In 1840, the fad in Paris was to stroll your leashd turtle thru the arcades. The clotheslines of nostalgia. You might can do that. Not this. These little sentences all surrounded by theory, fury. Opaque window of a bathroom glass. Pink tint to the puke signals red wine. The weight upon the pith blue helmet, the postman's shoulder shirt. Hard, by candlelight, to see brown eyes dilate. The number of rooms / filld by mirrors / is very old / folding in on one another / & forms a dance / of books in the head. It is not the communicability of your writing that is here at issue, because few will in any event ever comprehend, the distance between words & their causes, contexts, is too various, too vast, but the integrity with wch you approach this necessary limitation. Already paper was in the word. In point of fact. Amid birds foghorns twitter. In jogging, speed is not the point. Mags slip thru a slot to mail stoop. This sentence has no hidden meaning. The noun of an irrememberd is not religion. So finally we do get out of bed in time to see the sun set. Summer sun some

are with without. Languid duck. Thoughts of the instance you
sentence them recede. The metaphor of poker acquires senior-
ity. Men talk with horses in an old sushi bar. Drop chairs on
prose writers. The strain after in the morning balls. Down the
block a burglar alarrn goes off & stays on all night. I space like
white. Teleology loves a suffix. Hardwood on a barefoot floor. If
you flush, the pressure on the cappuccino machine drops like
that of your blood after a good hash brownie. Iced sausages
coffee & brunch cafe. We walkd into the wrong time. The bath-
room sounds from behind the door. I call in sick, then stay
home & write. By a tractor towd yellow tons of trucks.
Dreaming retroactively softens lines about the eyes. Shanghai
shoes for a peasant. The lens of the snapping photographer is
one type of aquarium wall. Its day without no mark. Good dog
book. It brings all this back. An attachment to concepts intro-
duces you to the crossfire. A head plodding the way. First they
painted the forest leaves with honey in the script of the army
descending from the north, then out came the caterpillars to
chew in the dewy night, then, when the invaders arrived, the
words eaten into the thick foliage read "Enter here & be
devourd." I can hear the page as it scrapes the pen. This wld be
an inkle strap. Fern filters grove in a light. Loudly, with an imag-
inary Thompson, he submachinegunnd Everyone in the deli.
The children shout of morning. No manuscripts need apply.
Instrumental land. Thunder thorns the storming air. The first
fog thru the blue. The point at wch this ceases to be a poem.
Cyprus, eucalyptus, pine of odors. All hells are private. The love
of any real hardship. I met an electrician who plays the clarinet.
Flat nets in clear air. This sentence stands out because of its
context. Next to Iowa, wch we do not believe, is Minnesota.
Pisan our. Glade fern & brown twig on the dust layer floor.
Basal. Small stool in a large bowl. Any long work makes read-
ing a struggle & the figure here of battle is no accident. Boar
brush hair bristle. At the dial's turn, there's a burst of flame.
Reading frenchroast in the aftertaste of paper, sipping break-
fast. This text might be a guide, but it is the route of your own
mind we are, both of us, in this instant, act, committed to

pursuing, following, tracing. Paper rush in gutter traffic's scatter. Color tv for the deaf. Simmering windows steam the soup. Watching Phil die, these days, we say goodbve, one by one, as best we can, or are else unable to lay these cards upon that table. Button sez 'press' toilet's metal handle. He can't even get to his own idea. I fact only smokes. These poems want to be liked. Against the possibilities of the driver & not as an aid directly behind the urban bus of life, as that cane he sits on directly between his legs in walking. One page each day devoted to the presentation of strips of comics, two to four frames apiece but always of identical space in a set order, with possibly a puzzle or the single rectangle of Dennis the Menace, as tho that rimed (!), always below horoscopes & one odd fact. Central Service Station City. Unexpected, love's rush obliterates daily business. Less I used letters in the angles to write. Where you swallow between the words. Moving separately as if two figures in wch a dance comes together. By & large, a nautical phrase, meaning encompassing both extremes. White tennies bleachd grey. The promise of promiscuity. Bruisd spoon scoops away banana parts. Atop, she arches her back while I lie flat until the topside of my prick rubs hard against the crossbone of her pelvis. Congas modern in the night. Backlit scrim at the stage front is what is heard in the word middleclass. Speech scars meaning. This cigar one can smoke for two hours. This will be on vacation shop. Poetry's uselessness as a commodity is in direct conflict with its necessity as a product. The inside of dry snot cakes on the nostril. The first blush of dawn light. Beer of fear cans. Your friend, Roy G. Biv. Killing gonna digest me yet. If today the sun rose behind this thick fog wch blankets all & is to be met, confronted, down every tilting narrow alley, where parkd cars rest wtih two wheels each up upon the curb, we have no evidence for it. She pulls the bus up onto herself. Two-ply kingdom. Kitchen shines on the sun sink. Try to read aloud while everybody's leaving. The steep green slopes of the fog behind changes means its hillside rises on. Tongue pushes hard against teeth & breath gasps over the rough surface of that fat flesh. Invoking realms, we enter the counterfactuals of possibilia. Say if I write the words "in love," only one person can in fact know what I mean. Hook hangs from his metal sleeve. The game of Hangman versus the game of Ghost. One the one pulse one at one the one base one of one the one skull one counts one & one one. Steamd bamboo makes me anxious. Apply to design small & penlike in wax. A conic tree constructed of cream-puffs. To have had have. Imagine thot congeals powder. As jaw's gum chews a she stick of motion. He likes to read ads in comic books. Plant stem of a rough spider. Leave articles out of sentence. Cut. One habit I have in speech is the announcement of lists, say of examples, with some heading such as "(a)," but to proceed then with no other items, or possibly to mark them by conjunctions, "furthermore." Jet thread of an ice trail. City prices in the country. Remaining the beer can to shake what gauges. My formalism marks a new content. Then orange's first white light is sunny. Anyone's possession of the universal equivalent is relative, tentative, temporary. Whooping amid traffic & blind to the wild gestures, he stumbled about the gesticulations, intersection, morning. Each word burnd into the paper. I insist you don't know why. Reading the ink in a ballpoint pen like mercury in a thermometer. The photocopy of uniform pressure. Once a novelist was simply a fallen writer, but even this is now no longer so. Unknown twitter of a familiar bird. A different style for reading titles. Pain in the lower after walking calves. You can't break in here to ask for an explanation. Cups soak in the sit, "sinking." Mabeline, Texas. Gather flagpoles about a pigeon. Just give me a half-block headstart on whatever is scratchin' to get out from behind that screen door. The parkd lowriders of civilization with the radio on: adolescents sitting in a car. Some articles are nearly pronominal. At chips war. An egg-beater stands in as a relic. The duty is on that stupid baby. If I step too close to this picture, the truth of its falsity just dissolves. Empty fish water stagnant bowl. If this is Paris, who won that war? Grey-gray & blue-green. Going on too long will give rise to a whole new sense of rhythm. We set conclusively toward the water of the sad. Tossing, with one hand, the cat from my lap. Its own time is sound. With the tip of my finger I write your name in the windowpane frost. Each asymmetry around its own form faces. Prose pores. Horizon on the writing line. Who knows what novels lurk in the hearts of men? If no hair burns, then side piece. How much are the Godzillas? A lighter bird that ignites like a cigaret failing to sound. Not used to the indoors, cats go manic with days of rain. Veins holding pen down stand up at the wrist. Have I time for coffee? Favors of ferns as shadowd forms. Curious as the FBI at a Mafia wedding, we come to see just who will attend the death of the novel. When we, too thin to see, go, clouds are where they are. Never met a Maoist that didn't love Dylan Thomas. & then went down to the shop, said he to the deadbeat. Up upon. Tie new faces with new shoelaces. You are implicated, responsible, for anything you read. The scrape of a fork eats a man alone. Radio culture. Aqui is Ponge. The interpretation of wolves. The total fog of logic. Wanting pets, the cat slaps at my pen to force attention. Whistle industrial lunch meaning. Her roommate's 4 year old puzzld by my presence at breakfast. The day's inertia on a cold body. Two small old women fussily pushing shards of glass into the gutter with their open-toed shoes. Quips in the players, blood in the diamonds. Learning the way you like your eggs. Each written demand be sentence. Horses of butter. Next the next teller hollers meaning. Reading this changes you. First she pens sentences, then removes paragraphs from them. Today I wrote eight pages. Near clues thereby are. To tell staff from clients, apply litmus paper to drool. Mermes. Already we are at war & sense it. Rain excitement is peculiar for summer felt. Readings & study groups may not be the workplace of literature, but, at minimum, they're its cafeteria. Some windows are curtains, others eyes. Dropping my gum wrapper into the mailbox. Every major French mansion in the ugliest consulate city. What you & I might share might only be the aloneness of our private lives, but even this between us will have a character wch is specific, wch we recognize & about wch a discourse cld be spun. This flowerpot is organizd by a desk in one corner of the room. An umbrella is first of all a sharp stick. Yet our exits do not form. Hey, Writer, put me in there, hear? The lamp of a fluorescent sound. Bourgeois order is the continuous subject. Rose stroll thru a wee garden. Do you believe in an alkaline stomach? A table is left on an apple. Was it Pound first heard the citational, swirl of words' eyes in air? For 3 full moons lightning stayd, followd by the days. Eye pockets. A small white foot at the basement of the office stairs. I will not be read in times of peace. Either nor that. A machine with one function: to stir gallons of paint thru shaking, an absorbing white turning light blue. Forward is pressurd by the follow of up. Aren't these all topic sentences? Baba me lu caw. You only think I don't notice how you cringe when I come in. Any eye on one side of the nose. Structuralism, another god. Stop renders an architect rest. Slips of speech slap together. In a clear plastic pom shop with the old magazines wrappt. People who wear watches with faces on the palmside. The storm into ourselves we saw driving straight. Mosaic of a satyr play rehearsal. Just this is one example. Police peer thru the curtains & field glasses in a corner of the Allen Hotel, down on the dealin & slow talkin, Leavenworth & Eddy. Tulip turnd to us, tunic, is not tulis unique, tuneup is not turnip, not tuna's Tunis. Stop reading this. Fast & hard. Semigloss. Bright pink "Gumps" shopping bag. Well, I hope your grandmother comes thru. Opacity of apropos. Lock that door, Rueben. Shake the waking brain. An excess of tuning begets poems like the polish wch brings the blue out in China. Skulls parallel to the ear. In one instant you can recall all you ever knew about how to break free from a full-nelson. Tish. Beetle bomb. A gin-imagind image. All writing cuts the reader. Each word wafer was a mind meaning meant. Cleverness will get you bullshit. Rash of cameras flash. Once each week for 22 months, he was sent into the Mekong bush to kill people & now all he has is a wife & baby in a one-room pad & this hangover that will never quit. Attempting to shut people, bus windows struggle. Words fall where phrases fold. Morning in the early brain. He pickt up a 20 foot ladder & tried to hit her with it. Imagines no water fish. Hey Writer, sez E.B., now you ever see a dealer? New words in a house. The child lay twisted in the intersection under the fender of the cab. One slice sees segments. A king &

his fool. It is nearly 9 at 9 o'clock. Flubadub soliloquy. I at pool's surface center. Medium pitted ripe olives. Out to pull shut the door a hand reaches. Rainbow's off her meds again. These words, these people, determine this room. You're my audience now, wch leaves me surrounded. We invent slowly the house. Electrician's tape censors what is no longer offerd on the menu. The lavender midway between dress & pink shirt. Trying to sleep while ice is melting. Bernal over lightning heights. These words are capturd only with rubber cement. Her heavy hair, her layerd eyes. Mud on a merchant's top-polishd shoes. The quantification of time into figures of theory surfaces in dance as a chance of rime. Pregnancy transforms your chemistry. Warp while on the loom taut. The time of the preterite is past. A jaw twice its size expanded into the vessel. Each day I have to decide whether or not to keep shaving. Just by the restaurant to get in working. Viet Vet Consultant 'Purged.' Eggs scrambld in milk means an excess runoff. Holding off on my orgasm until she's ready to come. Sentence self is it each. Eating chicken with a fork. Stomach knots the codeine. Anna pens "I linger in the slow coils of a moribund manana." Walking at dawn slowly home. No bicycles, no skateboards, no skates. The beard of the organization. What about people who write on only one side of the paper? There is no poem to the joke. He permits the unlit cigarette to just hang from his lips. Not that. What then? A glass cat meows at an orange door. Is this a Part One crime? A knows that list. I've long since forgotten these words you're reading, wch serve only to feign a union in the act of this instant, leaving each of us secretly in this place alone. Mode fogs western. Stirring my ice cream. Toes with more cats began to appear extra. 'I'm not Bill Berkson,' he screamd. Pour warmth into waking esophagus, coffee in the mouth. First you must melt the powder before you shoot it. Writes what writing. He likes to sit with his hands tuckd into his armpits. I can feel blood in my poisons. The idea of an equal distance between words. How one's figure arms in the dance. A poem with its zipper broken. A little swoop cessnas by. Blood pressure, body's barometer. Stick & dig. Dimples about the kneecap. At staring into the glass of the last bottom. We all talk about your paranoia. The cigarets of language lighting. The voice using your own name is seldom your own. Jaw in the law as a mode of vengeance swollen with pain. The fate of any former perfect apprentice. Curve a wicked mean throw. Writing in lines means space. Blotter over a traveld wedge. Descriptive of collage. One's time taken. The smoke in the room suckd words up like cotton. Sun is now where rain was. Bas-relief humbug. Scratch that. Althusser's Spinoza. Slow thought of forward motion. Life among the chronics. White garbd in tennis. His attitude toward the towel rack was strict. A gas way 'pops' the flame off. Chinese jumprope. Ing move keep. Mom's always known life was a construct. The morning of reason tilts. Blue flower clock face. A limp is her signature. Superfluid. Even that certain body of fever sensation meaning warrnth. Only by writing, an act, do I commit myself to my ideas. Ing ed kill dress. Absolutely no carts allowd in vanity dept. The thin ball of glass encased in a shoe snaps under the bulb of my foot. I am a gland. Camps there were recurrent sights. This is absolutely simple. Basketball sits at a busstop lap, boy in his trophy. In her hands she holds the luggage-colord vase. Suit he burden jump. You smell of cigars, Pop-pop. The silent witnesses of sight. You must first let the work exhaust you before you can really begin to read. Hard shrill watchtower breaks grip, back leap selling pedestrians. I swish lukewarm beer around in my mouth. On the sidewalk the mouth & eyes of the family gatherd in stress in front of the mortuary. When he calls her hair 'adorable,' he means 'cream-rinsd.' No neutral means sun is sky. Some people just sit with their mouths open. In the bass in the downstairs stereo flat. I hate thinking about wch side of the quotation mark to place the period. The public occasions of privacy. Now I look at bald spots with a certain fondness. From here I drive cars to watch the top of that hill. Thinking concretely of metaphor. The world before must conform to each inventing. At the back of the crowded reading two deaf men argue vigorously with their hands. The baskervilles of the type. The American most likely to be a victim of crime is a black male under the age of 30. Not this. Firm flawd faces form. Cld familiarity of problematic make this mode? Warp-face. Bags on the bus carried groceries. Where is the light source? Or is it compositional too. One page of note-book equals 1.8 pages of double-spaced type. Not that. Squirming on the edge of the seat until I find some place numb enough to relax. Word is the number of inverse. The heat of your body (at night (in sleep)). Where in the panhandle life began. This is not funny. Without the tooth ache tooth. Dingle peninsula. I smell senders. The disaster of a broken straw. To fixture a socket a render. James takes a plea for a two month county fall. A passing rain that mists in the sifting air. Lenin's Diderot, Mach's Berkeley. The electricity can see you sitting in the clouds. Philosophy is that strange theoretical site where nothing really happens, nothing but this repetition of nothing. Hegemony was the afternoon of this. The gardener's tools in the back of his pickup. Call break this day score. So that's what a decenterd narrative of emptied signifiers wld look like – a mess. The milk crushd its turndover truck cabin. Down in the nimbo-stratus, up above the fog. Dial a voice just to hear the weather. From the field, the world. One on the street sees windows, imag-ines thru them. The meaning of any term you can't understand turns out to be the reason it eludes you. Me fever to keep warm & sweaters. Economic difficulties have forced the Engels family to sell the textile factory that provided funds for the writing of Karl Marx's Capital to a real estate firm, wch plans to demolish it early next year. One's life feels violence, one described. Your failure to speak is a provocation. Small cloud of eyes behind the fog. STOP PAY TOLL. Not that. Entering any room, determine the number of exits. The inverse of word is number. People agree to be silent & listen. Fumbling with a street corner at an umbrella. Under one of about when a bit. A drunk gulps the cool air. There is not such a sentence F such that this is it. The dimple in her cheek when she sips on the pina colada. Back pries cat door ajar. Roundness of letters in a red neon script. See lump as muscle head. Fink sez you got a gun. All rubbd letters linger, on rub away. At least we'll get it thru the skylight. Cue curley. What's your trigger? Steams sink from a full rise.

Improv's message: keep busy. Yo bean soy. When the armless inebriate was askd to hush, he began to bang his head against the counter. Dry glass flowers in a blue. Disgusting potatoes. On a blue sink beneath a mushroom mounted on a postcard by the jay two chestnuts nibble fieldmice as the wall looks on. Cold air fractocumulus. Electric table in kitchen light. Decal duck on frozen pea. Hot sweeminy. Autobiography follows the shadow of thot. See in a mug thru coffee. Latin girls in their black satin tops. A blue nail sits next to an old sponge. Some brain. Violence like body to paragraph done. Underrupted. Dew suns the suck up. A limited option of numbers. In the street boards shush, birds go off, auto horns twitter, rain creaks in the tires. Balanchine's machine. Mind stops like time possessd of its own inertia. The door distinctly latches shut. Cat braces itself hisses. Authority of eye-contact fuses the beggar to his other. Red old star. They've got their brights on. Over first thot to fall at rocket. All wooden rulers warp. Chromatic speech reflects aberration. One side of each page gathers moss. Jack's Ike-o-grin lantern. Little chewing sounds she sometimes makes in her sleep. I am even something now thinking from these words quite different. The violence of just sitting still. Their inability of many lives to accept the. Words on windows do not go away. Thick from the underside of rain hang drops of phone water after wires. Fast pass. What then? Frieda is a trochee. Admit air words hammerd out of light. The hands on the pages on the lecturn on the plat-form on the carpet on the floor. Off in scrambled milk drains excess eggs. No pockets. Time your nostrils, one make at a flare. What a tape recording wld see speech as. Any are these days. REMs of the newborn present images of what? & are we here because might remain. Rubber Biscuit, by the Chips. To see the brown face of the t-shirt was to look closely at the polar smudges on his bear. Chandelabra. Speckld colby cheese processd with caraway melted into the sizzling oregano & eggs. Companies scramble to adjust. One there as shambling might get well. The sister is the real wrinkle. Because these cacti have the holder shape of candles. Fits & starts. First faces form voices. On the freeway people driving thru dawn fog to employments, left hand on the wheel, right on a coffee cup. The light mist mutes. Woman in a pink bathrobe on a front lawn, one storey houses on a treedotted street with no sidewalk. Moods energy "is." Sheer poetry's stocking cap. There is a poplar calld Alley St. In emergency lift this bar, push window open, exit. Is in his eptness. Tuba flesh. Sphincters to the signal. The Schleuter Family Son. Voice forgets others are not seen where one carries. In Gilroy, people go about their business as tho one existed. The melting red rug melted into the fibres of the wax. The rising clockwise curve of an on-ramp. Urn our journal. Asleep on the couch in Gitin's house, my dream imagines how the alarm will sound & then it does. Because here the flat snowtops are built & not for roofs. Rancho Motel. Of a match holding one's fingers at the tip. Cukes. Small upper ridges of a dry lip. Some story to that motorcycle abandond at the underpass. Cannot landings fire the Z-form rungs of escape. Video blue, dilly dilly. Any old think I can thing of. Rollerderby Urethane. Hushd scurrying voices downstairs footsteps. The slouch of the saxophones. The cat prefers to drizzle in sit. There's a proprietary quality to pain. Days eyes raises rise. There was this chick on the steps nearby & she was like paranoid, screaming. Faucets fasten. The failure of the mails is no accident, but thousands of dispatch clerks, sped up & spied on, tense & bored in the same instant, inventing games, inflicting sabotage, anything to get a hold on, to make it to that end-of-the-shift whistle. Till a ripple of listeners forms one light motion moves beer in a crowd, silence follows cigaret, opens others, settles. There he is, under the piano. Tart drink citrus. Born to be a t-shirt. In the red somber darkness of tennies. I want these books in trade. Between my caraway bursts teeth. Will build to suit. Stanza begins in a room. Early earlobes. The none too kitty smell of the subtle box. For want of better words. A specific relation demands ambition but calls size withinness. Twistoflex. Brown sprouts in an alfalfa jar. Imagine bongo. How force a trend. Slickers & parkas. A child hops as the smell of. My signifiers aren't empty, but they leak. Is the this road. I'm here as a potentially hostile audience. All sedans were the green enemy. Professional deli sausage slicer. Not this.

Cough mava sky. A boppo kangaroo. I just operated thru the mail. Nervous people rain into night, emerge, excess energy stops at sunset. Rime is an organizd violence wch proliferates meanings. How is oolong long? The table crowded with empty cups. A Chinese waiter with the quick dishes. Some desire to drink, others just the opposite. Inconsolable is dawn. A can in a bag in a corner of the doorway. What later will wonder brought that up. Bob swerves to save our lives. The low dark smoke of the clouds from wch that ship fell afire joind with the rain. We only speak to clear our throats. In chairs the chairs of noise. The depression is economic. Constant trickle left from my nostril. We love the untrue for its false tension. Glass is a conductor. Reading, this hallucination in front of an opend book. Cld I have been a cobbler? Over the heart of the plate. Never precisely center shade lamp. Each word is a land mark. One sentence I forgot, but later dreamt of. Moss spreads across the cornea. Jaw by ear begins. Aaron's lung. Old sunbathers on that rooftop will mean mattress later. Gratings over the class-room's airvents muffle a hushd hum. Up to alter street habit tears. Ten people, some kids. Something only recently dark, such as the known side of the moon. Actually I met a guy today that once I met before. Dillweed is daily & oregano information. The Jarmo Bums. In a sentence of place. The older persons were the geniuses. Certain neck means listen at angle. Precisely what we first wanted out of our poems, that language wch told us of our oppression without disowning it, wld later be exactly what we came back to, by study to destroy. I am about. The idea of a museum is overhead light. An up way of class indicates rolling sleeves. Civilization without plates. These blank lines can never again be green. Fate of prosoid. You cannot tooth down on one bite. Bob wants me to speak on my exclusion principle, mean-ing he thinks there shld be one. Narcotic is interest. A woman in spike heels skipping in the night rain across the spaced stages, spotlights, provided by the street lamps. That brings this to what? Relations proposd descend into a spiral, at first a stair-case, then a music box. Many little moves to trick it along. Handcuffs always dig painfully into the flesh of the wrist. Not this. Juggling open bottles of beer. It on don't count. Gravity strains at the muscles of the face. Can you finger a writer by the length of their tell. Purgolders. Even a sign is a skeleton of life. His pals call him Pooch. Opaque window steams. Jutting from her clenchd fist, the blue pen, jotting, scratches the page. This years a new mark. When you can't hear it, it's music. Smells: wet wood or pine smoke. Cat scratch fever. The bearded eyes / of the impossible lady / makes it crossd / for her to really see me. Burnt beans. Yellow-green painters above a scaffold window brush libraries. Man in a tie & down vest. In his weight pocket something coats him down. A row of trees to screen the field of not-yet-visible crops from wind's rough continual scrape. The traffic of this vocabulary is cars. Or ganic. I dream in a notebook of grotesque writing. Transistor pistol. Fire's cloud soakd up into fog's smoke. Median meaning. With age, the stooping habits of children extend themselves, small old men & women. The poetry of buttons. Clerks exchange in an elevator chatter. Each man holds a theory of sox. Not permitted, because one has leukemia, to touch a glass door, two cats play thru. Smoke lingers up from red clay ashtray. Jocks mill camera, windbreak-ers idle around in television station. Carrying a mattress is the polar opposite of carrying the bedsprings. Uses over wch we have had no say, the tyranny of their history is these words. Permitting the contact to drop from her eye. Any electrical city built of wires. Just how anyone crosses their legs. In the rain an old bear sits on the deck rug. Fiberboard. If it carries a tourist it's a map. Poets who read aloud from unbound typed pages. Chinatown wants directions to it. There's that damn pen again. Registerd as glare, the vulnerability one sees in the eyes of the particular, as she woman public emerges from a restroom in a hostile place. Can we get Fell off of Gough? The politics of his poetry ≠ even ask. No matter how many hands you've got, you reach a limit. The stone man is a new piece of paper. Midway thru its left turn, the auto pauses to let pedestrians pass. You ate it, barb life. In the land of sky blue waters (waters). The uniform town of the stern mining houses. Xmas tree lights blink in its antlers. Fragile that future's fern. Her hand shades her eyes indoors. What you do with prose is a typewriter. Off the highway an old farmhouse surrounded by tractors, pickups, sedans. A sick liquid gagging dropper, by wch to insert an eye into throat of vitamin cat. If I stare at his shoe, he moves it. Jack is my name hammer. His mind goes soft before our own eyes. Because alley & things are the only mice alive in that moss. Community garage & storage. Basement door in sidewalk opens to reveal store's steel trap. Pushpin—chic thumbtack. Candle wick wax of an unlit. Farm implements in fog. Breeze whips fish in the kite noon. After clarity the sleepless nights increases several. Word valences summd form the sentence. Are we who, are we how? Devo tea. My object with truces. Chairs in order note lack of use. Sit in beer, drink bus at a sun stop from a sack in a can. Let's get it right from Jump Street. Hard as cereal in raisins. Letting sea bass lie in the debris of its scales. Smoke head encircles cigar. P. C., protective custody, Punk City. In equivalence, what is the foghorn of Kansas? The rhetoric is they're selling fusion. Ear on one son, the shade in other. Leopardy. As tho there were an invisible crack on the tooth about to clamp it. A band of breaths. Fading appliances of store signs. Read aloud, all spacing reduces to before & after. Plant tall sturdy avocado. Direct current elevator sparks fire. No red blue white used plastic radio cars on a flags lot — negamos cred-ito — antennae (& tennis). Nomenclature sorts file cards by zipcode. My wound is a mouth. Folks who double-knot their shoelaces. Is this formal a vocabulary? Rip in my cheek's inner slope. More parts in some layers than others. Adulthood without earlobes. Lexemes of an afternoon. Yellow industrial extension cord taped to the rug. I rise when I write. Sticks a small gold star onto the dog's cool, always porous, black nose. What then? Bruce checks big round silver watch he keeps in a pocket. Carding heavy. But that mock yawn's arrogance drags me. Black fenders roar, Volkswagen mufflers out with a past. Senior eligibility worker's denial appeald. Mind comes to Mallarmé. Question of wch side of door to push. Their handbags holding women, arms must bend. Small tab inside collar reads 'M.' Thru the flame shot an arc of chromosphere. Bright pink kitty penis.

Egg shopping juts from carton bag. Virgin acrylic. Concerning the canal treaty route. Striped shirt rimes the spine. Truck old red newspaper. Plastic poker chips, overgrown tiddly-winks. These days are simple devices. Imagine the grownups play good-cop/bad-cop with real guns & mean it. Champagnes of the beer. Boxes along wall's bottom, in case of plugs. Edam smoked. – itus. Out meaning ekes. Sand City. Different rings move at Saturn's speeds. The idea over years of the sentence alters. Ball lizard pin. Common mouse-ear. All neato is not keeno. Scumbag. The marks of morning up. All in a seconal. Filters like a word. When the fridge's compressor gives out. Sleep curls halfway in the fingers. Mexican brown, two per cent. This small mission calld the valley. Now suction-tip arrows use cheaper 'rubber,' pillowy plastic. Ick if heights spec. When in doubt, pun. Big gulldance of the rains in sky. Credit for time servd. A word words to a point. Jacket sleeves always gray at the cuffs. They left nothing to ask & nothing left to say you have have. Typical turbine trip. Gutted the knot of muscle. This is the golden section. Then what this? Milk fits. As consequences to predictability haunt craft. Half-life at the containment core. Rich bush thick lush. Palatino or Bembo. Thot to make letters for stand. The blue wooden penises of one John Buck. Prism of the sun greend down. It did come out of a commuting experi-ence. From that square segment of the air is bay reds. Outside the hospital the liquid oxygen container is kept in a cage. Elephant rearing plastic head. Man in a phonebooth, waiting for it to ring. Entropic words thrust against body in air. Leaves always climb the stem in a fixd rotation. Human were specifically its eyes. The microphone was a symbol. As if to sentence the universe in states. A woman's hand pauses on a curtain. Cat's food while anxiety is readied. When the nail rusts, the wood streaks. Rotating the inevitable ventilation, the grind of the bad dryers—loud laundromat. The organization of any other person's bookcase is both lurid & neurotic. Head horse nebula. On Sunday, comics cover the front page. The winter weather was without this. Foxtail in my sox. Why not here these words & others? The archetype sun pasted against a blue sky. Each hinge framed inexactly to its door. I swallowd hard for us all. Here echoes siren farther. Who sees the infant as mother's phallus. Paint plainer than gray wood someone must have thought pretty. Energy / for a strong A / merica. Words can be flatness of infinite. The self is to language as sugar to my coffee. Consequences quickly to the choice narrow, one gets down. Little Miss Mixd-Messages. Rainy bells on Mission Sunday. After leaves drop, I wonder what held them. Backwards walking new to the straight Jerry. Is he pro nouns? Slipping about in kung fu pads. Raw sentence. Gestalt fails to collage illusional abolish. An old salad sits in its oils. What jackets refer to as grownups, derbies call kids poplin. Raise them for questions. Are these samples not? In the gutter leaves mush down into a red-brown paste. Early up, after time to get noon. Blood, money, sex, language. Ruling edges as the hedge of a hard class garden. George Segal's short people. Processd strong black Kaiser face collects at my Tuesday sliced sense of precondition redistrib- uted by Mother's fine ear, Man-naise will be lunch luncheon spread across strange thin self meats, always backward lips atop insides of a strange knowing coffee & solitude in the mirror. Eye is the sponge of sight. Ling this brist. Selected pronouns This blue is the wrong bathroom. I see in the squid's purple tenta- cles the formula of a flower. Never have my trousers learnd just how to wear long. We lie lazily among ixias & sage, consuming champagne & fruit salad in the warm morning breeze. In the park we read & sat. Stonemasons start on the northeast corner. What house wind does to the salt air paint. I is conglomerate. Old rain lays in the bear rug. Poets are Kallikaks. Antique windows shutter chandeliers. The statue of liberty is just visit- ing. Today no gray as true as sky. Lean up. Out of a water habit mineral. I made the flood. Cadabra candelabra. The squeak of windows pushd open, dawn of a spring day. Chip dime. Standing, toweling her long body off in the tub, steam curls up over the curves & planes of freckld ivory flesh. Mind's buzz a dull music. Assurances are one thing, possum's another. He socks time as others do purchases. Rapidly the bananas are going brown. Basket to hold wire garlic. In person, Dennis

Cooper is soft & cerebral. Cigar crushd box. I register the Filipino gardener to vote. Use not aimd at bourgeois decor. Turnd away twice from General, she had her baby alone at night in a residential hotel guestroom, meaning the nearest sink was behind the elevator at the end of the halflit hall. Washers of top-loading row chartreuse. What ratio—word to thot? I hear Peg in a far room cough. I bent over to pick up the Magic Marker. No heat with summer. Liver byproducts exhaust the cat. Rackd towels into their just jam. Political practice: walk into a roomful of strangers & start talking. At medium lies the edge of each theater. Oral B-40 yellow soft bristle toothbrush. Invisible jets describe lines in the sky. Las Vagueness. Got lip waves redder in the micro-era of stick. The fog's arrival like rush hour traffic. Always something going just straight up like a gravel mouth over mute roofs/rooves keeping smoke & gas shingles of pipes jutting from reason for from what? Prim it if. First tootsie-bottles disappeard, then milk rolls. Almond odor rubber cement. Words in hand in head. Keychain on beltloop, heavy jewelry. Were string pants then in draw fashion? A good sharp nonreproducible blue. Like schoolyards, vultures circld a gull. Life is just a cabernet. Freak airplane causd mountains to meet storms unexpected. The wet wooden walking boards under the bartender's feet. Now we house in Kit's life. White pus pushd the skin tight. What others wash about their do as they learn you. Pawprints about the lightswitch. Procedures for regular thot. Pink tissue, half-dissolvd into wadded fibre, froths up at sewer's mouth. I myself found the delta missing. Dog yaps warning of my approach. Inch forwards. Soft spots on the strawberries. The right asphalt came to the linoleum up. No front here. Occur within clouds clouds. Prosody of tennis. Just as if they had been hair wore their swimming people. Backside of a couch pushd up against bay window. More life wld be moons if we had richer. Puffin on an all-day cigar. All the middle arrived by the time you seemd to be in conversation. The chair is there / as there is not. How work the learn of one's own nature? Continual redistribution of categories on the shelves of the bibliopole. Conflict punctuates the words of limit. Something in this crisp dawn air recalls the Franklin wood stove we had on Misery St. Trucklike thru the alley, the garbage tank pushes forward. In the good years before it got heavy. All had begun to grow lawns imperceptibly quicker. RV, regardless of the hour, pulls up & honks for its rider to descend the stairs. Short seemd too night. L⊙⊙K. More dogs were easily provokd. I learn to marinate asparagus. Sun's own bay above that of the glare. Laugh in gull's throat. Even hieropaper newslines begin to look like head glyphics. With a push-broom sweep broken bottle into the gutter—song of a glass harmonica. Each sentence a few days. Verbs, years. day it was more steps to climb to the difficult house. Strobe whines as its flash dims. Wage hands with bare war. No one begins at Leisure World. The sound of primitive consonants had begun to drum like the rhythm of sounds. Do not disturb occupants. The second sweep of the circular hand. Lawn mowers are not a model Whimper was the intolerable of vowels. Colord chalk sign on butcher paper pushpinnd onto unfinishd wood-beam wall. Eye red. Noon on no one. Neighbors were the salsa constant. Teardrop moss bunches up in the patio's shadowy cracks. Water tongue dips into the cat's rain. Paint the balcony pink to the grey house. Took the street to you. A slight whistle in every 's.' Anchovy cock tip telescopes into smell of hardness as testicles tongue fingers touch. This box is sold by weight, not by volume. White-gray chance of light thun-dershowers. Because standing next to the spotlit chair, she is tonight's reader. The window in the shadow watches me. Class stand of baggy Levis. Wind dangling in the staind glass bangle. Fat cigar flaunts its waste. Design each sentence problem not hanging solvd, blister clog inexplicable in a different yellow sinus, mouth hanging rug room "the long way." My boss was a nut for dead-heading. Act of affiliation is a blue-gray lamp cover-ing class tv furniture. I'm not the rowdy I once was. Cough alters the body weather. Redwing ladybug. Ceramic biology of the dog. Radio chatters the ballgame as he mows the lawn. Lump defenestrators in gutter. Even tangled, the wind chime clamors. Paint fleckd tennies red. Our narcotics abatement program will proceed according to a flexible timeline.

Morning's small snowblack mousehead rattling a cat's gourd
she had threatend to let run in the rain, remember, maybe it
will all try to clear shirtsleeves with flat windows, fails to plaint
lightning & no sense of fall go down. RDERS. Words eyes is not a
heavy toy to let light drift in hurt to piss sockets like rain bill
weightless soft takes all gas one has to let nervous. The second
t cancels the first. Direction or other face in head. Pigeon
shuffles fast into the gutter's shelter, out of the path of my feet,
trotting past. Red light mechanism covers words shadow it
writes on page, green delayd yields grey. She snaps her wrist to
shake the thermometer down. All his casual migraine torque
covers silence. The audients of politics / in the -torium sounds.
Clown performer bulls interviewer. Tear a bulb plant, but break
the tiger lily. Stuff tentative title. I'll try to read around. One
face on wall sees into another third direction window stares.
Bicycles lean up against plastic trash cylinders by the taqueria
door. Bottle calistoga water. Any book itself is transparent. Fat
layer of puffy flesh. Doves make a home in the shell of a burnd-
out church. Head up you prefer straight ahead what the posi-
tion says of you. Jogging rimes the legs. Spine that fails to
stretch very far around, nails small & fingers wide, hand is
formal & essential. The blink of shade thrown by the passing
plane. My writing on the off-white wall is shadow. Red buttons
for a plaid shirt. Elm lozenge slippery throat. These hotels were
built quickly after the earthquake in order to house tourists
coming to the Panama Pacific Exposition, 1915, old brick, unre-
inforced concrete. Flat old brown cat chooses to sit atop paper
bag. Mooch City. Fine blahs since pharmeceutical blah. Sitting
in a hot cloud of MSG. Someone to clean up mouse noun puke,
cat filth, utter verb parts. No one is watching the tortillas.
Tobacco smell of his skull burnd right into his shirt, hair & eyes.
For a living she stands naked on a turntable carpeted lavender,
while men in small latchd booths deposit quarters for windows
to gawk thru, to the sound of course of disco music. Drop
modular stool. He sits on the beer-cooler, waiting his turn at
bat. By territory now familiar. The baby is on duty. To make
need do. This bears repeating. Little prisms' clouds sway on

rainbows until loom walls up. This is a Concord train. Nothing previous to do with the thing. Conversing lazily over espresso, saying hello to friends, watching pedestrians lean off-balance out into the street to see if their bus is visible amid the coming traffic, one is apt almost thoughtlessly to speak honestly to the most casual of strangers. Ingredients active. He punchd his fist thru the window, shouting he was Chairman Mao & had orgasms thru his feet. ¿Sabbath usted? Let your fingers do the talking. Meanings edge up to align with probable words. Sweatshirt logo: East Bay Aluminum. Thermal dates in an old plastic baggie, sesame socks in margarine progress, orderly consonant container, anything cld be in the described. The electrocuted robin clings to the wire. Progenitor wake-up, empty-headed contemplating. Have you stoppt flushing, my toilet? From into cold open air bursts cloud of mouth breath. Going to sort of wing it. 'Rock of winter' like 'ages of dead.' Leader is a type of tape. These many words in the other of place. There goes Peggy in overalls & purple t-shirt, carrying a gallon of water thru the morning traffic by the Hibernia Bank. Slight hand streaks tremor to shake the page. How green was my valium? Clear echo of skycraft fills the air. Waiting for the light to change. Traps speech but hate by thot. The last car of the subway, where the gangs hang out. Typical of achieving the status. Alone at home in our own civil war. Thing surges urgent toward some siren. The rump of sad weather squats. Early water light shine towers atop Potrero Hill. Simple sentences assert the inevitability of the world's order. The traffic of nearby gush. Candles of fat sheep. A determinate combination of infinite shape & no jigsaw. Dinner with Dick Higgins. Stand on the sake for the deck of it. First the shit, then piss flows. She sticks her butt out, all those tongues. Biker's hair in the wind blown back. Poplar pigeon thru alley pecks its way. The substation admits no windows. Cat blows little on the tuft of deck. Birds in the bank bark. Where a world continues in clothesline. Sound tech wanders around with cords in his mouth. Strands of jammd houses sag against each other, long wooden back steps wire top peeling fences. His poetry was an anthology of minor moves. My head right over 747. You hold the soft disk-like dish between fingers & ooze the jelly into it from a blue-white tube, smooth it around, then lean back, not looking now, eyes shut in concentration, folding the diaphragm almost closed, pushing it in slowly, gently, beyond my sight. Shut door pops with a sliding slip. No two sirens are identical. Cardboard slump after boxes rain. Short sentences. Morsel grinds the teeth. Brick red dogshit. Before catching the nervous & concernd hang-glider the air in parallel to watch the head face nosedive to the cliff. Post-neo-Afro-fusion drift. Cloths not quite cover the rare couch. Silence denounces the absence of its sign. Driftwood brings kerchief back in a wrap. I order stuffd cabbage, one scoop of mashd potatoes with just a little gravy, beets too red-purple out of a can, a stale roll & a stein of Hamms. Always a jar door closet. Just try to ignore all these video lights. Once we thought solid sought. No, your nose is not bent. Flames' shadows angle inexactly atop mock candles candelabra cactus flickers. You got this way one step at a time. Bird in the fridge calls. Come ye Masters of Rime, ye that make the big claims, with your egos sublime & your gossip that maims. One-half salad afloat in red sour cream will not keep snapper, marinated baked potato smells smoked. Waves flogged the beach. Ice are not ice will not plants burn. Those moments when, among the coarse & curly hair, you're moist & warm & open instantly to tongue or finger's touch. Sun in a flat round sky. What I mean. Receptive brown-feet lopes curiously up to a setter. Flurry of books here. My shadow saw I write this. The old gob re-ups. Simple facts settle sentences. Threading the heddle & sleying the reed. Ripe round olives behind the black pitted wall of that can. Analogy is my second line of defense. Nails can feel the finger stretch over the broad back of anyone. Life is horrible & we are stupid. Rain sides fallways. You look awfully cute in your pencil, tho. Silvie & Alphonse. These sentences are in chronic order. Alley truck the garbage width. In the shadows of the doorways, euphorians crouch together. Bench gives red way. Let's eat. Sit prisms spin in window & hung back. Are you watching all these audience tactics? All tendencies to desire slump with the modern. Soap sits in its damp dish. Arms into the bathroom over naked breasts she walks. Last year's dried gum now faintly stains the walk. Peeld orange eaten as grapefruit. Lots of sirens tonight. C's taken hatred of himself as fear of women. An history of water. That wheel wld arrange itself into a color. In lieu of our living together, you wld rather get engaged. All cloth, chairs, couches printed in draped tables. Dorothy droppd the phone & now it won't ring. Empty backpack leaning against the shapeless wood sun in the blue morning kitchen haze, envelope left upon the table wall. Arguments with my master's errors. Whose name is Rainbow & wears shoes & depends on Prolixin. Entirely by accident to get on Bart right after this year's first 'Day on the Green' rock concert, Oakland Coliseum, seis de Mayo, is to be sentenced, however briefly, one more time to high school. But all one's poem is a life not a life. She scolds her child's hunger. Black flowers fade to red. Dispatcher spreads calm out over the intercom. Jars filld with big seeds & brown flour. Cobwebs carry secret electrical impulses. That hillside, Clark, is calld a recipe for haze sorrell soup vapors on the east edge rattles of town as the head turns en espanol skyward & Holly Park orange juice favors its paw damp from the fresh earth never quite in sky's bran center means cat juts rhubarb brunch but this is a muffin. Use caution when you leave the train. What the perfect sentence wld be. Woman chews her gum vigorously, mouth open. Only one rest for the used reads, discarding the language. Staring at you in the doorway, blocking the sun, what I see is a great glare, that & your shadow. Jigsaw red telephone puzzle shoes scatterd on the Saturday livingroom paper floor. The appetite of my cat's come back. Shaping a cut of meaning, as if each solid word were a block. She grins back at the waving baby across the aisle of the train. Sky blue dusty tape measure guitar. Shaved his beard, then grew it back, only to discover it had 'gone gray.' Each operation marks an event. One has baggy, fuzzy sox, rising from slender blue running shoes, the other's sox are shiny, green, ankle's pink peeking thru, but the shoes, big gum soles, sit like aircraft on the rug. The stomach is not the same on a full writing. Shooting wolves in the moorland vs.

men in the street. Blisst. Fern's new fronds balld up like a baby's fists. Blood decay on the lid signs lower blister. Alleviate your dry mouth. Turning at the corner, shouting "C'mon, boy," she runs ahead of the slowpoke. Hyperventilation, second only to a Thai stick. Toy siren sounds like tiny pulse gun. These words have been tested prior to their current application. Keeps pop in old spice bottles. A master tenant will lease a fleabag hotel for 10, 12 years, managing it him / herself for a profit. The man at a desk works in a window. Pumpkin soup, lightly seasond with curry. Converts you hear too personal an embarrassment. Funeral version of Amazing Grace playd on bamboo flutes. Stick chap Suzy. The minute hand twitches forward. She inserts an s / m porn candle. Tennis ball in rain gutter rolls forth & back in the wind. She doesn't have a crazy, she's not even an excuse. Receptacles near exit. His voices is their idea. Oild, my finger slides all the way up your ass. The ceiling stops at smoke. Glutamic acid (15.84%), Serine (12.92%), Proline (9.14%), Arginine (9.00 %), Trionine (8.92%), Aspartic Acid (8.86%), Glycine (5.52%), Valine (5.12%), Alanine (4.32%), Lysine (3.52%), Cystine (3.20%), Leucine (2.54%), Isoleucine (2.40%), Phenylalinine (2.30%), Tryptophan (2.26%), Histidine (1.28%), Methionine (0.78%), Tryosine (0.78%). Looms leave. Sperm spills out of your mouth back down my cock. By her sleep can you tell with whom she hairs? Now we proceed without transition to the next sentence. Letters keep showing up in words. Already I've begun the composition of Force. This balk is a. Tuba belly. On so. The witness halted his car on the bridge & leapd out to run after you, but you, who were already over the railing, turnd to him, waving & smiling, then jumpd. To see it at last you just have to make it all. Danny always loved Ireland. He's in the head way back there. It might be quite. Fills a cookie jar with glass. Soft, solid sound the cat makes, dropping to the floor. Heads in the theater bob. Some little burnt toast college. Over that face I see shoulders. Bromige arrives late & eats a sandwich. Never east or west who some people face. Storm patterns from Tuba City. Head heat drains steam out. Helot for space there is in the confusion hegemony of art. Can I borrow your grey piece until tomorrow, hey? Foggy like a doggy. Oh see Poldy. Chalkd shadows of bison on the cave wall begin to stampede. Intestines of the wait. It's because he's your friend, old & dear, formerly your lover, that I want not to think of you, last night, sleeping soundly at his side. I, little big T, got in with an 'L.' Her legs spread awkwardly & both hands grasping the arms of the green metal lawn chair, Antoinette stared with mute horror at the dirt falling onto her husband's casket. Wire garlic gathers basket. Xerox it, Harley. So we three climbd the stairs of the flight. Every smell is a kiss on the nose. Stars patternd in the sky rose. Wet scab is flesh soup. Coffee thru the filter filld the cup. Strappd in so tight he was unable to move his head, eyes sad & helpless before the black hood was lowerd, he nevertheless clenchd his fists to the voltage so hard knuckles broke, 'body wastes' passing freely, until smoke rose from a singed leg, the skin on his hands starting to blacken, meeting the demands of the state. Fast off to a start. Soysters. At the end of the vision a household of escalator furnishings. He gobbld the bottle of tranquilizers to ease his long, slow drop from the bridge to the bay. Yet the plant is brown at the spider edges. The predawn light is without brilliance, flat gray cast to the valley of white houses. Bowls need to be both washd. More boring art-photos of families sitting on their front porch. I can hear them moving even on the day they shout. I like to read this even tho things have changed. You cld hear the garbage can at the winds. The secret mongols of the history. Military jets shook the small sky. Note at blue book's bottom: "please don't fluck me." She tackd the wrappy terrycloth about her robe. Jealousy's warm knot nauseates. Thunderbird flags at the base of the pole bottle. It's your fault if I burn the toast, confusing my mind with poetry. Yellow broom with a green brush handle. The great privacy of old age. Tongue hung flat on the words. Disc of white rubber, whose task it is to fit over the tub drain, plugging it. A space of events that are class forms a simultaneity. Today's first auto coasts silently down the hill, street of tiny houses. Pill in water floats down the throat. Please do. Drinking up the doorway, sitting in the liquor of the store. Steel door of the diesel repair garage rolls down. Think of dessert as salads. Serial monogamy. 3 Euclidean cats in a space sat. Brown rice, he mumbld, cattle food. Fear indexes dream. Keep your head about you. Each points to the next sentence. The last trimester of my wife's pregnancy. This completion tends to its own motion. In the tea garden's pine needle debris, old slips of broken out of fortune cookies. Between what organs in the body is not the body. 'Quiero hombres!' he shouted, pounding his fist on the bar. Can opener rears with a start, o cat's head. Pride of dada. In the house of the forest of the mountains of summer. Whose phone was busy for an hour when I tried to call back. Bent horsehead looks more like thumb nebula. Kora in Hayward. This what followd but. Premies in their isolets. Wld scrounger pimps look as male if they had a hustler. To smell, the candle must be snuffd. Smiling man at the bar motions baldly to you. Don't knock it if you haven't kickd it. Soothing music to savage the beast. Bell signals margin. Pops what out. Gate at the stairtop means children. Proposd not as a line of layers, but what thot of a mosaic emerges. Female image of the buttocks style, engraved on a baton of reindeer antler. More coming weather. May reduced to 2 pages. Your feet oud. What is that a transformation of? Layers build, as candles drip on tables. Earliest morning, when lights switch on in houses, when traffic first begins to fill the road. Above below mocks form see. A, semi, s, l, d, k, f, j. Contra bedrest naturam dictum, cat sleeps beneath the flickering car, heart to moonset if to party at curb, yet cops tapping front pane on the door on the glass porch. The mouth is the mouth pausing. Light in the shape of a kite shades the elephant. Standing on the Mexican beach, looking for the first time at the Atlantic Ocean, she said, "I expected it to be bigger." Rust wagon in the shaft of the airpit turns to red. W/M prof, 37, gd-lkng, jogger, seeks curvaceous, open, woman, 21-30, no children, for companionship & laughter, Pisces pref. Eye in the middle focuses just left of center of words. Green straps held the grey box suspended above the bottom of the grave, as first the rabbi, then the wife, gently spilld the first dirt from a shovel. To shoot it thru take time. If your nose is on strike, pick it. As the eye spells spelling. Coming in from the glare of day, I am momentarily blind in the kitchen. 4-space is a context. Dodekadent. On a hanger from a nail in the door, trenchcoat. Cocoanut oil on my finger as it slides deep up your anus. Zigs an ant & wiggles on the underside of the outside of the window, futile in a search. Revolting door. Flies fold in curtain's sleep. Earth silence. A trowel smoothing the sound of cement. Finances of the fountain district, Tom, spout hard water in a soft wind, yes. Revs engine up. How the heel bends & the ankle rises to carry the stair from one body to the next. To be a rain man in the garbage. She was a damaged unit, she was a bum child in a space. Boiling water fogs windows in a pot for coffee. To keep them from swallowing, to force them to surrender their catch, the fishermen's cormorants wear rings around their necks. They still have & she yanks undies from clothes-lines here in the rain. Idle men atop their cabin roofs, when the sunset is reflected at the point of low tide, play a dobro, a jaw's harp, a dark brown 12 string guitar, houseboats beachd only to float again. Old pigeons pop out eaves of backfire scatterd hotels. Potatofish, silverbugs. Jersey style football t-shirt. The western grain of blue-gray summer is what I want. Sea bass eats smoked butter. The subtle nurse, by a shift of text, moves in front of the words in order to more rapidly board my life. A rain of fraid. A wool box on top of the cardboard bookcase in order to indicate home sweaters. Its piece is each own. A day of June in the middle of rain. The ice of space. A caravan of silhouettes, horizons, wch to him appears to be a toy wagon bearing tamed ostriches, fringed tigers in hats, surreys of fellaheen, begins a slow circus vanishing to the migration point on the right object line. Head translates the visible to eyes. They ate us. Gaind to have 5 sure lbs. Water table. Sun falls on square of couch & rug. Walking amid alders, thistles, Queen Anne's lace. Wrapping the play cats in paper. The dest subtles. Traffic roar in the dull sky says air. Sacrolinguistic. Once tennies white. Salt of the ear. Front of free a bottle in me. The flames' heat warps the Coke sign across the street. A red-brown dog on a black stool flies shining blue. Sleep hath its own world. Hand comes to language. Having, just before sleep, devourd rex sole marsala, my dreams were my digestion. Feeding cookies to ginger mallards. The last quote came in the mail. For a fraction of a down tumbling sound second where silence shld follow pots pans dishes beyond wch drumroll song. Making a dye out of snake grass. One the other nostril clouded serene. The Germanies! Talking her cat to the tone. Lox from atop of. Some afternoons the morning is a kind of Sunday. What a lovely slice of moon! If Marlowe is Mitchum. Each insect has its own means of travel. Whose lake means names. You go to light a cigarette & find one already in your mouth. My mercy at the memory of all these days. Boy slides into geyser & is boild. Will I have this sentence to think out time? A wall is a bulletin board support-ing a roof. Brewer's goo in fish cat yeast. Too hot, muggy for her red ones, Kathy is hooking tonight in a green dress, sitting in the shade between tricks at Sam's Hofbrau, slicing a light cake with a fork, sipping ice tea. New words twist warpd thot where idea begins. Wet sand easier to walk on. One day just showd up. Language has not the power to speak what love indites: the soul lies buried in the ink that writes. Doing off putting taxes. Field grows faint as fog flows in. Sweet Kentucky horse, white-gray face for a walker. The shaming of the true. What you might not mix, samoyed expected with afghan. Privacy of concentration shared, love's exchange. That leaf has been eating something. Snakes slip away from beneath our feet. Head lush. Flares route the traffic. In generative state, America means you cld build a base in the military mid-east & call it Chomsky. Numbers defend cliches. A string in the plunk as you buzz it. As the walls of the hotel caved in to its flaming center, mixing billows of dust with smoke in the midst of a complex fountain, firehoses like seaweed all tangld in the street, electricity out for blocks & only the light of the moon, red flashes of the trucks & the glow of combustion, people sat on the hoods of cars or their own steps, leand out of bedroom windows, to make of the disas-ter a sober party. Text con constitutes. In the dream my lower jaw had been removed surgically, a portion of the brain draind away. Harmonicae. A tree grows in Bromige. Nosy blotch. No pitcher stays a stranger to the batter the second time up. What then? Not this. A splashing background of puddles. For 'court,' hear 'quart.' The sky comes & goes in clouds. This idiot studies idioms. She sd scratch, meaning let's start from scabs. While the lizard makes like lichen, an ant wanders up its tail. On the wall of the old glass bowl cakes porridge. If that's the bank building, tall dark shadow at this hour, this then is 22nd Street. Tuna about the room will follow open tin of cat. The sentiment of forms. I can no longer paint imagining. Dial tone, kind of Om. Disembodied plastic lives, using colord voices calld boxes, to negotiate their telephones. It went down the wrong goozle. I had not seen the blossom in that plum yard until it treed prematurely. The dorms are dark. This leaves a thinner pen. White socks & Birkenstocks. Our respect in lines demands thin leaves. Lynchburg News & Daily Advance. That sun sponges the cloud's light how? That green shirt you gave me, you know, the blue one. Cart wire to market to the drag. I love to hear the fractal music. Fingering shell-less prawns with our heads. Under a eucalyptus I read "Ode to a Nightingale" while a family of mule deer grazed nearby. Up from a water saucer cat laps rain. Lucky Tiger Butch Hair Wax. Four cosmics from out of five spaces are outer mu-meson rays. Wild succulents cling to the rock. Into a barrel spills a dumpster of bottles. Sad-eyed & silent, JW ladies stand in pairs in the shade of an awning by the entrance to Woolworth's, holding up identical magazines. Of white-orange veins with green rock. Music is no object. Many shades of sky in the blue. Security Mall. Wind raises gull & the wings lift it up. Three firs arc a cathedral, at whose top webs cob spidery delights, strands seen solely thru sun's inflection. Looking in my reflection I see the window & the world, but also my kitchen where it sits. Assembly unit whacks budget. Enjoying spiders' bash. Clarkwork. We never lived fully & months later unpackd that way. Dog & cat. I can buzz the hearing tenants in them prospective. Aggressivity. Communication of onion perfects salsaskin wall. Tooths Sheaf Stout. After sentence sentence. Let's play dinosaurs in the gas station. Image is language not memory. That there British hillbilly is a Finn! Sit in the back of the pickup, 3 dogs motoring thru the park. Motel art must not be subject to the desirability of theft. Chip in a hay horse. Applied futures. Writing across the prism casts a light. Infant chokes on a nipple, while Mother gulps a Bud. Time directs words' pose. Masochism is detail. Of water cooling & metal contracting in the heater sound. Gestaltifying. Smokelike clouds of puff. Saltwater honed this stone. Smell of burnt window by their toast. Kids in the forest playing Thog. Days it takes to attend that constant forgetting, weak, warm, too puffy, getting well again as if awaking to the body. Teenagers on the hard beach, playing football with a white frisbee. Spanish banter of rapid. A man & Amanda. Buggy back porch dying alone on the coleus. Mind is the thought of the body. I was still the only beard at that one who wore a reading. Sometimes, when she comes, tears pour down her face. Telephond for an instant by who he is at work, he forgets poets. The world is my newt. Scarecrows as antennas for rooftop tvs. At Mother's knee & other joints. The still birds chur the whistle air. What means something. Then one day dinner doesn't show up for the cat. Thought stops at the wall. You read you in front of themselves, while some books merely listen. American cigars like American beer. Grease converts to whim at hair. Coming from the Academy. Today the shapeless sky seems grey. Holding the phone away from my ear so as not to be implicated in conversation. Gesture reservd now for the truck jammd together whose intention is no longer garbage, behind alleyway houses rememberd together. Waiting for you to be ready. Pleasant social music enclosing San Salvador spills from the club of the foreign front. No other sentence cld have followd but this. Ali in his own defeat saw eyes. Blocks of condos proppd against the hillside Red-back & brick morning wch, each window out the building, stares back. Fat swell of amber pus of mosquito's suck thru red, dry, fever'd skin of sunburn, under the backpack's tight strap, will slow you down alright. Revolving slide won't door. Sea's salt, its own gestalt. Expect keeping the ease to turmoil up. Imitation of the tape. The right pen pressing into the paper. Fly upon tablecloth rubs hindmost feet together. Boston moves to

Anna. Gauge the runner's fatigue by inability to make a fist. Within yet above the microwave transmitters atop the hill jut a green grove of telephone trees. The dogs of art. Backpack is a kind of baby already in a hang-glider. Head O' gobbler. Doomd is salt in my ant shaker. Taste in my mouth after one too-hot sip of coffee is sense of taste burnd away. Coffee cans will rust, we too on a rooftop. Egret's legs rudder long wings as it soars off still lagoon. Shld hair smear, pentip drags word into shadow. At first the gray sky seems flat, but gradually eyes adjust, glare's difference articulating cloud shape. Not rain, tho it's sposed to look it. She spent the next decade pregnant. When tv elephant downs a pygmy, they immediately bull the cut tale off. University's a jail in utopian guise. Even to consider one's presence is to project the object inanimate into it. Palmer's Duncan. Exhaustion from writing. Behind the lens a finger rubbd his eye. Light moon by writing The switch to plastic soda bottles simplified the conversion to metrics. What begins as language perceives transformation into itself. Child-like stallion at the ocean's edge, permitting the limit of wave's cool froth to reach its hooves before scrambling up the sand. Night from the deck sounds back. I dream steam. There is always city in the traffic. I put Robyn in my poem. That dark light crossing the airplane is the sky. Latin curdles the air. Just above the soft glow of rooftops street lamps the sky half lights. Flushing cuts espresso's pressure. Someone I hear washing dishes across the metal alley. One taste of lox from atop your bagel. Dark shines in the hospital. Seaweed lasso. Barks dog. What urges wave's surge? At moment to be what do we couple cease. She walks with her hand in his back pocket. Some animal on the one is blocking for the next whistle. Boats on the horizon rise & fall. Some movies do sound just like in the planes. & there shall be/Beautiful things made new, for the surprise / Of the sky-children. Life strobes continual sentence — fading data of words frozen into sequence, then one before the next. The night is a monster. Knot this. Your basic classic tire-in-the-mudflat sunset. Then what? The will in the windows. Never a function more than you see. Curl of wave's scoop crashes down, disappearing

in a line of white froth. What we hold in imperfectness is our
common. How can I write when you're kissing my ear? An over
turns engine. Miss Otis, egrets. Return will my cat. Felt tip
syringe. The next morning might be the next day or even
sentences later. Newborn snake will lose its eggtooth. Candle
mess creates a drip. The flower is the sex life of the cactus.
Moving for the weight to bowels. Rockface bearded by lichen &
seaweed. This lion is the kitchen of our refrigerator. The old
woman wades ankle-deep thru the surf, as her daughters tip-toe
behind. Strategies of the town terminal. Voices aren't speaking.
In the arcade of the boardwalk only the salt ocean air is open
after dark. Thick rolls of baggies hanging over the fresh, damp
produce beneath the glare of fluorescent light. Banana of the
meat. Log-bearing flatbeds rumble into the past. Powder in the
haze is sun's rays' fire. Blood dries quickly, then flakes. Perfect
pure fog. Bronze buffalo on the lawn with an electric tail. Up
to the dull overhead eyes of phenothiazine, his whole left side
crumpld in candy spasms, we helpd him into the emergency
room, up the fluorescent pastel glare triage reaction of the
nurse's eyes. This is the way the word ends. Into a bowl of goug-
ing Familia. Paycheck to paycheck. Lips of others in own words
warp mouth. Five figures stand at the ocean's edge on the
balcony's ledge below the tavern window, a young couple with
sleeping bags, arrns about the other's waist, a fellow with a
Nikon, & an older pair, man in a blue-gray leisure suit & a
woman, perhaps wife, turnd away from him & the water, her
head cockd back over her shoulder, watching him. That fear of
their own kind for artists. BW: Rightness is all. Meant is of. Ten
years ago I sat on this same beach, a somewhat different man.
That sentences wld leap is connect of fate. Grey sea, gray sky,
envy all that flies. Real opposable tale calld larynx, throat with-
out a thumb. Dogs must be kept within the limits of these
signs. Box by the cat trowel. The way people hold beer cans
when they're out in the street. Last events of unknowable
Tuesday. Influences factoring the weather. Sterile is urine. One
thing, one vote. Each topic picks a word. Brave men to be in that
small boat, there on the horizon. Hands' little canals intercon-

nect lines of back. Brittle stick of stale gum. Blond sprouts fine hair. Pride's a good reading even when no one shows up. Nails from cuticles extend out. I can tell you're writing (Benny) by the way you bend your neck. A sliding helicopter blends by, above which the air. Reredundant. I, you see, don't know me & all this limit beyond wch in your eyes. Throwing dogfood to mosquitofish. Small terraces of houses together flatten sun & haze. Sky be my content, ocean my form. Fingers from the palm look shorter. Swimmers in the morning grunt for air. Splinters tweeze flesh for dredgers. Support epilepsy. Radio music full-blast in the Spanish alley. Melon coleus. Stroke of broom swish. Earless world of snakes. Wake dizzy but not groggy, some room about to swirl days continually. Intentionality wld be begging the question. Walk around the page, stare at stare, sit down at page again. Sphincter choking its own fart back. I don't rook to want you. Color the ducks yellow. Simultaneity not of nonco-incident inspection is open to direct events. Modernism reduces to consumption of effort. The order at first seems to be a syntag-matic in wch these planes occur in a specified word. Striped kitty is no panther. The indentations, curves, bumps we see later. RFP. Thots appear as word masses, into wch ellipses might point, but over wch leaps might vanish. Invasion of the Bromeliads. All I sequence is the determine. The acupuncture of sunburn. These regions exist in this thing. Anselm is out. This is typical is an orange sentence. Fish flops about on the rock (& spear) until stillness spells death. All thot quotes language. New hope for dwarves. Sentences are strict in the occasional sense. Last call, Eckbert, party of two, last call. This cloud is a chamber. Low over blue water, rescue copter raises a spray. Only this is what might not exist within one. New song of computerizd cash registers. Gesture strippt to thought. I love to put the whole half-cookd yoke into my mouth & let it burst. Narrow eons. Splash of swimmers doing laps fills the morning air. Text, drifting is suddenly aware that one has been thinking, one's completely preoccupied something continuing their methodi-cal anything other than the across-&-down reading, one, eyes. The washer hums into its next cycle. Waking not hungover as one sobers up. Ears of corn. Fish micro. Coated paper to make the image pop. Only reading old languages does one hear the newspaper in that voice. The girl on crutches on roller skates. One of goop half cloggd with head. Coming up from the dive her hair's reduced to the shape of her head. The image without its eyes. By now & save later. Wind braids storm chimes. Beauty of a small black box in realty window, red-orange neon script: notary. The woman with the eraserhead saved my hair, said the life with blue. Each day is specific. As if perhaps sometimes. Pelicans, by twilight, find a rock. Planet part of the clouds too. The steaming chocolate soothd me. Flying over oceans at a snow distance edge. Proofreading. Sun undisturbd by California. Constructing a voice with right angles. Air shivers in turbulent fuselage. Slice of lemon bobs among ice. Meadows squard into cities. Arbitrary, like a collar. What if the last person to bear me alive isn't seen yet? Cherry bomb in one's plumbing after tostadas. Monitors batter into babies like pluggery in the ICN. A succession of evenings & one afternoon. Ocean scoops hover in the air cloud. Flame fl-fl-fl-fl-flickersss. The skull pressurizes mucus. This Logomachiad. Noses begin to plane downward. The kitchen sink. A proof pops Wittgenstein's ear. From behind the clockface on the wall, a brown cord hangs down to the socket. La Jolla, hello. Thot, at the equator, changes direction. Seat use flotation for cushion bottom. "Thumb," sd the bottle, becoming uncorkd. Bet you. We are dealing with a very detaild molecular process, one of extreme analysis, capillary, whose docu-mentation consists of an overwhelming quantity of books, pamphlets, articles in reviews & journals, verbal conversations & debates wch are repeated infinitely & wch in their gigantic totality represent this long labor from wch is born a collective will with a certain degree wch is necessary & sufficient to deter-mine an action coordinated & simultaneous in the time & geographical space in wch the historical fact occurs. Con — not to fuse the solitude of literature with the literature of solitude. Hell has a ballad. Webs of townlights flying that night saw the dark shimmer in the later. Signs posted on the lockd doors of taverns. The arroyo of the bank changes, poetry falling in on her. The yo-yo at first a weapon. Drug is a hard coffee. Sheet count. Lose in one day your hearing for an ear. Even the shower is discontinuous. Play of catching hardball dream in the street. The fingers of writers seem soft. Stand up writing. Total noise deprivd on internal differences equals silence. Clarity night. Stawberry. Woman never calls, sez she will bring the cat over, has it, shows up. Big ball of blue flame burst where the house had been the instant lightning hit. Lives behind shades cast shadows. An end to rewriting. What then? 3197. 9962. A peen may be divided into a claw, wch then functions as a lever for the extraction of nails. Begonias supplement a drab conclusion. The yard consists of a few small squares of concrete, divided by clotheslines naild to a patchwork wooden fence, filld with old chairs, among wch you have to choose carefully before you sit down. The garbage man of words I am. I yam. Bic pentameter. Roll of paper towel still in its plastic wrapper props the window open, hot day. These petty continents are boats. An older man in a gray suit & a young woman with long hair in t-shirt & patchd Levis linger in the rear of the parking lot, passing a ciga- rette back & forth. The first small tufts of fog enter the air of the bay. Schema, schemata. Crossing the street—fording the river. These are the people we call section 8s. The chicken's history is diverted into cartons. One of the quarters is secretly a dollar, contracting. A word's meaning sums the labor of use others have put into it, against wch each utterance is tested, that new force be felt. Many small scratches on the face of the softball bat. The telephone squats in pastel anticipation. A civilization wch produces white refrigerators is not to be trusted. When form counterpoints content cats jolt up, dogs suddenly start to bark. A tuft of gray hair on the tip of his nose. See-thru mail chutes in highrise office bldg. At Judim Hadash's Pleasure Dome on Hollywood's flashy Sunset Strip, tramp fashions sell faster than Mercedes-Benzes to well-heeld & well-known customers. Bottle air. Walking the dog vs. string tricks. Larry gets off on good dish. I run into Deena on her way to work. You die for your politics. I sit in the sun, sip coffee & smoke my cigar. In the dream she begins her reading with cum still spilling down from the sides of her mouth. Madlock's whack helps Bucs embarrass Astros. A first edition of the Communist Manifesto is sold to a French industrialist for $60,000. An old drill rusted thoroughly, naild to the fence as decoration. Harsh overhead lighting generates saliva. Flip City. One who buys limes knows liquor. Four decades later, her description of Robert still applies. The shadows in the alley are more firmly its structure than brick walls. Gold cheques come on wch day of the month. Grammar operates to push the line. The eye's the hole into wch the handle is introduced, by wch to lift the hammer. Pilot fineliner. No two eggs are identical. Moppd floor dries by itself. I found my voice, pickd it up, lookd at it carefully. Mercator's orange. Unusual that it's a woman you see, puking between parkd cars into the gutter. Southern rural black dialect, with British spellings. There are only two straight-identified line staff at the Tenderloin Clinic. A teensy white dog in a red sweater. Cheek's shaved surface tingles. Haldol prevents throwing pots. Drinking Kefir from a milklike carton. The nego-tiations of traffic. It was the shallowness of his sleep more than the lack of it that made him restless. A walking cane with four rubber-glovd tips. A yellowish stool the length of my intestines. Having to frown to keep my glasses from slipping. Better depraved than saved. The low riders' long sedans bump & bounce slowly forward, radios to the full, maroon-jacketed, rouge-cheekd girls bunchd under the arc-light, pretending only slightly not to notice. Shoot the signifiers. Holding the page to the light, to read thru the white-out. Loyalties in quarterly payments. The First Lady crawld onto the trunk of the moving limo in a pink suit, vain search for the head of state. Yo soy one sentence. Later poses the alphabet under flashing lights. Quarterback's legs are governd by pulleys. In the small hotel the manager's office is no more than a counter made from a Dutch door, behind wch infants cry, voices drownd by the strong odor of curry. I read about 6 books of poetry per month & follow the work of perhaps 50 living writers. There are limits, e.g., sleep. Noises meant to be music sort up the airshaft. Viola, the pale south. Body's torque, the jaw deadend, on the end of a dental drill, feet raisd, head lowerd upon a pastel & mechanical chair. Short sentence, long paragraph. The noise of thought drowns the room. In the harbor boats awkwardly rock together toward a mean of average grace. Sadder Budweiser. Totally up in the air, excuse me, I see walls totally up in the air. The plum tree had been torn from the sidewalk & I thot to make of that an image. In the release of her orgasm the sum of the week's stress, that disorienting return to work after a brief vacation, was triggerd, discharged, sobs swelling loudly to fill the whole room, an uncertain fearful look in the bewilderd eyes of her lover. Don't touch that, it will electrocute you. In the morning, quietly, the depositors, if that's what they are, gather on the steps of the soon-to-open bank. Can you, later, see the seams of revision? Bow's string mediates the arrow. Cigar sizzles down into beer bottle. Nob your hobs with gobs of slobs. Leather Lovenest. I bite thru to the ink source. Backd into the figurative corner, you begin to understand her spaced-out behavior as ruthless, uncompromising manipulation. Gum in the pockets of old jackets grows brittle. The simple pressure of speaking before hundreds. Lid's flesh, always specific to the eye, delineates a "look." Shattering plate punctuates diningroom conversation. A midweek bar band. To have a birthday in the midst of family is to acknowledge obligation. The idle waiter slowly wiping his empty tray with a short white towel still tuckd into his apron. Twinge of the syringe. Don't talk to operator while cutting machine is in use! & pages to go before we sleep. I'm tired of having to lift the back of the toilent in order to play with the chain. Linguistics lacks a theory of the sentence. They sit in the lobby waiting to die, Grandmother says of the nursing home, pastel blue & deep shadows, & one woman hogs the tv all afternoon. Cat, dreaming, twitches. The ballistic threat posed by a bullet depends, among other things, on its composition, caliber, mass & impact velocity. The eye itself a form of filter limits the knowable to mark the known. I tip my cigar ash into the wrong beer bottle. A library copy from the X-8 collection. The stiff dignity of the young woman, briskly walking into the back entrance of Greyhound at midnight, no sunglasses to cover blue bruises ringing her eye. Sky clings to the trees, begetting rain. Larry said 'power failure,' but I heard 'poet.' Jaws of the cockroach. Red shingle rooves slant atop white stucco houses, large windows of tinted glass, lining the green waters of the bay. Who will judge the Pudge? We'd been looning for days. Between democracy & efficiency, she said, looking cooly over the half-moons of her reading glasses, I like to get things done. Lights reflected pulld together along the curves of the glass.When anyone other than the one he'd telephond pickd up the receiver, guilt passd thru him that it was not them he'd wanted to speak with. One week of nada, brothers, fathers my need. If I blow into it, flame extends from the far end of the cigar, lit match held slightly below. X-rays jaw thru a tubehead cone. According to code, lightwell becomes inner courtyard if windows opening out onto it belong to bedroom, livingroom, kitchen. Meaning passes from the sentence to the word. In grease-pencil on phone booth window: Gomez '79. Cockroaches nested, no swarmd, in the wainscot over decades of rotting National Geographics, all he owns besides hotplate, crutches, walker, the black ball glistening, pulsing along the wall. The prongs of the forklift slip smoothly into the slots of the flat. My love's no ignoramus / She even reads Albert Camus / She doesn't have to ask who / Will be the famous shamus. Weigh the group's value by the worst of its individual acts, the killer, say, or quisling, whatever deed for wch the restd argue the absolution of personal responsibility, fragmentation of function. T-shirts visible under summer formal wear. Painting isobars by number. A day of rain on the verge of September. My slumlord, who owns 30 buildings & manages more than 100 others, has no home of his own, sleeping in his suit on a couch in his office or in vacant units here & there about town. A schizophrenic is never alone. Under grey ash an orange glow lingers at the end of the cigar. Tom & Jerry & Jane & Linda, pop opportunism has got to stop. Only 8 centuries since the word sentence comes up & for 3 meant Opinion. Azure, as sure as ever, is over all. If everyone in India wants only one more child. 874 & counting. Pulling forms from a hat. That's why we talk language. All that aside! Gas up. I like my hat. The aorta in the coffeehouse. Categories & dogmas. Any minimum complete string of formatives. In the blue of Rayleigh scattering. Ammoniacal, the thick smell of restaurant kitchens before dawn vents. Relaxd, like a jellyfish on the beach. Heygood shakes a finger at the brother, calling him a Ho-ho. Kite & wheelbarrow, Chinese inventions. One small jet, insect crawling blue wall of sky, air filld with pure roar. Be sure to call the roshi, dear. One thing to write the work, another to hustle it. I stare at my new Nike running shoes, blue nylon with black waffle souls, full of secret, just-purchasd pride. Days later, the after-effects of one sleepless night ebb. Here in the ghettoes of my mouth. Documentation decorates. Earwig scrabbles across red metal lawn chair. Metaphor is pressure. One mike to amplify, one to record. Baseball, a secondary sex characteristic. More important than these marks is the grain of the paper on wch they're printed. To use any word is to submit it to grammar, an analysis both instant & linguistic. The bar by the street light's shut, but its vent fan still runs. The swoosh stripe is a trademark. The book itself is just an excuse for the exchange of capital. A copter that low must be searching for something. Good booze goes down smooth before you know it. A large poster creates need. Noun verbs noun. Sipping from a bottle of Old Sox. Phil is alive again, hair slickd back & black vest heavy with oversize white senior power buttons, & we're eating sandwiches in George's grocery wch somehow now includes a long picnic table. All I saw was glare. Meters on your tuner. Women sit with knees together or, if apart, let skirt fall (demure) between thighs. Press brand desired. A black hole has no teeth. Can I trust these words to be my thoughts? Incomplete sentence base. Preeludes. Flies talk to plastic soldiers. Cops sprinted up the apartment steps as we leand & lounged up against Eddie's puce Cad. Tags in shirt collars curl up. Hair always expresses a theory. Eye contact amid strangers emits electrical storm. There is no sentence but a detemminate sentence & that fixd by a period. Half the park is the sky. Tiny fuzzy toy bears, seals & tigers bunchd in the rear window, tinted blue, of the Dodge jackd up on mag wheels. The doves start their depressing coo. The secret of potting lays in the glaze. Words here are treated as objects. Leaves closest to the root will be the first to fall. An old black trunk, turnd on its side, becomes ad hoc lectum. Long flat brown mound. Not tannd where she wore sunglasses, this freckld blonde looks like a raccoon. Hammer in a holster hung over the belt. The worms are unspeakable today. Sentences legislate the possibility of content. Slim, dark & mannish. From the rear the huge church has the personality of a gymnasium. The simile of the evening. A shock of white stains his beard. One blank page is itself sufficient to convict a society of literate regrets. Ears ornament cheeks. Telepathetic. Let's go out on the deck & watch the freeway. We force open the back door of the bus & pull ourselves aboard. Hombook. The thrill is not the stitch. Rarely is a sidewalk all one shade of grey. Let me read you my dreams. More numbers are becoming unlisted. Works wch are new & don't have titles. Sometimes birds are not omitted from a sentence. Ragged pocket. Red hair of Mary Butts. Metaphor sublimates analysis. Oh golly. X over easy. Examinine. The nostalgia of reading. The toilet is a tool. Our eyes are as hours. Regional poetics. The linoleum surface blisters under the heat of the spillt ash. She married well. I only take super. Longtail kites stretch out in the air over the harbor. Max has mother's face, into wch is placed father's nose. Carried to the tens' place. Rumpld chic of punk. Air-conditioning makes 'em sleepy. Consider the images of women here. Anger equals longer sentences. & then went down on the sheep. Out please. Small Asian man in wide-brim straw hat. Is that your Dream Whip? Nothing resembles it in properties or composition or is comparable to it but itself. Porn is the presentation of an unequal power relation between partners in the act of sex for purposes of commerce. Backing out of the parking lot of ideas. Amazing Mouse / How sweet the cheese / To feed a rat like me / / I once was thin / But now I'm round / Had Swiss / But now I've Brie. Night has no reason. As he reads aloud, droning, everyone sits there, staring at their pens. Sexism is not erased. Wittgenstein proceeds by metaphor. Twists her hair into a ponytail, long & blonde. Standing on the island in the middle of the street, waiting for the light to change. In Gary's story the parents are "silent as forest bats." The baby is still growing fingers. Waving her transfer, woman in blue slacks runs after the bus. The SWAT team bursts in, only to find the sniper sleeping in a fetal position. Poetic Procedures (supercedes all previous manuals & memoranda). People keep their dogs in / the night / garbage is collected. The erection of the Theatre of Representation in the place of production. You obey the sound of your name. Wittgenstein is "in pain." Set sentences circle syntax. This is not encouraging. What then? Pie-cards stifle rank & file. Literature is the writing of the dominant class, of those in a position to perpetuate their writing. Any profile depersonalizes the image, blocking the illusion of eye-contact. These authors may be the children of the bourgeoisie, but adulthood finds them growing poorer & some are confused to discover their class in such flux. Spontaneity is the enemy of a conscious practice. A cup, to become round, must first be centerd. Secret ballots alienate you from any responsibility to your neighbor. Three cans of water to one of concentrate. & sentences to go before I sleep. Words, like a shadow, passing over this field under the gaze of your reading eyes. Muscles, as you stretch in a well-deservd yawn, want to cramp. Roots are red wch hold the eye to its socket. An egg with no shell, precarious. A gull throws its voice. No, a gull throws its shadow up against the wall of cloud, gray on grey. A connection between sentences is projected. Helicopters are freed of syntax. Small bees swarm in the Christmas tree. To bury the dead, the followers of Zarathustra trade up from vultures to a microwave oven. Each new thread is tuckd in at the edge. Your hot soup shatters the cold glass bowl. The cat stands up on its hind legs to peek in at the garbage. Each of us stunnd at the thot of a new week. The bug pulls up in front & honks. Prosecution cuts prose. You are getting sleepy, drowsy. I scramble up the scaffold to wash a window. Thru the past tense a continuity emerged. The mayor stood stiffly on the City Hall steps, feigning ease. Bulb poppd. Clay dinosaurs live amid magnified ferns. The small white ball stoppd dead before it rolld foul. We rose to our feet. Red brick skyscraper collapsd into the dust of its own muffld demolition. A bird on a branch is heard calling. Our friends are the people we permit to disappoint us. He gives a two-fingerd salute. Synonyms against the polysyllabic. Black ten on a red jack. The dull morning light of autumn. The ropers. To build strong bodies 57 ways. Bill Berkson was Bolinas. Instantaneous triple click of the lens. I flick the cockroach from the surface of the bar. Blotter nostalgia. A weeklong series of nights. Here you are. Wives of the Pirates dance on the dugout roof. Gene Autry hugs Dick Nixon. Duncan hugs a koala. These ratty little words. Her boyish face with those incredibly female eyes. Grid of pipes along a ceiling's beams. My search for Patti Smith. The gelatin comes in on the next line. Adrenallin, bruises, categories, dogmas, excess. Bebop was thot music. I.e., to think by. Hold pen's cap in my mouth, to scribble in notebook. Someone in this room is smoking grass. Frost in a forest for a rest rusts. Scrape of sulphur head against matchbook. The cathedral of memory. Coathanger reduction of shoulders. Noun phrase. Beneath the brown-black flesh of her vaginal lips, the soft inner surfaces are bright pink. You have to imagine shoes before you can buy them. So poetry dies, but we turn out not to be victims, but executioners. Live ash sizzles, droppt in the wine glass. Wrong, capital raw. Up the thin wooden steps to the manager's office, shadowy corridor, checkout time in crayon on wall, an Indian woman opens the upper half of the dutch door, curry's thick odor flooding the mildewy air. Call me Ralph. Open here. Who first thot to number pages? Bricks punctuate the mortar. Long limbs packd into a hunch over book at table. The percolator happily grows quiet. Silliman, a word I've never used in a work. A child in a parka, hooded, barefoot, on the sidewalk, in the rain. Folk music: listen to / the sounds of syntax. Sir lamps aloft. New shoots jut from the tree top. Obnoxious stage, when child first learns social function of spit. Spelunking hints Orpheus. He tucks hair behind those pink ears. Whose cough ski? One sentence with two main verbs evades commitment, the boy stares at his shoes. Sea below. Not aware of the light till it dims. Bricks approximate a wall. Who is

Floyd? Leisure people speak of art, sport, politic. The old women just sit in the lobby, staring into space. In the middle of elaborate soul handshake dollars & balloons flash & disappear. Cardinal numbers tend toward maroon. When first you crush the cigar smoke billows up. Trimming one's beard is all guesswork. Objectivity = subjectivity—perception of distance. I said that. To build 57 bodies strong ways. Stargell hits a wall job. Chair focuses spine. Topology of connotations. Jet heard but unseen might be tree falling in forest. Bourgeois literature argues universality of audience. People sitting, legs crossd, often flex their ankles. Getting out of bounds stops the clock. Doubt is between two words. Pin the tail on the honkey. Veggies sizzle in the oil of the wok. An athlete's knees are money. Almost all at once, stars fill the sky. It gets cold & I go back into the kitchen. The model here is not psychology. The telephone cord is inevitably tangld. Under the syntax meanings hover & slide. Thursday is the trough of the week. People manifest anxiety toward their cars. All repetition functions as anaphor. We crawl into bed the minute we get home, too exhausted to do anything but sleep. The blue rabbit pulls even with the XL at the curb, before swerving back to park. The keychain of the postperson. No one expects ballplayers to comprehend the implications of their work. Hey man, you want to buy this radio? Maybe a third of the bricks around the garage door were candied up red, green, yellow or black. The jogger's progress thru the light rain. The fly lights on the lip of the cup. Law is a language that denies connotation. When finally the sun first tips over the rooftops all the red-orange goes out of the clouds. I sense grief at the impending finish. Impossible, at speaking distance, to see whole face, but eyes or lips now moving, round & serious. Who are you being being here? What does a question mark? Soon the swoon of words in a room will bloom. Politics of staple guns. Sister morpheme. When Jujube meets his connection, everyone in front of the so-calld Deli takes notice, forgetting for a moment pitchd pennies & baggd bottles of beer, getting ready instead to casual-like stop by to say Hi, soon as that long maroon Lincoln pulls out of sight. A day's work, a way's dork. He sits quietly in the cafeteria, swearing softly into his soup. Old Samoan man in a print skirt, sweeping the sidewalk in the rain. The limit of knowledge is demonstrated by chairs. Dawn on a grey day is by degrees. The clerk in lingerie casually wears home two bras. Three year fall behind a bank job. The tiny drill-like needle scouring abcessd pulp from the nerve, there was no pain to the root canal therapy, merely the dull sound of somebody somewhere scraping a blackboard deep inside his head. This began at a table in a yellow room. Bellflower is X. Dogs & vinegar. What are reasons? Enola D. Maxwell wants to be your voice in the back room. This image, screend & croppd. People love to inform you that the pen in your pocket has leakd. Sadness fills the red wagon. In Rome or in logic. I came from a peasant background & here were these great words. In media see. Although written in 1967 these essays are as fresh as tomorrow. Old man using broom as a cane. The correct line goes to the margin. Women find it easier to share the adventure of sexual plots. Before language, only dreams were conceivd; later, pocket calculator supplants slide rule. Small animals are perfect for bondage. Look feverish. Meditations in a barber's chair. Sooner or later a cowboy comes off his horse. Alas abalone. In order to refill the sandbox we go to the beach. Grandmother, waking, calls for 'Daddy,' husband dead for nine years. That man is snapping thin wood sticks in half. Painfully, I inscribe this book to you. An image of the unfathomable in under-the-hood-of a car. Such continuity effaces hesitation, revision & doubt. I run into Watten in a lumber yard. When you get near the bottom the newspaper droops. The dog is happy rolling in the dirt. I am rapidly running out of lines. Small stainglass frog hangs in the window. Meat by-products. Education designs the brain. Education redesigns the brain. Dry petfood is cereal. Ibid. A man tunelessly whistles, lugging garbage down three flights of backstairs. Jars, cans & spray-bottles sit in a kitchen window. I slap my hands clean. What you can determine from the sound of unseen traffic is the general size of vehicle. Old broomsticks rotting on the porch. Think of stitching as a mode of margin.

Children scavenging crushd cans as scout project. One million pennies from the National Endowment. Chickenwire on the fencetop to prevent entry. Direct-mail brochures targeted to fear-defined groups Vote No. Gas vents jut from brick chimney. White numbers stencild on the side of red dumpster. Four-wheel plastic duck. Language occurs by division of labor. Elizabeth Bishop is dead. Only some of the people went to work expecting rain. Each night defined by the sleep I didn't get. The dog is bland. Bookstore clerks have no greater function than punch the register. A trace of supplementary deconstruction. Across the plaza, grey as the November sky, trees trimmd to skeletons, members of the Tac Squad in black jumpsuits watchd the parading Irani students, idly slapping batons into their palms. In the argot of drags, real women are "fish." Utility lines sway in the breeze. There is nearly always room to stand at the rear of the bus. Education teaches, regret the jobs you don't get. A heavy rain half-dissolves the coils of dogstuff abandond on the curb. Lawyers believe in their power. Hark— pigeons in the park. The primary issue is the election of business agents. Nine percent money is getting hard to find. Watermarks stain the ceiling. Leaves closest to the root die first. Special staples to attach the phone line to the wall. The joy of a big closet. The cat scratches vigorously at the base of its ear. Such poets are said to show contempt for meaning. The flower of the coleus is blue. Capitalists are conditiond not only to work against the other classes, but against one another as well. My intention is to write until the rain stops. The prism house of languish. T-t-t-t-t-t-tenderloin man. Smack runners often carry cans of Tab in case they have to swallow their balloons in a hurry. Does your mother know? That's not music, she said. Roar of the porcelain elephant. Spider plant's new shoots arc up. What is grungier than an old sponge? Sculpted heads. 100% Pure Natural U.S. Fancy Grade. Don't fuck with the Wongs. Plum leaves in the gutter become a purple mash. The cat first attempts to kill the sausage. An evening with Sam 'n' Ella. People who live on the top floors seldom pull their shades down. A separate key to open the mailbox. Only way to untangle the windchimes now wld be to cut the strings. Someone has ravaged the bananas. A splint in wch to set the Althusserian break. The refrigerator freezes everything, milk spilling splinters of ice to cool the steaming reboild coffee. Tiger brand olive oil. This cigar's wrapper leaks smoke. I pour a 2nd cup of boiling water's worth thru these grounds. Plastic coin purse starts to crack. My love is a grump / I take her to the dump / I tell her where to jump / doo wah. Any book of matches with its cover torn off. Shld I type up these notes or just write letters? Sound of a vacuum in the next flat. Old woodframe house groans even under softest footsteps. Every great fortune is built on a crime. Ream lover, so I don't have to ream alone. At the pay phone her free thumb plugs her ear to street noise, a cigarette lodgd between the first two fingers of the same hand. Harder not to make typos on a cold day. Nightness. As the bus approaches my stop, I pull up my socks. The salt shaker sits atop the table, half filld with its grainy crystal: if some hand were to shake it the salt wld even off, becoming level, but set down carelessly it slants. The pull of gravity is felt as peace, in both one's spine & intestines. But when I am tired I sense it in the muscles of my face, wch sag with exhaustion. These muscles are simplified in the make-up of a clown. Any noun mentiond twice carries special meaning. If some hand were to shake this, connotations wld even off. The carries in my smile have been filld now with silver. The dentist's face is magnified by its very lack of distance. The table sits in a wood-frame house, 100 yards from ground zero. What then? I retire to the mirror to admire long black gloves against my face. I retire to the mirror to admire long black gloves against my fish. In a fire compressd butane lighters go off like dynamite. The history of silence. This ego is an open wound. Naval shipyard, fluorescent night. The dog-like anxiety of the cabbie. The words are attentive. Curses sing to laughter. Once the mailing, wch had gotten out late due to a confusion as to the allocation of tasks, faild to arrive in time, civility between them dissolvd quickly. If there's a urinal, it's the men's room. By the time I got to work people were already spilling out to the catering truck for the morning break. Groans of a typo. Motorcycle roars up to the back steps, foll,owd by shouting in Spanish. The function of the hat indoors is a signature. The dude is in pocket. Don't drive, never remember the names of cars. Not all stores stock the same cigars. The women were getting brazen, working the dark peepshow aisles in the rear of the bookshop. The words are a tent in wch meanings hover. Arc hates / heartaches. Goodbye to impulse. Cardboard boxes labeld Fusion. Standing in the elm-lined dark, I see shopping carts abandond in the yellow light of the entrance to the 4-story green brick condo. Who will write of shoelaces? Even before the accident FOH had grown silent. At night shadows pass rapidly thru the front seat of the truck. Anxious owner will carry second. Danger in that four-plex, black-n-white angled up on the curb, empty, lights flashing, doors open. Pushing on the garbage to make room for more. I step inside a laundromat to wait for the bus. Sienna is burning. Idly, she fingers a lock of her hair, curling, uncurling, exhausted. Parsley in a glass, alas. Still-life with ashtray & styro-foam cup. Umbrellas on the N-car are shut & dripping. Somethin arcane, passe, to heroin sez the first, the other nodding. Office life. The "loaded notes of the dulcimer." Yosemite Sam, Wiley Coyote. She holds her shoulders stiff when she jogs. The cabbie leans across his seat, trying to read the house numbers. Anything I hear is fair. White clay mime mask hangs above the clock. The Sunday supps strewn over the kitchen floor, chippt linoleum tile. Each new gray book lessens his sense of urgency, the line taught loosens, the life livd looks increasingly back. Poor blue Dodge van, hoisted half off the asphalt by that yellow tow truck. Her head surrounded by curls in programmd wildness. Write poetry, sell novels. The spoon is sticky. 3 cars of police & the baby blue coroner's wagon to carry the man out who left his gas on & 2 doors up these brothers cld care less, shouting loudly over their bottle of port. On the bus discuss manners of the driver. Shut door to closet before mist-ing plants. I hear the water getting ready to boil. This tooth is not dead, it's killing me. She gets up each day at eight, walks long & thin in plain view picture window (walld-in old back-porch) naked to the can, owns an Afghan & Fiat, has a black lover (male), jogs on the weekend & is registerd as a member of the A.I.P. Doors of the bus creak open slowly. Empty produce scale registers quarter pound. All the false detail of "competent verse." The heart in the head in its hands at arms' ends bends down. Sugar on that storebought granola makes milk at bowl's bottom register sweet. Jim again: "the haiku of Ohio." Revisions of Cody. Work at any job 4 years & you'll be theirs forever (not these bosses— any). Cheap wine in tiny bottles. One bite on the granola & tooth implodes. The truth is no defense. Traffic slows, up ahead lights flashing, red flares in the dark, trouble. The silence in the laundromat of night. All look the same, sheet over head. The small, rented cement-mixer squeaks as it spins. Brushing on silicon to waterproof boots. The tooth is no defense. Cat sits at the window & sings at the rain. What is this you? Large loud dark radio-cassette player, attache case of the young. Pushing a lit cigarette thru the wall of a styrofoam cup. The hammer filming itself. The moth on the window as if under glass. Texxt. Heed cats. On the tarrd roof an old rug beside the overturnd pink easy chair begins its slow dissolve in the rain. Nicotine fingers turn the page. A brown film grows inside the toilet. No bars on Oak Street. This back tooth, square molar, crackd open, one spot of wch wakes, waits for a touch, morsel or toothpick on its blind probe, to burst, suddenly, into a full rose of fire. 12 points to a pica? Bigfoot & Thud. The continuous breath of gas heat. The author is in the livingroom. Consonant clatter. The patter (pattern) of the saxophonist's fingers. Rug-wrappt kitty condos. In the rain sawdust becomes red mud. Mounth. The slow approach a car makes, seeking a place to park. Implicit construction of the self. The scissors have sat for weeks atop the kitchen table just because no one has thot of a place for them. In a land of flat rooftops, do not expect snow. When I teach poetry old women dredge wadded posters for past tea dances, their backs filld with crampd rime, up from deep within satchels they call pocketbooks. On the window rain-drops cluster at the bottom. Old eggs clutter my gums. Tempo reality. Marxist Literary Group cash bar (Potrero Room, Hyatt) at the MLA. Seal the char truce. Brave Cowboy Bill. Ghede (pronounced gay-day) shows up, wearing wire-rimmd dark glasses with one lens missing. Drops of rain plop down gas vent's pipe. A piece of paper towel lies crumpld on the table. The powder bubbles, melting in the spoon. Now I'm out of lined pages, writing on the back cover. Alone in the old house, rainy December, we put Rubber Soul on the stereo & hold to each other thru a sort of waltz. The cat in its chair sleeps the day away. Thank you, Jerry, for the gift of this pen. Maya Deren wades into the sea. Rats live smug on no gums evil star. Breaking apart the meat of the flea. The butter in its glass coffin. The girl who died of the blackwidow in her beehive was just a parents' fable. The wax keeps the dye from spreading, leaving a line, a remainder. None but official cars. Little Hitler in your stocking. The smell of the inside of a tent. Lightning! Bob's earliest memory is the word 'tremendous.' In accepting this discipline the progressional reality of my activity has become increasingly clear—that being: the reality of my work can be viewd as an investigation as to the meta-implications of principle information—as it pertains to the dynamic funda-mentals wch solidify what a given information line means in its expanded sense (its actual physical universe effect as well as its spiritual assignment) & what this implies for the formation of a possible alternative world music. Pood! Pulpstone. Beam me up, Olson. This means you. Untenantable. The soybeam futures trading pit. Aluminum piano, Hindenburg stateroom. Ocarina lullaby. The superstructure can throw you in jail. Rubber leaves chemical taste to the cock. Lionhead pillowslip. In the Halpern anthology, 47 of the 76 refer in their bios specifically to jobs teaching (another dozen are too shy). Moth jaws. Wakeing. After rain, digested paper froths up at sewer lips. But you already said that. The new noon whistle. From the flat's far end the long buzz of the alarm clock is inaudible. Suction pup. The mind always reduces the distance between two sentences toward a minimum limit. My yellow dingdong. Island of the Moon apiaries. When father went off to war, I was eating a cream-coverd bowl of peaches, mother crying on the bed, & he saying Goodbye & going. The poems are really there. A salt. It thinks.

January 1, 1980: full moon. Trillions, deacon, trillions. Scientific, a word that never means itself. Clothes on a makeshift line, 3rd storey backporch, soakd with rain. That most butch but hetero woman. No hyphen in rip-off when used as a verb. What is the half-life of that salad in the fridge? We reserve the right to refuse service (meanings). In the shadowy grain of the old Movietone News of the big dirigible bursting you can make people out dropping to the New Jersey earth from the flaming tip, starting to run just before the whole hull, one fireball, settles down. In structions. In the tooth's chamber grew calcium deposits, oyster wedgd into root canal. For Barrett Watten, a sense of rigor playing back. Geologic map of the Cassini Quadrangle. Sleeping moth tucks its antennae between its wings & the windowpane on wch it rests. Vowels /valves. This crater's named Saussure. The embarrassment one feels, reading Creeley's letter to Blackburn, describing the death of his daughter. Into info. I clarify clarity. Root doctor. Articu'lating papers— carbon squares to chew down on. So sentences are forming (word bubble). Decades early, decays late. Gotta quit talkin in regular rhythms. Pood, pood! The art & arc of my life is across time & in time. Shaped white bubbles pressd into styrofoam cup. Marx was a Taurus. A pond of riddles laying back. Nor a pound of rattles playing rock. The garbageman always wears gloves. Catnip is a mint. Don't look at the camera. What makes this political? The clerk typist determines the linebreaks. Unwarranted leisure, undirected education. I can see the top frond of the palm over that tip of red shingle. She never quite puts out her cigarette. Even Trigger cld compose in syllabics. Jay Gutz? This piece doesn't quite fill your present needs, but I'm sending it anyway. Selfhatred in politics is the image of correctness. Reading the New Yorker, waiting for the next cab fare to turn up. A man is shot dead for no reason under the bright overhead lights of Doggie Diner. A case of acid indigestion causes the cocaine smuggler's balloons to burst in his stomach, great rush before convulsive death. The flag slaps about wildly in gusts of rain. Jim Goldstein wants credit: the haiku of Ohio. Killer titles. Is that how you write it? No trace of commie. Little

Indian cigs calld bidis. Eggwhite goes opaque with heat. Swing vote. What makes you want to read words? Ash sprinkles on shirt. Lap valley. Anxiety as to just when that left shoelace is going to break. What I sought & saw. People spilling down the street, jumping over the tangle of large cream-colord hoses, the gutters flooding, covering noses, mouths, with kerchiefs & coats, t-shirts pulld up, black billowing acrid smoke not rising, but rolling down across the intersection. Paper with little napoleonic bees. Art fights space. Max begins to comprehend the individuation of fingers. This thought has new meaning. Store at room temperature. Write that down. Shoes are bondage. Dollars per column inch. The warm wet indoor odor of ducks. At night, shouting at the mustang to turn its lights on. Orange snake extends into open manhole from rear of phone truck. Now is the weather for leather. First thot, next thot. He squats. Reading even your own handwriting aloud will be filld w/ blips, gaps. Bitter lemon smell of cat spray. Wipes his glasses with his tie. Solitary Instances, Migratory Instances, Striking Instances, Clandestine Instances, Constitutive Instances, Conformable Instances, Singular Instances, Deviating Instances, Bordering Instances, Instances of Power, Instances of Companionship & of Enmity, Subjective Instances, Instances of Alliance, Instances of the Fingerpost, Instances of Divorce, Instances of the Door, Summoning Instances, Instances of the Rod, Instances of the Course, Doses of Nature, Instances of Strife, Intimating Instances, Polychrest Instances, Magical Instances. No ped crossing. Writing a poem in wch 'you' means 'I.' Snoweling thru the bargain bin. Facial quality bathroom tissue. Surprise reprise. Not this (what then?). Marble burnd returns to lime & in the first rain collapses. Words scar the page. Steve's unit is the sitting. From atop the rear of the truck the gun fires water into the center of the black smoke, billboard cracking, crumbling over, fireman / gunman looking idly on. The finish on the dancer's floor. Rollers & stops embedded into the floor of the rear of the hearse guide & hold many a pine box. This thought has no meaning. The paranoia of the man at the metal detector. Star Spring Fruit Box. A garage band is tuning up. Jam her off / jam her off / jam her off / her buffalo. Saidism. You don't exist. Please take a number & be seated. The early surveyors named the streets for themselves. The grease in the towel is from human hands. Direct sun brings the red in the coleus out. The motion fails for lack of a second. The house shudders under the reverberations of the hovering copter. The lens focuses on an expression of surprise. Layers of cigar smoke hang still in the air. Parallel syntax reduces the space between statements. These nails thru my lips are words rusting. Old shirts naturally gather in certain chairs. I slap myself awake between statements. Basically, this is a sonnet. Behind every exploited worker stand ten superexploited peasants. Imagine what these running shoes wld cost if they hadn't been made in Korea. Sometimes I stand paralysd before a choice of frozen juices gleaming in the supermarket freezer. Readers of poetry fall into 3 main groups: students, writers & a certain sector of the proletarianizd petty bourgeoisie. There is a problem of space in this notebook, the result of false starts. Walter Benjamin is stoppd at the border. Waxd shoelaces are best. The sky more pale towards the equator. No peace can be made with capital. We prefer to read the dead, because their lives point towards our own, lending the comfortable air of a false inevitability. Diamonds in the blood, embolisms. 4001. Stitching. Composition vs. construction. A fell swoop. "Meow," screams the child into the face of the cat. Carol sat in the waiting room, listening to the gunfire. Not all yellow stripes atop phone poles are coach stops. A round L. Birds of a mailbox. Persian dust. If I mention Alcibiades wch reader do I lose? A bead of sweat slowly makes its way down his cheek. 3 cops pointed pistols into the blind alley, bystanders frozen, the young man crouching behind a parkd car who might or might not also have a gun. Dumb dog, no fun. Hit Sign Win Suit. The Balinese mask with blue eyes. "Oh yeah," says Eigner, "you guys can write in the dark." Euphausia is krill. The short form. A single file of wives, waiting patiently to pass thru the metal detector. While she jogs the sheepdog lopes half a step behind. Gas station keeps bowling trophies in window. Capitalism depends on your emotional anarchy. Colostomy & stratification. Seersucker dental apron. A work in wch each paragraph begins "The next day." May I help you? He pickd the smashd bulb up & ground the glass into his own eyes. The world is merely a recess in the wall. Hanging out on the corner, waiting to cop. Everybody nods to form & content, but nobody invites it home. Fang Bwiti. A perfect pocket notebook. "Motherfuckin' nigger," the balding plainclothes cop screamd, snubnose gun at the base of the suspect's neck, "Motherfuckin' nigger, motherfuckin' nigger." Wch way shld the toilet paper roll? Popular Poetix. Simmon tree. He expects to hear his own words. Her program is that there be no program (all spontaneity is reactive). Do I contradict myself? The centerfuge of paranoia. Able to smell the sea, unable to see it. The atmosphere of a highschool shop class that never lets out. Whang Way. Give me liberty or give me glue. Filming the gamelon worlds meet. Your mother eats kitty litter. Reform is itself a form of danger, Quaker. Sat in type. To little. Sentimental Detroit t-shirt. The cat never looks like a cartoon of the cat. After he was handcuffd, subdued, they beat his head against the prowl car until blood maskd the distorted face. Sullair Sulliscrew 160 (what makes a jackhammer jack?). Sunset View Cemetery. Quote this, Soldofsky. All along the dingo fence. You put the cat out & now it's raining. Rabbit's a prisoner prone to escape, a mule bears contraband. All the body rests on feet. Some stuff magazines into their shirts, that a chance shank might not penetrate deeply. 'Years & Flowers.' Balinese dancer, backstage, walks as if feet hurt. Zen commitment to hair. ℒ . Motorscooter sounding like wings of a giant moth. Morning, the first lights go on in the bathroom. A rooster on the sidewalk. But the next page is the first. The people a board & I a hammer. Reading the Cantos backwards. Antarctic, ten percent of the earth's surface, holds more than 85% of all its fresh water, caked in ice. The function of the visiting poet is to breach the scene. Not this. Zone row. Paint changes shade as it dries. 2 kinds of banana. The porous mother. I'm filld with artificial closures. Banging the filter & old grounds out of the coffee cone. Disguise delimit. Quit claim.

Whacka-mole. The Chief Information Officer, going to the social concerns committee of X church to speak of the 'unpleasant-but-necessary' task wch society has given the Department of Corrections, brings with him his six-year-old son. Write that down. Stanley Kunitz' stainless steel stove. The middle of somebody else's winter. Defense of the Code. Hangnail throb. Two men with the same nose walk into the cafe. 'E' in Notley. Design to confine. That hill to the east a silhouette means the high sun still ain't visible on its west slope. People always gauge one another's shoes. When you say Elvis, he thinks Presley. Quiet poem back file. Taiwan tobacco & wine monopoly bureau. A simple single gaze at traffic involves translation. Jack Benny's Rochester. Thomas Merton's socket. What causes you to trust the chair? Dog's name is Bijou. A staple wounds the page. Time flies like an arrow, fruit flies like a banana. Used coffee grounds turn into a paste. Grammar, a tragedy. She abandons the agenda at the slightest pressure. I make sure to sign out. 'I want you to write down "The crystal brick" (you can always edit it out later).' Fingersmelling blues. Skunkd, lil Bobby begins to tear his christmas presents open with his teeth. Dixon Ticonderoga 1388-2 (soft) yellow pencil. Make a partial deposit. A room in wch 30 makes a crowd. Rubbing the jelly around the diaphragm. What is a full stop? Not this. Seeing Creeley's Pieces in a used bookstore, I long to buy what I already own. Clogs are shoes rumord to be comfortable. This kid, driving under the influence, DUI. I want you to look at the hinges. Ionizer in law firm's office neutralizes word processor's static electricity at doorknob. Less cash receivd. What, on any plate, a person saves to eat last. Big dog has right-of-way. The alphabet is your fate. Piss-elegant. Wicker hamper. Waiting for mung bean soup. In the realm of the kittens. All those pens, a case of writer's pocket. Oh no, now I did it too much. Do not break this chain! The name of other things. Morning's first sound, brush of streetsweeper's broom. He won't talk about his problems until they're too big to handle. There's more to romantic love, says F, than sucking a woman off. While Michael reads aloud, Eileen braids her hair. The deficit of Air France. Jobs Now. On the wall of the bathroom behind the restaurant kitchen, dozens of blueblack flies struggle against the hanging strip of sticky, poisond paper. Freedom from causal bondage. This penny is cold to step on. To turn the page is to climb a wall. Wear safety glasses to cook bacon. 7-Up & Coke logos adorn signs of small markets. Horns passing in the night. Here's the problem of scale. Are you frightened of finishing? The description is the thing. What is less eerie about a pigeon, newly dead on the sidewalk. Part-time work is disguisd unemployment. The cat prefers to sleep in doorways. To construct models from the outside is to view them with guilt. I didn't say that. Robins begin to gather on the telephone wire, staring in at me thru the window. It's spring again. His chair tips back & he falls to the floor. The coleus sits on the sill awaiting the sun. The avocado plant has grown to the ceiling. "Tenure!" shouts B. Forty-three percent of the world's paper is produced in North America. A 12 year old patrols the street with a loaded submachinegun. Helicopters buzz about the accident, flies at a carcass. The mayor views it all thru a pair of field glasses. Opera of demoralization. These are our baby pictures. I help you lift off your blouse. In America's 213 major manufacturing industries, the top 4 companies in each field control an average of 42% of the market. They love to polish & putter with their RVs on the sidewalk. A greek chorus with wah-wah pedals. Condos, like a pueblo terraced on the hillside. Flat facts allign assertions. Shelf-life of a book. I want to hear the terms of your resistance. Vertical gravel. If we all sleep together now, we'll remember this moment forever. Punctuation is mortar. The song of the sprinklers on these well-trimmd lawns presents a false surface. What then?

6.27.77–3.9.80

Lightning Source UK Ltd.
Milton Keynes UK
UKOW03f0137020217

9 781876 857196